T0031293

HOLY GHOSTS

HOLY GHOSTS

Classic Tales of the Ecclesiastical Uncanny

Edited by
FIONA SNAILHAM

BRITISH LIBRARY

This collection first published in 2023 by
The British Library
96 Euston Road
London NW1 2DB

Selection, introduction and notes © 2023 Fiona Snailham
Volume copyright © 2023 The British Library Board

"The Cathedral Crypt" © 1935 The Estate of John Wyndham/John Beynon
Harris. Reprinted with the permission of David Higham Associates.

Every effort has been made to trace copyright holders and to obtain their
permission for the use of copyright material. The publisher apologises
for any errors or omissions and would be pleased to be notified of any
corrections to be incorporated in reprints or future editions.

Cataloguing in Publication Data
A catalogue record for this publication is available from the British Library

ISBN 978 0 7123 5413 4
e-ISBN 978 0 7123 6885 8

Frontispiece illustration based on a sketched view of a crypt, *c.* 1780. The original work
bears an inscription stuck on the verso which reads "I think the Crypt Canterbury
Cathedral", though it remains uncertain whether this is the crypt depicted.

Illustration on page 287: "The Inside of the Crypt, underneath the
East End of Hythe Church in Kent" by Thomas Russell, 1783.

Illustration on page 288: etching of the effigy of a knight on an "Ancient
Tomb in Norbury Church" produced for *The Topographer, c.* 1790.

Cover design by Mauricio Villamayor with illustration by Sandra Gómez

Text design and typesetting by Tetragon, London
Printed in England by CPI Group (UK) Ltd, Croydon, CR0 4YY

MIX
Paper | Supporting
responsible forestry
FSC
www.fsc.org   FSC® C171272

CONTENTS

INTRODUCTION

"... at one bound he was in the church, holding up the young girl above his head and shouting with terrific voice—'Sanctuary! Sanctuary!' This was all done with the rapidity of lightning.

'Sanctuary! Sanctuary!' repeated the mob, and the clapping of ten thousand hands caused Quasimodo's only eye to sparkle with joy and exultation."*

In a memorable scene in *The Hunchback of Notre-Dame*, Quasimodo seeks sanctuary in Notre-Dame, claiming the cathedral as a place where his beloved Esmeralda may find refuge. Whilst the sanctuary granted to La Esmeralda is only fleeting; the notion of ecclesiastical refuge reflects a long history in which consecrated spaces, situated outside secular authority, provided safety to those seeking to escape persecution. In this anthology, spectral apparitions suggest that holy settings are not always able to provide such protection: spirits of those who have passed reveal holy sites as the setting of horrifying deaths, and malevolent phantoms threaten the safety of those visiting hallowed ground.

Of course, physical safety is not the only protection offered by a church. Spiritual salvation is a key tenet of most religions. This is certainly true in Christianity, the faith which underpins the religious spaces represented in the English, Irish and American stories collected in these pages. The New Testament is clear in its teaching that followers "should not perish but have everlasting life",† an

---

* Victor Hugo, *The Hunchback of Notre-Dame* (London: Bentley & Sons, 1833), 310.
† John 3:16, The King James Version of the Bible.

assurance founded on the premise that part of the believer will live on once their physical body has failed. The separation of spiritual and physical selves embedded in the concept of eternal life is echoed in the phantasmal apparitions that appear throughout the stories in this collection, for what is a ghost if not a manifestation of the spiritual self? Historically, this question has caused tension: how does one reconcile the notion of eternal salvation (or damnation) with accounts of the continued earthly presence of those who have passed? Are phantasmal apparitions manifestations of evil or are they merely innocent souls unable to reach a place of rest? These are not issues that can be resolved by reading the stories collected here, but the ghosts encountered in the pages that follow do each have something to reveal about the relationship between the individual and their faith. In different ways, each asks what salvation looks like and how it can be obtained, whether sought during life or from beyond the grave.

Holy Ghosts: Classic Tales of the Ecclesiastical Uncanny presents a collection of stories published between 1851 and 1935. The tales offer accounts of holy places filled with horror and believers tormented by terrifying ghosts. The spectres enclosed in this volume invite us to explore the relationship between the church and the individual, whether living or recently deceased. The majority of the stories in this anthology offer narratives that in some way reinforce church teaching: some reiterate the promise of redemption, others warn against a life of sin. A few depict evil acts committed by natural or preternatural perpetrators, presenting stark depictions of the horrors against which the church can offer protection. At the same time, each one, by revealing phantasmal presence in holy settings, raises questions about the sanctuary—physical and spiritual—offered by faith.

Some of these tales demonstrate a Church's failure to offer sanctuary to the living. In both "In the Confessional" and "A Story Told in a Church", ghostly visitors offer accounts of horrors perpetrated in sacred spaces. Spectral appearances reveal acts of historic human wickedness against which the walls of the church were unable to protect. Of course, these stories are not the first to suggest human transgressions within consecrated sites. One only has to look to earlier Gothic tales to see a line of literature in which the church is infiltrated by the sins of humankind. In *The Monk* (1796), Matthew Lewis introduces Ambrosio, a murderous monk whose acts of sexual violence are perpetrated within the crypt of the convent of St Clare. Lewis also introduces a Prioress whose heartless behaviour leads to the death of one of the novices in her care. Similar human villainy is presented in *The Italian* (1797), a text commonly discussed as Ann Radcliffe's response to Lewis's novel. Where Lewis and Radcliffe offer accounts of human transgressions at the time they occur, the apparition of the ghost in the short fictions included in this anthology suggests the continued presence of earlier sin. Writing about the haunted house, Emma Liggins asserts that "haunting in its broadest forms not only denotes the appearance of ghosts but a sensation of being troubled, discomforted and trapped in the past".* In the pages that follow, the persistence of phantasmal menaces in holy sites might be read as an indication of spiritual dis-ease; a means through which the wickedness historically perpetrated by humankind might be brought to the attention of the living in order that prior transgressions might be atoned.

* Emma Liggins, *The Haunted House in Women's Ghost Stories: Gender, Space and Modernity, 1850–1945* (London: Palgrave Macmillan, 2020), 6.

A similar plea for redemption occurs in "The Parson's Oath" in which a spirit is unable to rest until buried in consecrated ground. Rather than questioning the church's ability to afford salvation to the living, Mrs Henry Wood's tale reinforces the doctrine of spiritual salvation. In foregrounding the deceased's desire for a Christian burial, the story aligns itself with Victorian beliefs in the sanctity of holy ground. The importance of being laid to rest in a sanctified site is signposted in other mid-century fiction, notably in *Bleak House* (serialised 1852–3*) where Lady Dedlock voices concern about the consecrated status of the pauper's grave in which Captain Hawdon (Nemo) has been laid to rest. In contrast, the salvatory nature of a Christian burial seems to be of little interest to the spirit depicted by Marguerite Merington in 1899. In "An Evicted Spirit", the phantasmal narrator is less concerned with their own posthumous status, choosing instead to focus on the comfort that the burial rites bring to those she leaves behind. Although Merington's attention shifts away from the salvation of the deceased soul, the tale's depiction of religious comfort aligns with Wood's implicit presentation of the church as a place of comfort.

In other mid-nineteenth century stories, sacrilegious spectres offer the living reader warnings about a life of sin. In this collection, the presences portrayed by Sheridan Le Fanu and Elizabeth Gaskell address the sins of extravagant intemperance and witchcraft. Each author presents a tale in which sinful behaviour can be seen as an impediment to eternal salvation, although only Gaskell clarifies that a life of atonement will bring redemption. The fate of the sinful Sexton in Le Fanu's narrative is less clear, although the story offers a vivid depiction of the cleric's earthly attempts to avoid relapsing

---

* Charles Dickens, *Bleak House* (London: Bradbury & Evans, 1852–3).

into the wicked behaviour of his earlier years. A similar battle is faced by the patient in Robert Hichens's tale: a man haunted by a monastic double who feels the impact of every sin he commits. Both Hichens and Le Fanu present behaviours which must be avoided, depicting uncanny apparitions as a means of manifesting the demonic forces sent to tempt humankind into sinful transgression. In different ways, all three stories use the ghostly to reiterate Christian teaching about the temptation of evil, its impact on the offer of salvation and the need to atone for wrongdoing.

Where Gaskell shows that sincere repentance can lead to eternal life, Nesbit and Wharton bring into question those who attempt to purchase redemption. While wealth might pay for the erection of posthumous memorials in holy sites, the terrifying movements of the life-size effigies in "Man-Size in Marble" suggests that familial investment in a church is meaningless without the personal atonement of those who have sinned. Nesbit's marble knights continue their reign of terror for centuries, the holy site in which they are entombed unable to contain the evil residing in their unrepentant souls. Equally lacking in remorse, the Duke in Edith Wharton's tale uses wealth to memorialise the passing of a family member. Where Nesbit's statues torment the living for their own nefarious amusement, the horror in Wharton's tale lies in the effigy's attempts to convey the truth about its namesake's demise.

I have suggested that most of the stories in this collection in some way reinforce Christian teachings, demonstrating the dangers of straying from the path and highlighting the promise of spiritual salvation for those who do not err. The final two tales, however, move away from the notion of holy deliverance, instead presenting stories of malevolent forces residing unchecked within holy sites. M. R. James presents evil in the form of a cursed carving in "The

Stalls of Barchester Cathedral", while innocent tourists witness a fatal procession in Wyndham's "The Cathedral Crypt". The latter might be read in conjunction with "The Earlier Service" (1935), Margaret Irwin's tale of a ghostly Black Mass anthologised in Tanya Kirk's *Haunters at the Hearth*, also published in the Tales of the Weird series.* For Irwin, Wyndham and James, malign encounters occur on hallowed ground, leading to potentially fateful outcomes which open up questions about the power struggle between good and evil.

The Hunchback of Notre-Dame, referenced at the start of this introduction, also raises questions about the battle between the benevolent and the malign. It is a story in which the church offers temporary sanctuary but also houses an obsessive Archdeacon with malevolent intent. Although not a supernatural story, the novel houses a suspected phantom when children mistake the injured Gringoire for the ghost of an ironmonger. Despite being in a consecrated space, the youngsters are open to the possibility of a resident spirit. Their perceptions of the cathedral allow room for the presence of one who has passed and their imaginations create a ghost story of their own. Contemplating her production of supernatural fiction, Edith Wharton set out the role of the reader in meeting the writer "halfway among the primeval shadows" in order to fill in narrative gaps "with sensations and divinations akin" to the author's own.† As they approach the stories in this collection, I urge the reader to heed Wharton's words and, regardless of individual belief, keep open minds as they seek to meet the writers of these tales in the "primeval shadows" of the churches they explore.

---

* Tanya Kirk (ed.), *Haunters at the Hearth: Eerie Tales for Christmas Nights* (London: British Library, 2022), pp. 141–162.
† Edith Wharton, *Ghosts* (New York: D. Appleton & Company, 1937), Preface.

A NOTE FROM THE PUBLISHER

The original short stories reprinted in the British Library Tales of the Weird series were written and published in a period ranging across the nineteenth and twentieth centuries. There are many elements of these stories which continue to entertain modern readers; however, in some cases there are also uses of language, instances of stereotyping and some attitudes expressed by narrators or characters which may not be endorsed by the publishing standards of today. We acknowledge therefore that some elements in the stories selected for reprinting may continue to make uncomfortable reading for some of our audience. With this series British Library Publishing aims to offer a new readership a chance to read some of the rare material of the British Library's collections in an affordable paperback format, to enjoy their merits and to look back into the worlds of the past two centuries as portrayed by their writers. It is not possible to separate these stories from the history of their writing and as such the following stories are presented as they were originally published with minor edits only, made for consistency of style and sense. We welcome feedback from our readers, which can be sent to the following address:

British Library Publishing
The British Library
96 Euston Road
London, NWI 2DB
United Kingdom

THE SEXTON'S ADVENTURE

Sheridan Le Fanu

Born in Dublin in the early nineteenth century, Joseph Sheridan Le Fanu (1814–1873) was originally destined for a career at the Bar. Turning instead to journalism and fiction, he entered a profession more closely aligned with his family's established literary heritage: his grandmother, Alicia Sheridan Le Fanu, and great uncle, Richard Brinsley Sheridan, were both playwrights, his mother wrote the biography of Dr Charles Orpen. In due course, his niece, Rhoda Broughton, would enjoy a successful career as a novelist.

Le Fanu wrote prolifically, producing work across a range of genres. Whilst his early novels were historical in focus, he is now more frequently discussed in relation to his sensation novels and supernatural horror. Key texts include *The House by the Churchyard* (1862–3), a dark murder mystery later alluded to in James Joyce's *Finnegan's Wake* (1939); *Uncle Silas* (1864), a sensation novel with Gothic undertones; and *Carmilla* (1871), a novella which presents a predatory vampiric woman.

The story that follows is one of many spectral tales penned by Le Fanu, a writer praised as one "who stands absolutely in the first rank as a writer of ghost stories" in M. R. James's editorial preamble to the posthumous *Madam Crowl's Ghost and Other Tales of Mystery* (1923). Other notable collections include *In a Glass Darkly* (1872) and *The Purcell Papers* (1880).

"The Sexton's Adventure" first appeared in *Dublin University Magazine*. Published in January 1851, it formed part of "Ghost Stories of Chapelizod", a longer piece consisting of three haunting tales which run from one into the next, set in an area introduced as one of "the village outposts of Dublin". The setting of Chapelizod draws on Le Fanu's family's clerical connections: as a young boy he lived in the adjoining Phoenix Park when his father acted as Military Chaplain to the Royal Irish Artillery in the Hibernian Schools.

Those who remember Chapelizod a quarter of a century ago, or more, may possibly recollect the parish sexton. Bob Martin was held much in awe by truant boys who sauntered into the churchyard on Sundays, to read the tombstones, or play leap frog over them, or climb the ivy in search of bats or sparrows' nests, or peep into the mysterious aperture under the eastern window, which opened a dim perspective of descending steps losing themselves among profounder darkness, where lidless coffins gaped horribly among tattered velvet, bones, and dust, which time and mortality had strewn there. Of such horribly curious, and otherwise enterprising juveniles, Bob was, of course, the special scourge and terror. But terrible as was the official aspect of the sexton, and repugnant as his lank form, clothed in rusty, sable vesture, his small, frosty visage, suspicious grey eyes, and rusty, brown scratch-wig, might appear to all notions of genial frailty; it was yet true, that Bob Martin's severe morality sometimes nodded, and that Bacchus did not always solicit him in vain.

Bob had a curious mind, a memory well stored with "merry tales," and tales of terror. His profession familiarised him with graves and goblins, and his tastes with weddings, wassail, and sly frolics of all sorts. And as his personal recollections ran back nearly three score years into the perspective of the village history, his fund of local anecdote was copious, accurate, and edifying.

As his ecclesiastical revenues were by no means considerable, he was not unfrequently obliged, for the indulgence of his tastes, to arts which were, at the best, undignified.

He frequently invited himself when his entertainers had forgotten to do so; he dropped in accidentally upon small drinking parties of his acquaintance in public houses, and entertained them with stories, queer or terrible, from his inexhaustible reservoir, never scrupling to accept an acknowledgment in the shape of hot whiskey-punch, or whatever else was going.

There was at that time a certain atrabilious publican, called Philip Slaney, established in a shop nearly opposite the old turnpike. This man was not, when left to himself, immoderately given to drinking; but being naturally of a saturnine complexion, and his spirits constantly requiring a fillip, he acquired a prodigious liking for Bob Martin's company. The sexton's society, in fact, gradually became the solace of his existence, and he seemed to lose his constitutional melancholy in the fascination of his sly jokes and marvellous stories.

This intimacy did not redound to the prosperity or reputation of the convivial allies. Bob Martin drank a good deal more punch than was good for his health, or consistent with the character of an ecclesiastical functionary. Philip Slaney, too, was drawn into similar indulgences, for it was hard to resist the genial seductions of his gifted companion; and as he was obliged to pay for both, his purse was believed to have suffered even more than his head and liver.

Be this as it may, Bob Martin had the credit of having made a drunkard of "black Phil Slaney"—for by this cognomen was he distinguished; and Phil Slaney had also the reputation of having made the sexton, if possible, a "bigger bliggard" than ever. Under these circumstances, the accounts of the concern opposite the turnpike became somewhat entangled; and it came to pass one drowsy summer morning, the weather being at once sultry and cloudy, that Phil Slaney went into a small back parlour, where he kept his books, and which commanded, through its dirty window-panes, a full view of a dead wall, and having bolted the door, he took a loaded pistol, and clapping the muzzle in his mouth, blew the upper part of his skull through the ceiling.

This horrid catastrophe shocked Bob Martin extremely; and partly on this account, and partly because having been, on several late occasions, found at night in a state of abstraction, bordering on insensibility, upon the high road, he had been threatened with dismissal; and, as some said, partly also because of the difficulty of finding anybody to "treat" him as poor Phil Slaney used to do, he for a time forswore alcohol in all its combinations, and became an eminent example of temperance and sobriety.

Bob observed his good resolutions, greatly to the comfort of his wife, and the edification of the neighbourhood, with tolerable punctuality. He was seldom tipsy, and never drunk, and was greeted by the better part of society with all the honours of the prodigal son.

Now it happened, about a year after the grisly event we have mentioned, that the curate having received, by the post, due notice of a funeral to be consummated in the churchyard of Chapelizod, with certain instructions respecting the site of the grave, despatched a summons for Bob Martin, with a view to communicate to that functionary these official details.

It was a lowering autumn night: piles of lurid thunder-clouds, slowly rising from the earth, had loaded the sky with a solemn and boding canopy of storm. The growl of the distant thunder was heard afar off upon the dull, still air, and all nature seemed, as it were, hushed and cowering under the oppressive influence of the approaching tempest.

It was past nine o'clock when Bob, putting on his official coat of seedy black, prepared to attend his professional superior.

"Bobby, darlin'," said his wife, before she delivered the hat she held in her hand to his keeping, "sure you won't, Bobby, darlin'—you won't—you know what."

"I *don't* know what," he retorted, smartly, grasping at his hat.

"You won't be throwing up the little finger, Bobby, acushla?" she said, evading his grasp.

"Arrah, why would I, woman? there, give me my hat, will you?"

"But won't you promise me, Bobby darlin'—won't you, alanna?"

"Ay, ay, to be sure I will—why not?—there, give me my hat, and let me go."

"Ay, but you're not promisin', Bobby, mavourneen; you're not promisin' all the time."

"Well, divil carry me if I drink a drop till I come back again," said the sexton, angrily; "will that do you? And *now* will you give me my hat?"

"Here it is, darlin'," she said, "and God send you safe back."

And with this parting blessing she closed the door upon his retreating figure, for it was now quite dark, and resumed her knitting till his return, very much relieved; for she thought he had of late been oftener tipsy than was consistent with his thorough reformation, and feared the allurements of the half dozen "publics" which he had at that time to pass on his way to the other end of the town.

They were still open, and exhaled a delicious reek of whiskey, as Bob glided wistfully by them; but he stuck his hands in his pockets and looked the other way, whistling resolutely, and filling his mind with the image of the curate and anticipations of his coming fee. Thus he steered his morality safely through these rocks of offence, and reached the curate's lodging in safety.

He had, however, an unexpected sick call to attend, and was not at home, so that Bob Martin had to sit in the hall and amuse himself with the devil's tattoo until his return. This, unfortunately, was very long delayed, and it must have been fully twelve o'clock when Bob Martin set out upon his homeward way. By this time the storm had gathered to a pitchy darkness, the bellowing thunder was heard among the rocks and hollows of the Dublin mountains, and the pale, blue lightning shone upon the staring fronts of the houses.

By this time, too, every door was closed; but as Bob trudged homeward, his eye mechanically sought the public-house which had once belonged to Phil Slaney. A faint light was making its way through the shutters and the glass panes over the doorway, which made a sort of dull, foggy halo about the front of the house.

As Bob's eyes had become accustomed to the obscurity by this time, the light in question was quite sufficient to enable him to see a man in a sort of loose riding-coat seated upon a bench which, at that time, was fixed under the window of the house. He wore his hat very much over his eyes, and was smoking a long pipe. The outline of a glass and a quart bottle were also dimly traceable beside him; and a large horse saddled, but faintly discernible, was patiently awaiting his master's leisure.

There was something odd, no doubt, in the appearance of a traveller refreshing himself at such an hour in the open street; but the sexton accounted for it easily by supposing that, on the closing of the house for the night, he had taken what remained of his refection to the place where he was now discussing it al fresco.

At another time Bob might have saluted the stranger as he passed with a friendly "good night"; but, somehow, he was out of humour and in no genial mood, and was about passing without any courtesy of the sort, when the stranger, without taking the pipe from his mouth, raised the bottle, and with it beckoned him familiarly, while, with a sort of lurch of the head and shoulders, and at the same time shifting his seat to the end of the bench, he pantomimically invited him to share his seat and his cheer. There was a divine fragrance of whiskey about the spot, and Bob half relented; but he remembered his promise just as he began to waver, and said:

"No, I thank you, sir, I can't stop to-night."

The stranger beckoned with vehement welcome, and pointed to the vacant space on the seat beside him.

"I thank you for your polite offer," said Bob, "but it's what I'm too late as it is, and haven't time to spare, so I wish you a good night."

The traveller jingled the glass against the neck of the bottle, as if to intimate that he might at least swallow a dram without losing time. Bob was mentally quite of the same opinion; but, though his mouth watered, he remembered his promise, and shaking his head with incorruptible resolution, walked on.

The stranger, pipe in mouth, rose from his bench, the bottle in one hand, and the glass in the other, and followed at the sexton's heels, his dusky horse keeping close in his wake.

There was something suspicious and unaccountable in this importunity.

Bob quickened his pace, but the stranger followed close. The sexton began to feel queer, and turned about. His pursuer was behind, and still inviting him with impatient gestures to taste his liquor.

"I told you before," said Bob, who was both angry and frightened, "that I would not taste it, and that's enough. I don't want to have anything to say to you or your bottle; and in God's name," he added, more vehemently, observing that he was approaching still closer, "fall back and don't be tormenting me this way."

These words, as it seemed, incensed the stranger, for he shook the bottle with violent menace at Bob Martin; but, notwithstanding this gesture of defiance, he suffered the distance between them to increase. Bob, however, beheld him dogging him still in the distance, for his pipe shed a wonderful red glow, which duskily illuminated his entire figure like the lurid atmosphere of a meteor.

"I wish the devil had his own, my boy," muttered the excited sexton, "and I know well enough where you'd be."

The next time he looked over his shoulder, to his dismay he observed the importunate stranger as close as ever upon his track.

"Confound you," cried the man of skulls and shovels, almost beside himself with rage and horror, "what is it you want of me?"

The stranger appeared more confident, and kept wagging his head and extending both glass and bottle toward him as he drew near, and Bob Martin heard the horse snorting as it followed in the dark.

"Keep it to yourself, whatever it is, for there is neither grace nor luck about you," cried Bob Martin, freezing with terror; "leave me alone, will you."

And he fumbled in vain among the seething confusion of his ideas for a prayer or an exorcism. He quickened his pace almost to a run; he was now close to his own door, under the impending bank by the river side.

"Let me in, let me in, for God's sake; Molly, open the door," he cried, as he ran to the threshold, and leant his back against the plank. His pursuer confronted him upon the road; the pipe was no longer in his mouth, but the dusky red glow still lingered round him. He uttered some inarticulate cavernous sounds, which were wolfish and indescribable, while he seemed employed in pouring out a glass from the bottle.

The sexton kicked with all his force against the door, and cried at the same time with a despairing voice.

"In the name of God Almighty, once for all, leave me alone."

His pursuer furiously flung the contents of the bottle at Bob Martin; but instead of fluid it issued out in a stream of flame, which expanded and whirled round them, and for a moment they were both enveloped in a faint blaze; at the same instant a sudden gust whisked off the stranger's hat, and the sexton beheld that his skull was roofless. For an instant he beheld the gaping aperture, black and shattered, and then he fell senseless into his own doorway, which his affrighted wife had just unbarred.

I need hardly give my reader the key to this most intelligible and authentic narrative. The traveller was acknowledged by all to have been the spectre of the suicide, called up by the Evil One to tempt the convivial sexton into a violation of his promise, sealed, as it was, by an imprecation. Had he succeeded, no doubt the dusky steed, which Bob had seen saddled in attendance, was destined to have carried back a double burden to the place from whence he came.

As an attestation of the reality of this visitation, the old thorn tree which overhung the doorway was found in the morning to have been blasted with the infernal fires which had issued from the bottle, just as if a thunder-bolt had scorched it.

The moral of the above tale is upon the surface, apparent, and, so to speak, *self-acting*—a circumstance which happily obviates the necessity of our discussing it together. Taking our leave, therefore,

of honest Bob Martin, who now sleeps soundly in the same solemn
dormitory where, in his day, he made so many beds for others, I
come to a legend of the Royal Irish Artillery, whose headquarters
were for so long a time in the town of Chapelizod. I don't mean
to say that I cannot tell a great many more stories, equally authentic and marvellous, touching this old town; but as I may possibly
have to perform a like office for other localities, and as Anthony
Poplar is known, like Atropos, to carry a shears, wherewith to snip
across all "yarns" which exceed reasonable bounds, I consider it,
on the whole, safer to despatch the traditions of Chapelizod with
one tale more.

Let me, however, first give it a name; for an author can no more
despatch a tale without a title, than an apothecary can deliver his
physic without a label. We shall, therefore, call it—*

---

* In the original publication, this story's final line begins an invocation of
the title of the final story of "Ghost Stories of Chapelizod", "The Spectre
Lovers".

1855

THE PARSON'S OATH

Mrs Henry Wood

The daughter of a Worcester glove manufacturer, Ellen Price (1814–1887) chose to publish under her married name of Mrs Henry Wood. A prolific novelist who owned and edited *The Argosy* from 1867 to 1887, Ellen's writing career began with the publication of short stories written whilst living in France with her husband and young family. Many of these early tales appeared in *Colburn's New Monthly Magazine* and *Bentley's Miscellany*, periodicals then under the control of author William Harrison Ainsworth. Mrs Henry Wood's first novel, *Danesbury House* (1860), was published after the family's return to England. The text won first prize in a literary competition organised by the Scottish Temperance League, but the author was not widely recognised until the publication of *East Lynne* (1861), a bestselling sensation novel that sparked numerous stage adaptations.

Like Sheridan Le Fanu, Mrs Henry Wood is an author with Church connections: she was born into an Anglican family and her father, Thomas Price, was a favourite of Robert Carr, then Bishop of Worcester. First appearing in *Bentley's Miscellany* in January 1855, "The Parson's Oath" offers a conservative haunting in which the spectre seeks eternal salvation through a Christian interment.

The day was drawing towards its close, and the young charity-school children, assembled in the newly-repaired schoolroom of the small village of Littleford, glanced impatiently through the windows at the shadows cast by the declining sun, for none knew better, by those shadows, than they, that five o'clock was near.

"First class come up and spell," called out the governess, from behind her round table, by the window.

"There ain't no time, miss," replied one of the girls, with that easy familiarity, apt to subsist between scholar and teacher, in rustic schools. "It's a'most sleek on the stroke o' five."

The governess, a fair, pleasant-looking young woman, dressed in mourning, and far too ladylike in appearance for the paid mistress of a charity-school, glanced round at her hour-glass, and saw it wanted full ten minutes to the hour.

"There is time for a short lesson, children," she said. "Put aside your work, and come up."

The first class laid their sewing on the bench, and were ranging themselves round the governess's table, when a young lady, in a hat and riding-habit, followed by a groom, galloped past the windows, and reined in.

"Governess!" exclaimed a dozen voices, "here's Miss Rickhurst a coming in."

"Go on with your work, children: what do you mean by pressing to the window? Did you never see Miss Rickhurst before? Jane Hewgill, open the door."

"How d'ye do, Miss Winter?" said the young lady, carelessly nodding to the governess, as she entered. "How are you getting on? What class have you up now?"

"Spelling," replied Miss Winter. "Jane Hewgill, why don't you shut the door?"

"Cause here's Mr Lewis and his aunt a coming up," answered the child. "I'm a keeping it open for them."

Miss Rickhurst hastily rose from the governess's seat, which she had unceremoniously taken, and sprang to the door to meet the new comers.

It was the clergyman of the parish who entered, a meek, quiet man of thirty years. It is certain he was not ambitious, for he felt within him an everlasting debt of gratitude to the noble patron, who had stepped forward and presented him with this village living and its 150*l.* per annum. He had never looked for more than a curacy, and half the sum. His father, dead now, had been a curate before him, and he, the son, had gone to Oxford, as a servitor, had taken orders, and struggled on. And when the Earl of Littleford, who had silently been an eye-witness of the merits and unassuming piety of the poor young curate, presented him, unexpectedly, with the little village church on his estate, John Lewis raised his heart in thankfulness to the earl, who had thus, under God, put WANT away from him for his span of life.

Once inducted into the living, the Reverend John Lewis worked indefatigably. Amongst other good works, he re-established the girls' charity-school; an anciently-endowed foundation, which had fallen nearly into abeyance—like many other charities have, in the present day. The old mistress of it, Dame Fox, was eighty years of age and blind, so Lord Littleford and the clergyman superannuated her, and looked out for another; and whilst they were looking, Miss Winter, the daughter of Farmer Winter, who was just dead, went up to Littleford Hall and asked for it.

The whole village liked Regina Winter: though she had received an education, and, for five years of her life, enjoyed a home (with her dead mother's London relatives) far above what Littleford thought suitable for a working farmer's daughter. They likewise took numerous liberties with her name. Regina! it was one they could not become familiar with, so some called her Gina, many Ginny, and a few brought it out short "Gin." After her father's death, she found that scarcely any provision was left for her, and, as she one day sat musing upon what should be her course, the servant Nomy, a buxom woman of forty, who had taken care of the house since its mistress died, now ten years, suddenly spoke, and suggested that she should apply for the new place.

"What place?" asked Regina.

"The shoolmissis's," replied Nomy. "The earl and the parson are a wanting to find one, and they do say, in the village, it will be a matter of thirty pound a year. Surely you'd do, Miss Gina, with the grand edication you've had."

"Too much education for a village schoolmistress," thought Regina. "But it would keep me well, with what little I have besides."

"Go up to Littleford Hall, go right up yourself, Miss Gina, with your own two good legs," advised Nomy. "Nothing like applying to the fountain-head oneself, if business is to be done," added the shrewd woman.

"Apply to Lord Littleford myself!" ejaculated Regina.

"Why not? Ain't he as pleasant a mannered man as ever one would wish to come across? One day lately, not three weeks afore poor master died, the earl was a crossing our land a horseback, and he axed me to open the gate o' the turnip-field, and he kept on a cutting of his jokes wi' me all the time I was a doing of it."

The servant's advice was good, and proved so. Miss Winter made her own application to the Earl of Littleford, and she got the place. Though the earl demurred to her request at first, for her own sake, telling her she was superior to the situation, and that the remuneration was very small.

As the clergyman came into the school this afternoon, he shook hands with the squire's daughter: he then advanced and held out his hand to Miss Winter. Miss Rickhurst followed him with her eyes, and curled her lip: what business had their vicar, *their* associate, to be shaking hands with a charity governess?

"I was going to hear the class, Mr Lewis," said the young lady, after some minutes spent in talking. "Jane Hewgill, tell my servant he may go on with the horses: I shall walk home. Pray, Miss Winter, where did you say they were spelling? Three syllables! how very ridiculous! Cat cat, cow cow, that's quite enough learning for them."

"Do you think so?" returned Regina, in a cold tone, for she did *not* like these repeated interferences of Miss Rickhurst.

"Highly ridiculous," snapped Mrs Budd. "What can such girls want with spelling at all? If it were not for reading the Bible, I should say never teach 'em to read."

A very domineering widow was this aunt of the clergyman's. Upon his appointment to the vicarage, down she came and established herself in it, assuring him the house would never get on without somebody to manage it. He had a dim perception that he and his house would get on better without her, but he never said so, and she remained.

Miss Winter went to the mantelpiece, and turned her hour-glass. It was five o'clock, and the children flocked out of school. The vicar, Mrs Budd, and Miss Rickhurst followed.

"Mr Lewis," began the young lady, in a confidential tone, "don't you think your schoolmistress is getting above her business?"

"In what way?" he asked, looking surprised.

"There is such a tone of superiority about the young woman—I mean implied superiority," added Miss Rickhurst, correcting herself.

"I have always thought there is a tone, an air, of real superiority about her," replied the vicar. "But I have never known any one who, in their manners and conversation, gave one less the idea of *implying* it. And she gets the children on astonishingly: one might think, by their progress, she had taught them two years, instead of barely one."

"It is of no use to argue with John about Miss Winter," interposed Mrs Budd. "He thinks her an angel, and nothing less."

"No I do not," laughed the Reverend John. "I only think her very superior to young women in general;" and Miss Rickhurst once more curled her haughty lip.

Meanwhile, Miss Winter left the schoolroom, with Mary Brown, a sickly-looking girl of fifteen or sixteen, who was her assistant. Regina lodged at a farm-house near, occupying a parlour and bedroom, and was partially waited on by the people of the house. As soon as they got in, Mary Brown, whose weak health caused her to feel a constant thirst, began to set out the teacups and make the tea.

"Mary," observed Miss Winter, when the meal was over, "you had better go up to your brother's for the calico, and to-morrow set about making his shirts: you know he was scolding you yesterday at their not being begun. Start at once, or you will have it dusk. I will wash up the tea-things."

Mary Brown put on her things, and departed. But not long had she been gone, when the parlour door opened, and a tall, fine young man, about six-and-twenty, walked in. He was dressed in a green velveteen shooting-jacket, leather breeches and gaiters, and a green kerchief was twisted loosely round his neck. Altogether, there was a careless, untidy look about him. The face would have been handsome (and, indeed, was) but for the wilful, devil-may-care expression that pervaded it. His complexion was fair, his eyes were blue, and his light hair curled in his neck. This gentleman was Mr George Brown, universally known in the village by the cognomen of "Brassy." He had acquired the appellation when a boy, partly because he was gifted with a double share of that endowment familiarly called "brass," and partly because in his boyhood he displayed a curious propensity for collecting together odd bits of brazen metal. Once, when a young child, he had stolen a small brass kettle, exposed outside a shop for sale, lugged it home, and put it in his bed; and when his mother, on going to her own bed at night, looked at Georgie, there he was, sleeping, with the brass kettle hugged to him. He would be "Brassy Brown" to the end of his life, and nobody ever thought of calling him anything else.

Mr Brassy Brown did not enjoy a first-rate reputation. He had inherited a little land from his father, on which was a small house, where he lived, called "The Rill;" and though he certainly could not subsist upon its proceeds alone, and had no other visible means of support, he lived well, and never seemed to lack money. He was upon friendly terms with the whole neighbourhood, from Squire

Rickhurst down to the worst poacher in it: indeed, so intimate was he with the latter suspicious fraternity, that some said he must be a poacher himself. Until recently his sister had lived with him in his cottage, no one else; but when Miss Winter found she wanted some one to assist her in the school, she thought of Mary, compassionating the girl's lonely life, want of proper society, and weak health, and Mary came to live with her. It may be questioned, however, if Miss Winter would have made the proposal, had she foreseen that they should be inundated with visits from Brassy.

Miss Winter put down the book she was reading, when he came in, poured out some hot water, and began to wash up the tea-things.

"Where's Poll?" began Brassy.

"She is gone to the Rill for the calico," rejoined Regina. "What a pity that she will have her walk for nothing!"

"Stretch her legs for her," returned Brassy, sitting down in the chair from which Regina had risen, and extending his own long legs across the hearth. "Now, Regina," he continued, "I want a answer to that there question of mine."

"What question?" she inquired, a crimson hue flushing her face.

"Don't go for to pertend ignorance, Gin, for it won't go down with me to-night," was Mr Brassy Brown's rejoinder. "You know what I have been asking you this year past: we are by ourselves to-night, and I'll have it out. Will you come up to the Rill and make your home there, and be my wife?"

"Why do you persist in persecuting me thus?" exclaimed Regina, in a tone of vexation. "I have told you, already, that I could not be your wife. You behave like a child."

"Why don't you say like a fool?" rejoined Mr Brassy. "'Twould be as perlite as t'other. What fault have you got to find of the Rill—or of me? Perhaps you think I can't keep you there like a lady, but

I can. Never you mind how, *I can*. You shall have a servant to wait upon you, and everything as comfortable and plentiful about you as you had in your father's home. I swear it."

Regina shook her head. "I would not go to live at the Rill—I could not be your wife, Brassy, if you offered me a daily shower of gold. And if you continue to pursue this unpleasant subject, I shall send Mary home, and forbid your entrance here."

"So ho, my fine madam! it's defiance between us, is it?" uttered Brassy, rising and grasping Regina's arm in anger, "then may the devil take the weakest. I have *sworn* to marry you, and I'll keep my oath, by fair means or foul."

At this moment, after a gentle knock, the door was pushed open, disclosing the person of the vicar. He saw the angry look of Brassy Brown, and his hold upon Regina's arm.

"What is the matter?" he exclaimed. "What game are you after now, Master Brown?"

"None of yours, parson," returned Brassy, flinging aside Regina's arm. "She affronted me, and I had as good a mind to treat her to a shaking, as ever I had to treat anybody to one in all my life."

"He will kill me, some of these days, with his shakings," interposed Miss Winter, laughing, and trying to pass the matter off as a joke, for she was vexed and annoyed that the clergyman should have been a witness to it. "If he does, sir, I shall look to you to give me Christian burial. Will you promise to do so?"

"Yes," said Mr Lewis, falling into the joke.

"You had better swear to it, parson," added Brassy, with a sneer. "It may be more satisfactory to her."

"I swear it," returned John Lewis, giving no heed to his words, for he was thinking of other things. A flush rose to his brow when their purport came to him—he, a minister, swear!

"Mind you keep your oath, parson, as I'll keep mine," said Brassy Brown, swinging out of the room. "Do *you* hear, Miss Winter?"

"Regina," said the vicar, looking after him, "he is not a desirable visitor for you."

"No," she answered, "and I wish he would not come. Not that I think there is any real harm in him, but I dislike his conversation."

"The plain fact is," resumed the clergyman, speaking with agitation, as a hectic spot appeared on his cheek, "your situation is too unprotected. Regina! you must suffer me to provide you with another."

Oh, deeper than the one Brassy Brown's words had called up, was the rosy blush that now dyed her face. *Neither*, for some little time past, had been unacquainted with the heart of the other.

John Lewis took her hand. "Regina," he said, "you cannot be ignorant that I have loved you. Will you take pity upon a lonely man, one who has had but few ties hitherto to care for him, and be his wife?"

"But—I—" she stammered, her trembling hand lying passively in his, "it will be said I am not your equal—that my birth does not qualify me to be a clergyman's wife."

"Not my equal!" repeated the astonished vicar, who was surely one of the most unworldly wise. "You are so far my superior, Regina, that I have hesitated to ask you. And it was but the thought of your unprotected state here that gave me courage to speak now."

"I was but the daughter of a small working farmer," she persisted, the tears filling her eyes with the extent of her emotion: "I am but the paid teacher of a charity-school."

"*I* was but the son of a working curate," he whispered. "We were four children and my father and mother, all to subsist upon

70*l.* per year. I am indebted to charity, who helped to educate me, for being in the position I now am. A working farmer was immeasurably above *us*, Regina. We are both alone in the world: we have no ties or kindred to consult: from this time forth let us be all in all to each other."

The news travelled forth to the village, throwing up a fine hubbub in its wake, that the Reverend John Lewis was about to marry Regina Winter. Mrs Budd was pleased to be satirical over it, Miss Rickhurst was indignant, and Brassy Brown furious.

"What on earth possessed you to do it, John?" exclaimed Mrs Budd to her nephew, when he came into the vicarage at dinner-time, the day she first heard the tidings.

"Do what?" cried the Reverend John, with a conscious look, and that suspicious hectic rising to his cheek.

"You have been offering yourself and your name to the charity schoolmistress, they say," retorted the aunt, who feared the introduction of a wife might lead to her losing her snug home at the vicarage. "You must be out of your senses, John."

"We shall be able to find another governess for the school," answered John, evasively. "It is past one, aunt. Is not dinner ready?"

"Dinner! You'll get bread and cheese to-day for dinner, if you get anything," retorted Mrs Budd. "I and Betty have been too much upset this morning to think of cooking. Oh, John, you are a great fool! you might have had Miss Rickhurst."

"Miss Rickhurst!" exclaimed the vicar, opening his eyes at the assertion.

"Miss Rickhurst, yes," mimicked the lady, "if you had not been more blind, more simple, than anybody ever was yet."

"I don't want Miss Rickhurst," answered the young clergyman.

"Let her marry in her own sphere of life: she would have domineered me out of house and home."

These events happened in March. The vicar proposed being married in May, until which time Regina was to retain her place in the school. One day in April, as she was walking home from its duties, she suddenly came upon Brassy Brown, who was looking over the hedge.

"I have been a watching for you, Gina," he said, very quietly. "I want to hear, from your own lips, whether it's true that you have promised to marry that cursed parson?"

"Yes, it is true," she timidly answered, not seeing how she could deny to him what was public news.

"How come you to conceal it from me, all the time you were fooling me on?"

"*I* fooling you on!" uttered Regina, in surprise.

"Well—let that pass. Why did you not tell me you loved the black-coat?"

"I—could not tell you what I—did not know," stammered Regina, a blush dyeing her cheeks.

"Bosh! don't make lying excuses to me. I'd stake my Skye-terrier again his holding-forth sermon-book, that there has been love between you two this many a month past. What is it you have got in that paper parcel?"

This question made Regina's conscious blushes grow more conscious. How could she tell Brassy Brown it was new linen she was preparing against her own wedding?

"Oh, it's a secret, is it?" he went on, eyeing her covertly. "One would think it was a bird, got on the cross, that you were smuggling home for the parson's dinner. He'd enjoy it as well as not, I'll lay."

"It is only some work," said Regina. "Good morning, Brassy. Mary is gone home already. She will wonder where I am."

"Let her wonder. I say, Regina, you remember what I told you—that I'd took an oath. I'll keep it yet, and have you, sooner or later."

The words might have imparted to Miss Winter a sort of dread, but that Brassy Brown was smiling as he spoke them—and a pleasant smile was Mr Brassy's, with all his imperfections. Her spirits rose at seeing that smile, and she arrived at the conviction that he had overcome his preference for her. She was delighted. Setting these persecutions aside, and a few slips of language he was wont to indulge in, she did not dislike Brassy, and had never thought so ill of him as some were disposed to do.

"Won't you shake hands before you go?" asked Mr Brassy.

She held out her hand over the gap in the hedge. He shook it warmly, and away she went, silently thankful that all animosity between herself and Brassy Brown was over.

Nomy, Farmer Winter's old servant, had lately married the under-keeper of Squire Rickhurst, a widower, with some grown-up sons. They lived in a cottage, about half a mile beyond the Rill, following the high road. That same afternoon, on coming in from school, Regina told Mary she thought, as it was so fine, she should go and see Nomy. "Do you feel well enough to accompany me?" she asked.

"No," replied the girl, "my breathing is very oppressed to-day. I feel I could not get so far. Do you mind calling in at the Rill, Regina?"

"What for?"

"To get my cotton shawl. This is such a weight, now the spring weather's coming, I can hardly drag to school in it. If the door should be open, and Brassy not just in the way, you can get it yourself: it's lying on the middle shelf of the press in the keeping-room."

Regina started on her walk, and had nearly gained the Rill, when who should come swinging down the road, in front of her, but Brassy Brown.

"Hallo, Regina! where are you off to?"

"I am going to see Nomy. The afternoon is so fine, I quite longed for a walk. And I want something for Mary from your house, Brassy. Can you come back and give it me?"

"Oh, bother," was Mr Brassy Brown's rejoinder, "I have not got a minute to lose. Ted Timms is waiting for me down yonder in the gap; and he is such a shuffling cove, he'll make it an excuse to slink off, if I'm behind time. What is it you want?"

"Mary's cotton shawl. Her woollen one is too warm for this weather. Do you know, Brassy, Mary seems to me to get weaker."

"'Taint no fault o' mine if she does. Have the doctor to her. I'll pay."

"Can you bring the shawl down to-morrow?"

"I don't know as I can. If I get what I want from Ted Timms, I am going off for a few days. You can call in for it as you come back from Nomy's. I shall be at home."

"Very well," rejoined Regina.

Mr Brassy Brown went on his way, and Regina on hers. She found Nomy up to her eyes in work, brewing. She was delighted to see her young lady, and hastened to set out the best china for tea, in the little keeping-room, darting away every five minutes to her wort in the brew-house. Nomy had heard of Regina's new prospects, and, in talking of them, the time slipped away unheeded, Regina forgetting the hour, and Nomy her brewing. The former at length started up.

"I dare not leave the wort, Miss Gina," exclaimed the woman, as she attended Regina to the door. "To think that you should have come this very evening, of all others, when I can't see you back safe to the village."

"Oh, I shall soon be there," rejoined Regina, speaking valiantly. "The moon is shining; and I have to call in at the Rill for Mary's shawl, that will break the way. Good night, Nomy."

"The Lord be wi' ye, dear Miss Gina."

The evening grew late, and Mary Brown sat on, in Regina's lodgings, shivering and trembling. She was a nervous, timid girl, and feared to be alone at night, her imagination always running on some absurd ghost or vision story. Some thought that the nervous dread she experienced, when left so much alone at the Rill, had been the first cause of her failing health. Where could Regina be? Mary had expected her home by eight o'clock, and now it was nearly ten. The people of the house, who had been in bed long ago, slept in a remote part of it, and their presence there gave no courage or consolation to the timid girl. Mixed up with her own imaginary terrors, came fears for Regina's safety. What if a stray shot from some poacher should have struck her as she came by the copse? Suppose anything had happened to prevent Nomy walking home with her (and the reader has seen it did), she might be lying in the road wounded. The girl half resolved to go out and look for her: she *dared* not stay much longer alone where she was: yes, she would, she would go out and meet Regina.

Throwing on her bonnet and shawl, Mary tore along the passage as if a spectre were at her heels, and out at the house-door, taking the precaution to lock it after her. Once out, her superstitious fears were over: and robbers, poachers, any tangible cause of dread, brought no fear to the mind of Mary. Reared in the country, amidst the solitude of its woods and dales, she thought not there of fear, and could have walked about, in the open air, from night till morning. It was only in the silence of a midnight chamber that her ghost-terrors occurred to her.

She continued her way beyond the village, but could see no trace of Regina. She did not meet a soul. The early moon, drawing towards its setting, was often obscured by clouds, but the night was light. At length she came to her brother's house, and sprang forward to open the gate, hoping Brassy was at home.

What a curious thing! the gate was fastened! Never had Mary known that gate to be locked before. The key of it had hung up, untouched, on a nail in the kitchen, as long as she could remember. Brassy must be out.

But, as Mary leaned forward on the little gate, for she was tired with her walk, she detected a light glimmering through a chink in the shutter of the keeping-room. And, at the same moment she heard, or thought she heard, a movement in the garden, on the right side of the house. She shook the gate and called out.

Was it her fancy? Mary thought she saw a low, dark form creep from the middle of the garden towards the back-door: but the house cast it shade just there. "They are getting ready for a poaching expedition," she mentally concluded. "Perhaps Smith, or Timms, or some of them chaps are up here." She shook the gate again.

"Who the devil's that?" cried Mr Brassy Brown, poking his head, enveloped in a cotton nightcap, out at an upper window, his bedroom. "It's not you, is it, Timms?"

"Brassy, it's me," responded Mary. "The gate's locked."

"*You!*" echoed Brassy, in a tone of the most unqualified astonishment; "what the fiend brings you here, a knocking people up at this time o' night?"

"I am looking for Regina," answered Mary. "She went, after school, to see Nomy, and she has never come back. I got frightened, stopping there all alone, and frightened for her, so I came out to meet her."

"Why, what a confounded little stupid you must be," ejaculated Brassy, "to come out upon such a wildgoose-chase as this! While you have been blundering up here, she's no doubt gone home by the other road."

"She never takes that road," rejoined Mary, "it is such a round, and very lonely. I was afeard lest some stray shot might have took her, coming by Poachers' Copse. You remember the horse as was shot down, going by there?"

"There ain't no poachers out to-night, you simpleton—it's too light. Miss Regina's walked home with her black-coat: gone round the longest way to enjoy his company. I'm up to her. I see, by the moon, it's hardly half after ten: just the hour for sweethearting. What a frightened fool you be, Poll!"

"Do you really believe she has gone that way with him?" returned Mary, wonderfully relieved.

"I am not a going to stop prating with you any longer, that's what I believe," retorted Brassy. "Just take yourself off. And never you come waking me out o' my first sleep again, or you'll catch what you won't like."

"Brassy, there's a candle burning in the keeping-room."

"Who says so?"

"I can see light through the chink. Did you forget to put it out?"

"There was a log on the fire, half burnt, when I came to bed. I suppose it's flickering up again. So much the better: hope it will stop in till I get up in the morning. Come, be off."

"You could not come down and give me my cotton shawl?" asked the girl. "The walk tires me so much, I don't know when

I can get here again. It was the excitement that helped me on so quick to-night."

"Cotton shawl be burnt, and you with it!" roared Mr Brassy, wrathfully. "Do you think I'm a coming down, out o' my bed, for a cotton shawl?"

"Regina said she would call for it," answered the girl, in a deprecating tone. "Did she?"

"No, she didn't," replied Brassy. "I've not seen the colour on her, since I met her this afternoon. She couldn't call here, not she, if she went round, with her parson, t'other way."

"Good night, Brassy."

Mr Brassy Brown vouchsafed no reply, but banged-to his casement. Mary had got some paces from the gate, when she turned back, shook it, and called out. Once more the window was thrown open, with an impatient anathema, and the white cotton nightcap extended itself out, as before.

"Brassy," she said, lowering her voice, "I forgot to tell you I saw something in the garden. It seemed to be making its way to the back-door."

"Saw what?"

"I don't know. It looked like a great black dog, or else a man on all-fours."

"Don't you think it was a cat?" rejoined the gentleman, sarcastically.

"No," said the girl, shaking her head, "it was too big for a cat—if it was anything. I'm not sure about it, Brassy. It might only have been the shadows, or my fancy."

"It would be a good riddance if you and your fancies were buried with the shadows," answered the irascible Brassy. "You want to be shut up in a 'sylum for lunatics, I think. Get along home with ye."

Mary turned finally away, and walked home as fast as her troubled breathing would let her, fully expecting to find Regina and the Reverend Mr Lewis waiting at the door. What excuse could she make for her folly? She never could tell of her superstitious fears to the parson.

No one, however, was there. And the girl, all her fears renewed, sat down on the doorstep. She did not dare to enter, and take solitary possession of their chamber. A thousand surmises crowded to her mind. Could Nomy be ill, and Regina have stayed to nurse her? She had a desperate illness the previous autumn. But, then, the keeper, or one of his stalwart sons, would certainly have brought her word, when they got home from work. Could Regina have gone home with the parson, and be staying to sup with Mrs Budd? That was not likely, and, if she had, she would not stay so late as this. Or could she have sat down, on her homeward walk, to rest (poor Mary had a great idea of people being fatigued), and so dropped asleep? It will scarcely be believed that the poor girl sat on that doorstep till morning. She did: it was a fact well known afterwards to the village. Sometimes dozing, wandering in spirit, always shivering, the long night slipped away.

With the morning light and the awaking village, Mary's courage returned to her. She thought Regina had but stayed somewhere to sleep, and would soon be in, and explain. The first thing she did, upon entering, was to make a fire and put on the tea-kettle. By seven o'clock breakfast was ready, and after drinking one cup of tea, for she wanted it badly, she sat down and waited for Regina.

Regina never came. Before long, the whole village was aroused with the news of her disappearance, and nearly the whole village did something towards searching for her. Houses, forests, glens, lanes, for three days every spot was looked into, every exertion made to find her, but in vain. No person had seen her, so far as could be learnt, after she left the under-keeper's cottage that night. Nomy deposed that she watched her as far as the turning in the road (about forty yards only), walking at a brisk pace: and Mr Brassy Brown asserted that she never reached his house, or, at any rate, that she never entered it. He was sitting in his keeping-room, smoking, a good part of the evening, expecting Timms to drop in, and he neither saw nor heard her pass. Regina had told him, in the afternoon, that she should call for his sister's shawl, and he looked for it, and laid it out ready, but she did not come. When asked if her non-appearance struck him as singular: "Not a bit of it," he answered; "what was it to him? If he thought of it at all, it was that she had gone home the longest way, to steal a walk with the parson."

Amongst the universal perplexity, none were so much affected by this mysterious disappearance as Mr Lewis: for none had regarded Regina with feelings akin to his. He left not a stone unturned to find her. He turned about in his mind every probability and improbability that could bear upon the case: at rest or in action, in his daily duties and his midnight chamber, he was ever dwelling on it. A vague suspicion, he scarcely knew why, rose, like a cloud, in his mind, a suspicion of Brassy Brown. But what suspicion? The clergyman could not define it to himself. Mr Lewis thought he had heard of such things as young girls being stolen away, and married against their will: and it was known that Brassy Brown had long wanted to marry Regina. But Brassy could not have ventured at a feat of the sort, in this instance, because Mary found him in his own house soon after what must have been the hour of her disappearance, quietly sleeping in his own bed. The joking words of Regina occurred to him: "He will kill me, some of these days, with his shakings. If he does, sir, I shall look to you to give me Christian burial," and he remembered his rash promise, and shuddered. The fourth day after Regina's disappearance, Mr Lewis went again up to Brassy's. The latter was in his garden, planting cabbages. He came forward when he saw his visitor, invited him into the house, and set a chair.

"Mr Brown," began the clergyman, "I have come up once more to talk with you about this mysterious affair. Will you swear to me, before Heaven, that you have no idea what has become of Miss Winter?"

"Won't do anything of the sort," said Brassy, coolly. "I have had an idea from the first."

"How, what idea?" cried the clergyman, eagerly.

"I suspect as you took her off for a moonlight walk that night yourself, parson, and that, maybe, you have got her hid, against taking her for some more."

"This levity ill becomes you, Mr Brassy Brown."

"Levity!" uttered Brassy. "I don't mean it as levity. Who else is likely to have got hold of her, but you?—you had the best right to her."

"Did *you* get hold of her?" asked the clergyman, looking at him keenly.

"If I did get hold of her, I shouldn't be likely to have kept her," retorted the imperturbable Brassy. "Here was Nomy here, the next day, a sobbing her eyes out, and a looking all over my rooms and into my cupboards. When she had done, I asked her if she thought I had locked her up in one on 'em. My opinion is, parson, that you and Nomy and Mary is all a going cracked together over this matter. What do I know of Regina Winter—or want of her? Not so much as you."

"Where *can* she be?" bewailed the clergyman, in his perplexity. "On what mysterious spot of this fair earth can she be hidden? Is she dead or alive?"

"She's not in my pocket," returned Brassy, "and I'm sure you are welcome to search everything else that's mine. Because I may have got the character for having took a hare, or so, you must go, slap off-hand, and suspect I'd take a woman! The two ain't the same articles, parson."

Nothing more satisfactory could be got out of Brassy Brown, and the affair remained as unfathomable as at its first onset. A new mistress was procured for the school. Mary Brown, whose health was growing rapidly worse, returned home to the Rill to die. Brassy continued to pursue his free-and-easy sort of life; and the village, in time, ceased to think and speak of Regina. But there were two hearts in which she was never forgotten—that of poor, faithful Nomy, and of the Reverend John Lewis.

II

The Reverend John Lewis lay on his bed, in Littleford vicarage, tossing and turning from side to side. The cheek's hectic spot, of which many had predicted mischief, in the earlier part of his clerical career, had at length shone out in its true nature, and John Lewis was dying of decline. Seven years had elapsed since the now nearly-forgotten disappearance of Regina Winter, and he had been an ailing, fading man ever since.

The years had brought several changes to the village. Mrs Budd was dead, and Nomy, whose husband had been killed in an affray with poachers, was now the housekeeper and general servant at the vicarage. It had been a desperate conflict, this affray: two gamekeepers were shot dead, and others badly wounded. Several lawless characters were committed for trial, on suspicion of being concerned in it, one of whom was Mr Brassy Brown. But when the trial came on, at the assizes, the suspicions could not be converted into proofs, and the men were discharged. Brassy Brown felt, or affected, great indignation. They had treated him like a low, common poacher, he raved, instead of a gentleman, as he was, by descent, and he declared he would not stop amongst them. He was as good as his word: advertised his small estate for sale, pocketed the money, and took ship at Liverpool. Some thought he went to America, some to Australia (not then flocked after as it is now), and some to the coast of Africa; but Brassy himself never said where, and after his departure he was never more heard of.

The Reverend John Lewis lay on his bed, tossing and turning. His restlessness that night was not wholly the result of his feverish, sick state. He had just woke up from a disagreeable dream. He thought that Regina Winter came to him dressed in white, with a pale, sorrowful face, and gently reproached him with neglecting his oath, and suffering her to lie in unconsecrated ground. He thought he asked the question, Where are you lying? and she glided on before, telling him to come and see. He seemed, after they had gone some way, to lose sight of her, and to have halted, himself, on a spot of ground familiar to him. But just then he awoke, and, try as he would, was unable to recal the features of the place, which he had seemed, in his sleep, to know so well.

With this dream, all the old trouble came back again, the painful feelings, the yearning after Regina, which he had, in a degree, outgrown. He had long been very ill; for many months had daily looked for death; his hours were passed in great pain and weariness; yet death came not: and the somewhat visionary idea now rushed over his mind, was it that he *could not* die—that he was not permitted to die till he had fulfilled his oath to Regina, found, and buried her? No wonder, with these thoughts haunting him, that the vicar slept no more that night.

He retired to rest the next evening, thinking of his dream, wondering whether it would visit him again. Not precisely that, but one bearing upon it did. Could it have been but the sequence to his waking thoughts? He thought he stood upon a plot of ground, a green plot of ground, about two yards square, and all around was cultivated land. He appeared to know, beyond all doubt, that Regina was lying buried in this spot, and again all the features of the place seemed perfectly familiar to him, but when he awoke, they had, as on the previous night, faded from his recollection.

None can tell how the vicar longed, all throughout the ensuing day, for night to come. A conviction lay strong upon his mind that the real spot of Regina's resting-place would be revealed to him. He had not, during these two days, spoken to any one of these singular dreams; not even to Nomy, or to the young clergyman who had come to do his duty for him, and who was to him like a brother. The reader may be disposed to doubt that such dreams ever had place, but that they had, and that the murdered body was found in consequence, is an authenticated fact.

The third night came and passed, and with the first faint glimmering of morning light, Mr Lewis summoned his housekeeper, who dressed herself, and hastened to his room.

"Nomy!" he exclaimed, "I have a strange trouble upon my mind. I cannot rest."

"Dear master," she said, "what is it? I am sure trouble's bad for you."

"These last three nights I have been dreaming of Regina. I thought she came and pointed out to me where she was lying, and though I saw it, and stood upon it, though all around the spot was familiar in my dream, I cannot recal it when I awake. This last night it seemed the plainest, and the place where I stood I now know was a garden, for I saw the vegetables, not a ploughed or pasture field, as I had thought yesterday. And I don't know why, but Mary Brown seemed in some way to be mixed up with this last dream."

"You had better call to mind all the places where you have ever seen Mary Brown, master, or where she ever was, to your knowledge, with Miss Regina," whispered the woman, after serious thought. "It may afford some clue, maybe."

The vicar lay back on his bed, remaining silent, his hand shading his eyes, as if he would shut out outward things. The woman stood watching him.

"Where is there a privet-hedge, Nomy?" he said, after a while, without removing his hand—"a privet-hedge, and potatoes planted under it, with a path running across to it?"

"A privet-hedge and potatoes growing by it," uttered Nomy: "there's many such in this neighbourhood, master."

"The kidney-beans lie in this way," he added, making a movement with the unoccupied hand, "and the peas—they are just coming up—are lower down. The cabbages are close under foot— Oh, Nomy!" he cried out, with a positive shriek, "I recollect—I see it all."

The servant drew nearer to the bed, and grasped hold of the counterpane. A nameless terror was stealing over her.

"It is Brassy Brown's garden," gasped the invalid; "I see every part of it, as I used when I went to read to Mary, in her illness. The green spot—but the green was only in my dream—is on the right of the narrow path leading to the back-door, along the side of the house. Cabbages were growing on it the spring I used to go to Mary. I saw Brassy transplanting them there, the very day I went to ask news of Regina. I believe solemnly," uttered the clergyman, with emphasis, "as truly as that we must all one day come to the same earth, that Regina lies there. Call Mr Hampton."

The young curate was summoned out of his sleep, and came. Mr Lewis related his extraordinary dreams to him, and his sacred conviction that, in this particular spot, the remains would be found. Before midday, not less than twenty inhabitants of Littleford had listened to these dreams, from the vicar's own lips.

He could not go himself, he was too weak to get there, and to risk the agitation it would entail, but he took a piece of paper, and drew a plan of Brassy Brown's garden, minutely marking the precise spot where he believed the body would be found. A company—such a company!—armed with spades, pickaxes, and shovels, and headed by Squire Rickhurst and the Reverend Mr Hampton, flocked to the Rill in the afternoon: the new owner of the place willingly granting them leave to turn up his garden.

It was in spring, just about the time of year she had disappeared, and the spot was now planted with broccoli. They rooted them up, and dug and dug, and a few feet below the surface, they came upon the mouldering remains of Regina Winter. Dressed as she had been dressed that evening: a black dress, a black and white plaid shawl, a white lace collar, and a straw bonnet, trimmed with black. The bonnet and shawl were torn and tumbled, as if in a struggle, and lay upon her.

A coroner's inquest was held, and the cause of death proved at it. She had been shot in the left breast, in, or close to, the heart.

The verdict was "Wilful Murder against George Brown;" though some of the jury were for bringing it in "Manslaughter," believing it might have been the result of an accident. Brassy always kept loaded guns about his house.

Then came a contention: between the vicar and Nomy, between the vicar and his curate, between the vicar and the squire: he insisting upon officiating at her burial, and they saying he was not fit to do it. But on the afternoon appointed for the service, the vicar struggled up out of his bed, and dressed himself. "I took a rash oath, during her life, that I would give her Christian burial," he answered to their remonstrances, "and I must fulfil it."

There was scarcely moving room in the churchyard: all Littleford, and its neighbourhood for some miles round, flocked thither to witness that singular interment. The remains of the once happy girl, about whose ill fate there could now be no doubt, whatever may have been its mysterious details, brought, after the lapse of seven years, to their home in consecrated ground; and the weakened frame, the wan, attenuated face of him who stood there, in his white surplice, reading over her! Many who witnessed that funeral are dead, but, of those who remain, not one has forgotten the scene, or ever will.

With the last word of the burial service, the Reverend John Lewis's strength, so artificially buoyed up with excitement, deserted him, and it was feared he could not walk back to the vicarage, short as the distance was. Leaning on Squire Rickhurst, on one side, and on Mr Hampton, on the other, he at length gained it. Before he had well reposed an instant on the sofa, preparatory to being taken back to his bed, Ted Timms, the man who had been the intimate associate of Brassy Brown, put his head into the room, and asked to speak with the vicar alone.

"Be quick in what you have to say, Timms," panted the vicar, "for I am very ill."

"I thought it my duty to come in and make a clean breast of it, sir," began the man. "I have been away from Littleford, till to-day, since the body were found, or I should have been here afore. I think I hold the clue to this murder."

"Speak up," breathed the vicar. "My hearing is growing dull."

"The night afore Brassy Brown went away for good, the very night afore it, we was a drinking together at my place, and Brassy got a drop too much, which is what he didn't often do. We got a talking about a many things; a bragging what feats, for good or for bad, we had done in our career; a boasting, as it were, one again the t'other. Brassy at last hiccuped out that he had, one night, decoyed a girl into his house at the Rill, and ill-used her; and afterwards, when he swore he'd marry her, she burst out with such a flood of despair and scorn and loathing, that it drove him mad, and he put a bullet through her. I didn't pay much attention to him then, setting it down to the boastings of a man in his cups; but, sir, I now think it were nothing but the truth, and that he spoke of Miss Ginna. He must have killed her, and buried her in his garden that same night. If you remember, sir, Mary Brown told folks she was frightened by fancying she saw something black a creeping from that spot into the house, while she was a shaking at the gate. It must have been Brassy a digging the grave then."

"Make ready with the sacrament," murmured John Lewis to Mr Hampton, as he feebly resisted their wishes to carry him upstairs, after the departure of Timms; "I feel my time here is growing short."

Sure enough that night he died. It indeed would seem as if he had only been permitted to linger on earth for the purpose of burying Regina Winter.

THE POOR CLARE

Elizabeth Gaskell

Elizabeth Gaskell (1810–1865), a celebrated author who spent much of her life in the North of England, was mourned by the *Manchester Guardian* as one whose "death leaves a blank that will not easily be filled". An established writer in her own right, Gaskell enjoyed friendships with a range of celebrated authors including Charles Kingsley, John Ruskin and Charles Dickens, in whose periodicals she published a series of short stories. Gaskell was also a close associate of Charlotte Brontë, writing her friend's posthumous biography, *The Life of Charlotte Brontë* (1857) at the request of Brontë's father.

In 1832, Elizabeth (née Stevenson) married William, a Unitarian Minister. She soon became involved in the daily missions of her husband's Church, teaching in the Sunday School at Cross Street Chapel and visiting the poorer communities in local Manchester areas. Desire to bring attention to the plight of those she met led to the anonymous publication of *Mary Barton* (1848), an industrial novel that sets out the social problems faced by mid-century mill workers. The novel brought Gaskell to the attention of Charles Dickens, for whom she then wrote numerous stories.

"The Poor Clare" was first published in three instalments in Charles Dickens's *Household Words*. It is a tale which both presents the repercussions of sin and interrogates the notion of Christian service as a means of salvation for those who have wronged. Gaskell's sympathetic presentation of the sisters of the Order of Saint Clare is notable given the publication of the story at a time when the Roman Catholic church was decried by many members of the Anglican faith.

CHAPTER I

December 12th, 1747.—My life has been strangely bound up with extraordinary incidents, some of which occurred before I had any connection with the principal actors in them, or indeed, before I even knew of their existence. I suppose, most old men are, like me, more given to looking back upon their own career with a kind of fond interest and affectionate remembrance, than to watching the events—though these may have far more interest for the multitude—immediately passing before their eyes. If this should be the case with the generality of old people, how much more so with me!... If I am to enter upon that strange story connected with poor Lucy, I must begin a long way back. I myself only came to the knowledge of her family history after I knew her; but, to make the tale clear to any one else, I must arrange events in the order in which they occurred—not that in which I became acquainted with them.

There is a great old hall in the north-east of Lancashire, in a part they called the Trough of Bolland, adjoining that other district named Craven. Starkey Manor-house is rather like a number of rooms clustered round a grey, massive, old keep than a regularly-built hall. Indeed, I suppose that the house only consisted of a great tower in the centre, in the days when the Scots made their raids terrible as far south as this; and that after the Stuarts came in, and there was a little more security of property in those parts, the Starkeys of that time added the lower building, which runs, two stories high, all round the base of the keep. There has been a grand garden laid out in my days, on the southern slope near the house; but when I first knew the place, the kitchen-garden at the farm was the only piece of cultivated ground belonging to it. The deer used to come within sight of the drawing-room windows, and might have browsed quite close up to the house if they had not been too wild and shy. Starkey Manor-house itself stood on a projection or peninsula of high land, jutting out from the abrupt hills that form the sides of the Trough of Bolland. These hills were rocky and bleak enough towards their summit; lower down they were clothed with tangled copsewood and green depths of fern, out of which a grey giant of an ancient forest-tree would tower here and there, throwing up its ghastly white branches, as if in imprecation, to the sky. These trees, they told me, were the remnants of that forest which existed in the days of the Heptarchy, and were even then noted as landmarks. No wonder that their upper and more exposed branches were leafless, and that the dead bark had peeled away, from sapless old age.

Not far from the house there were a few cottages, apparently of the same date as the keep; probably built for some retainers of the family, who sought shelter—they and their families and their small flocks and herds—at the hands of their feudal lord. Some of them had pretty much fallen to decay. They were built in a strange fashion. Strong beams had been sunk firm in the ground at the requisite distance, and their other ends had been fastened together, two and two, so as to form the shape of one of those rounded waggon-headed gipsy-tents, only very much larger. The spaces between were filled with mud, stones, osiers, rubbish, mortar—anything to keep out the weather. The fires were made in the centre of these rude dwellings, a hole in the roof forming the only chimney. No Highland hut or Irish cabin could be of rougher construction.

The owner of this property, at the beginning of the present century, was a Mr Patrick Byrne Starkey. His family had kept to the old faith, and were staunch Roman Catholics, esteeming it even a sin to marry any one of Protestant descent, however willing he or she might have been to embrace the Romish religion. Mr Patrick Starkey's father had been a follower of James the Second; and, during the disastrous Irish campaign of that monarch he had fallen in love with an Irish beauty, a Miss Byrne, as zealous for her religion and for the Stuarts as himself. He had returned to Ireland after his escape to France, and married her, bearing her back to the court at St Germains. But some licence on the part of the disorderly gentlemen who surrounded King James in his exile, had insulted his beautiful wife, and disgusted him; so he removed from St Germains to Antwerp, whence, in a few years' time, he quietly returned to Starkey Manor-house—some of his Lancashire neighbours having lent their good offices to reconcile him to the powers that were. He was as firm a Catholic as ever, and as staunch an advocate for the Stuarts and the divine rights of kings; but his religion almost amounted to asceticism, and the conduct of those with whom he had been brought in such close contact at St Germains would little bear the inspection of a stern moralist. So he gave his allegiance where he could not give his esteem, and learned to respect sincerely the upright and moral character of one whom he yet regarded as an usurper. King William's government had little need to fear such a one. So he returned, as I have said, with a sobered heart and impoverished fortunes, to his ancestral house, which had fallen sadly to ruin while the owner had been a courtier, a soldier and an exile. The roads into the Trough of Bolland were little more than cart-ruts; indeed, the way up to the house lay along a ploughed field before you came to the deer-park. Madam, as the country-folk used to call Mrs Starkey, rode on a pillion behind her husband, holding on to him with a light hand by his leather riding-belt. Little master (he that was afterwards Squire Patrick Byrne Starkey) was held on to his pony by a serving-man. A woman past middle age walked, with a firm and strong step, by the cart that held much of the baggage; and high up on the mails and boxes, sat a girl of dazzling beauty perched lightly on the topmost trunk, and swaying herself fearlessly to and fro, as the cart rocked and shook in the heavy roads of late autumn. The girl wore the Antwerp faille, or black Spanish mantle over her head, and altogether her appearance was such that the old cottager, who described the procession to me many years after, said that all the country-folk took her for a foreigner. Some dogs, and the boy who held them in charge, made up the company. They rode silently along, looking with grave, serious eyes at the people, who came out of the scattered cottages to bow or curtsy to the real Squire, "come back at last", and gazed after the little procession with gaping wonder, not deadened by the sound of the foreign language in which the few necessary words that passed among them were spoken. One lad, called from his staring by the Squire to come and help about the cart, accompanied them to the Manor-house. He said that when the lady had descended from her pillion, the middle-aged woman whom I have described as walking while the others rode, stepped quickly forward, and taking Madam Starkey (who was of a slight and delicate figure) in her arms, she lifted her over the threshold, and set her down in her husband's house, at the same time uttering a passionate and outlandish blessing. The

Squire stood by, smiling gravely at first; but when the words of blessing were pronounced, he took off his fine feathered hat, and bent his head. The girl with the black mantle stepped onward into the shadow of the dark hall, and kissed the lady's hand; and that was all the lad could tell to the group that gathered round him on his return, eager to hear everything, and to know how much the Squire had given him for his services.

From all I could gather, the Manor-house, at the time of the Squire's return, was in the most dilapidated state. The stout grey walls remained firm and entire; but the inner chambers had been used for all kinds of purposes. The great withdrawing-room had been a barn; the state tapestry-chamber had held wool, and so on. But, by-and-by, they were cleared out; and if the Squire had no money to spend on new furniture, he and his wife had the knack of making the best of the old. He was no despicable joiner; she had a kind of grace in whatever she did, and imparted an air of elegant picturesqueness to whatever she touched. Besides, they had brought many rare things from the Continent; perhaps I should rather say, things that were rare in that part of England—carvings, and crosses, and beautiful pictures. And then, again, wood was plentiful in the Trough of Bolland, and great log-fires danced and glittered in all the dark, old rooms, and gave a look of home and comfort to everything.

Why do I tell you all this? I have little to do with the Squire and Madam Starkey; and yet I dwell upon them, as if I were unwilling to come to the real people with whom my life was so strangely mixed up. Madam had been nursed in Ireland by the very woman who lifted her in her arms, and welcomed her to her husband's home in Lancashire. Excepting for the short period of her own married life, Bridget Fitzgerald had never left her nursling. Her marriage—to one above her in rank—had been unhappy. Her husband had died, and left her in even greater poverty than that in which she was when he had first met with her. She had one child, the beautiful daughter who came riding on the waggon-load of furniture that was brought to the Manor-house. Madam Starkey had taken her again into her service when she became a widow. She and her daughter had followed "the mistress" in all her fortunes; they had lived at St Germains and at Antwerp, and were now come to her home in Lancashire. As soon as Bridget had arrived there, the Squire gave her a cottage of her own, and took more pains in furnishing it for her than he did in anything else out of his own house. It was only nominally her residence. She was constantly up at the great house; indeed, it was but a short cut across the woods from her own home to the home of her nursling. Her daughter Mary, in like manner, moved from one house to the other at her own will. Madam loved both mother and child dearly. They had great influence over her, and, through her, over her husband. Whatever Bridget or Mary willed was sure to come to pass. They were not disliked; for, though wild and passionate, they were also generous by nature. But the other servants were afraid of them, as being in secret the ruling spirits of the household. The Squire had lost his interest in all secular things; Madam was gentle, affectionate and yielding. Both husband and wife were tenderly attached to each other and to their boy; but they grew more and more to shun the trouble of decision on any point; and hence it was that Bridget could exert such despotic power. But if everyone else yielded to her "magic of a superior mind", her daughter not unfrequently rebelled. She and her mother were too much alike to agree. There were wild quarrels between them, and wilder reconciliations. There were times when, in the heat of passion, they could have stabbed each other. At all other times they both—Bridget especially—would have willingly laid down their lives for one another. Bridget's love for her child lay very deep—deeper than that daughter ever knew; or I should think she would never have wearied of home as she did, and prayed her mistress to obtain for her some situation—as waiting-maid—beyond the seas, in that more cheerful continental life, among the scenes of which so many of her happiest years had been spent. She thought, as youth thinks, that life would last for ever, and that two or three years were but a small portion of it to pass away from her mother, whose only child she was. Bridget thought differently, but was too proud ever to show what she felt. If her child wished to leave her, why—she should go. But people said Bridget became ten years older in the course of two months at this time. She took it that Mary wanted to leave her. The truth was, that Mary wanted for a time to leave the place, and to seek some change, and would thankfully have taken her mother with her. Indeed when Madam Starkey had gotten her a situation, with some grand lady abroad, and the time drew near for her to go, it was Mary who clung to her mother with passionate embrace, and, with floods of tears, declared that she would never leave her; and it was Bridget, who at last loosened her arms, and, grave and tear-less herself, bade her keep her word, and go forth into the wide world. Sobbing aloud, and looking back continually, Mary went away. Bridget was still as death, scarcely drawing her breath, or closing her stony eyes; till at last she turned back into her cottage, and heaved a ponderous old settle against the door. There she sat, motionless, over the grey ashes of her extinguished fire, deaf to Madam's sweet voice, as she begged leave to enter and comfort her nurse. Deaf, stony and motionless, she sat for more than twenty hours; till, for the third time, Madam came across the snowy path from the great house, carrying with her a young spaniel, which had been Mary's pet up at the hall; and which had not ceased all night long to seek for its absent mistress, and to whine and moan after her. With tears Madam told this story, through the closed door—tears excited by the terrible look of anguish, so steady, so immovable—so the same to-day as it was yesterday—on her nurse's face. The little creature in her arms began to utter its piteous cry, as it shivered with the cold. Bridget stirred; she moved—she listened. Again that long whine; she thought it was for her daughter; and what she had denied to her nursling and mistress she granted to the dumb creature that Mary had cherished. She opened the door, and took the dog from Madam's arms. Then Madam came in, and kissed and comforted the old woman, who took but little notice of her or anything. And sending up Master Patrick to the hall for fire and food, the sweet young lady never left her nurse all that night. Next day, the Squire himself came down, carrying a beautiful foreign picture—Our Lady of the Holy Heart, the Papists call it. It is a picture of the Virgin, her heart pierced with arrows, each arrow representing one of her great woes. That picture hung in Bridget's cottage when I first saw her; I have that picture now.

Years went on. Mary was still abroad. Bridget was still and stern, instead of active and passionate. The little dog, Mignon, was indeed her darling. I have heard that she talked to it continually; although, to most people, she was so silent. The Squire and Madam treated her with the greatest consideration, and well they might; for to them she was as devoted and faithful as ever. Mary wrote pretty often, and seemed satisfied with her life. But at length the letters ceased—I hardly know whether before or after a great and terrible sorrow came upon the house of the Starkeys. The Squire sickened of a putrid fever; and Madam caught it in nursing him, and died. You may be sure, Bridget let no other woman tend her but herself; and in the very arms that had received her at her birth, that sweet young woman laid her head down, and gave up her breath. The Squire recovered, in a fashion. He was never strong—he had never the heart to smile again. He fasted and prayed more than ever; and people did say that he tried to cut off the entail, and leave all the property away to found a monastery abroad, of which he prayed that some day little Squire Patrick might be the reverend father. But he could not do this, for the strictness of the entail and the laws against the Papists. So he could only appoint gentlemen of his own faith as guardians to his son, with many charges about the lad's soul, and a few about the land, and the way it was to be held while he was a minor. Of course, Bridget was not forgotten. He sent for her as he lay on his death-bed, and asked her if she would rather have a sum down, or have a small annuity settled upon her. She said at once she would have a sum down; for she thought of her daughter, and how she could bequeath the money to her, whereas an annuity would have died with her. So the Squire left her her cottage for life, and a fair sum of money. And then he died, with as ready and willing a heart as, I suppose, ever any gentleman took out of this world with him. The young Squire was carried off by his guardians, and Bridget was left alone.

I have said that she had not heard from Mary for some time. In her last letter, she had told of travelling about with her mistress, who was the English wife of some great foreign officer, and had spoken of her chances of making a good marriage, without naming the gentleman's name, keeping it rather back as a pleasant surprise to her mother; his station and fortune being, as I had afterwards reason to know, far superior to anything she had a right to expect. Then came a long silence; and Madam was dead, and the Squire was dead; and Bridget's heart was gnawed by anxiety, and she knew not whom to ask for news of her child. She could not write, and the Squire had managed her communication with her daughter. She walked off to Hurst; and got a good priest there—one whom she had known at Antwerp—to write for her. But no answer came. It was like crying into the awful stillness of night.

One day, Bridget was missed by those neighbours who had been accustomed to mark her goings-out and comings-in. She had never been sociable with any of them; but the sight of her had become a part of their daily lives, and slow wonder arose in their minds, as morning after morning came, and her house-door remained closed, her window dead from any glitter, or light of fire within. At length some one tried the door; it was locked. Two or three laid their heads together, before daring to look in through the blank unshuttered window. But, at last, they summoned up courage; and then saw that Bridget's absence from their little world was not the result of accident or death, but of premeditation. Such small articles of furniture as could be secured from the effects of time and damp by being packed up, were stowed away in boxes. The picture of the Madonna was taken down, and gone. In a word, Bridget had stolen away from her home, and left no trace whither she was departed. I knew afterwards, that she and her little dog had wandered off on the long search for her lost daughter. She was too illiterate to have faith in letters, even had she had the means of writing and sending many. But she had faith in her own strong love, and believed that her passionate instinct would guide her to her child. Besides, foreign travel was no new thing to her, and she could speak enough of French to explain the object of her journey, and had, moreover, the advantage of being, from her faith, a welcome object of charitable hospitality at many a distant convent. But the country people round Starkey Manor-house knew nothing of all this. They wondered what had become of her, in a torpid, lazy fashion, and then left off thinking of her altogether. Several years passed. Both Manor-house and cottage were deserted. The young Squire lived far away under the direction of his guardians. There were inroads of wool and corn into the sitting-rooms of the Hall; and there was some low talk, from time to time, among the hinds and country people whether it would not be as well to break into old Bridget's cottage, and save such of her goods as were left from the moth and rust which must be making sad havoc. But this idea was always quenched by the recollection of her strong character and passionate anger; and tales of her masterful spirit, and vehement force of will, were whispered about, till the very thought of offending her, by touching any article of hers, became invested with a kind of horror: it was believed that, dead or alive, she would not fail to avenge it.

Suddenly she came home; with as little noise or note of preparation as she had departed. One day some one noticed a thin, blue curl of smoke ascending from her chimney. Her door stood open to the noonday sun; and, ere many hours had elapsed, some one had seen an old travel-and-sorrow-stained woman dipping her pitcher in the well; and said, that the dark, solemn eyes that looked up at him were more like Bridget Fitzgerald's than any one else's in this world; and yet, if it were she, she looked as if she had been scorched in the flames of hell, so brown, and scared, and fierce a creature did she seem. By-and-by many saw her; and those who met her eye once cared not to be caught looking at her again. She had got into the habit of perpetually talking to herself; nay, more, answering herself, and varying her tones according to the side she took at the moment. It was no wonder that those who dared to listen outside her door at night, believed that she held converse with some spirit; in short, she was unconsciously earning for herself the dreadful reputation of a witch.

Her little dog, which had wandered half over the Continent with her, was her only companion; a dumb remembrancer of happier days. Once he was ill; and she carried him more than three miles, to ask about his management from one who had been groom to the last Squire, and had then been noted for his skill in all diseases of animals. Whatever this man did, the dog recovered; and they who heard her thanks, intermingled with blessings (that were rather promises of good fortune than prayers), looked grave at his good luck when, next year, his ewes twinned, and his meadow-grass was heavy and thick.

Now it so happened that, about the year seventeen hundred and eleven, one of the guardians of the young Squire, a certain Sir Philip Tempest, bethought him of the good shooting there must be on his ward's property; and in consequence he brought down four or five gentlemen, of his friends, to stay for a week or two at the Hall. From all accounts, they roystered and spent pretty freely. I never heard any of their names but one, and that was Squire Gisborne's. He was hardly a middle-aged man then; he had been much abroad, and there, I believe, he had known Sir Philip Tempest, and done him some service. He was a daring and dissolute fellow in those days: careless and fearless, and one who would rather be in a quarrel than out of it. He had his fits of ill-temper besides, when he would spare neither man nor beast. Otherwise, those who knew him well, used to say he had a good heart, when he was neither drunk, nor angry, nor in any way vexed. He had altered much when I came to know him.

One day, the gentlemen had all been out shooting, and with but little success, I believe; anyhow, Mr Gisborne had none, and was in a black humour accordingly. He was coming home, having his gun loaded, sportsman-like, when little Mignon crossed his path, just as he turned out of the wood by Bridget's cottage. Partly for wantonness, partly to vent his spleen upon some living creature, Mr Gisborne took his gun, and fired—he had better have never fired gun again, than aimed that unlucky shot, he hit Mignon, and at the creature's sudden cry, Bridget came out, and saw at a glance what had been done. She took Mignon up in her arms, and looked hard at the wound; the poor dog looked at her with his glazing eyes, and tried to wag his tail and lick her hand, all covered with blood. Mr Gisborne spoke in a kind of sullen penitence:

"You should have kept the dog out of my way—a little poaching varmint."

At this very moment, Mignon stretched out his legs, and stiffened in her arms—her lost Mary's dog, who had wandered and sorrowed with her for years. She walked right into Mr Gisborne's path, and fixed his unwilling, sullen look, with her dark and terrible eye.

"Those never throve that did me harm," said she. "I'm alone in the world, and helpless; the more do the saints in heaven hear my prayers. Hear me, ye blessed ones! hear me while I ask for sorrow on this bad, cruel man. He has killed the only creature that loved me—the dumb beast that I loved. Bring down heavy sorrow on his head for it, O ye saints! He thought that I was helpless, because he saw me lonely and poor; but are not the armies of heaven for the like of me?"

"Come, come," said he, half remorseful, but not one whit afraid. "Here's a crown to buy thee another dog. Take it, and leave off cursing! I care none for thy threats."

"Don't you?" said she, coming a step closer, and changing her imprecatory cry for a whisper which made the gamekeeper's lad, following Mr Gisborne, creep all over. "You shall live to see the creature you love best, and who alone loves you—ay, a human creature, but as innocent and fond as my poor, dead darling— you shall see this creature, for whom death would be too happy, become a terror and a loathing to all, for this blood's sake. Hear me, O holy saints, who never fail them that have no other help!"

She threw up her right hand, filled with poor Mignon's life-drops; they spurted, one or two of them, on his shooting-dress,— an ominous sight to the follower. But the master only laughed a little, forced, scornful laugh, and went on to the Hall. Before he got there, however, he took out a gold piece, and bade the boy carry it to the old woman on his return to the village. The lad was "afeared", as he told me in after years; he came to the cottage, and hovered about, not daring to enter. He peeped through the window at last; and by the flickering wood-flame, he saw Bridget kneeling before the picture of Our Lady of the Holy Heart, with dead Mignon lying between her and the Madonna. She was pray-ing wildly, as her outstretched arms betokened. The lad shrunk away in redoubled terror; and contented himself with slipping the gold-piece under the ill-fitting door. The next day it was thrown out upon the midden; and there it lay, no one daring to touch it.

Meanwhile Mr Gisborne, half curious, half uneasy, thought to lessen his uncomfortable feelings by asking Sir Philip who Bridget was? He could only describe her—he did not know her name. Sir Philip was equally at a loss. But an old servant of the Starkeys, who had resumed his livery at the Hall on this occasion—a scoundrel whom Bridget had saved from dismissal more than once during her palmy days—said:—

"It will be the old witch, that his worship means. She needs a ducking, if ever a woman did, does that Bridget Fitzgerald."

"Fitzgerald!" said both the gentlemen at once. But Sir Philip was the first to continue:—

"I must have no talk of ducking her, Dickon. Why, she must be the very woman poor Starkey bade me have a care of; but when I came here last she was gone, no one knew where. I'll go and see her to-morrow. But mind you, sirrah, if any harm comes to her, or any more talk of her being a witch—I've a pack of hounds at home, who can follow the scent of a lying knave as well as ever they followed a dog-fox; so take care how you talk about ducking a faithful old servant of your dead master's."

"Had she ever a daughter?" asked Mr Gisborne, after a while.

"I don't know—yes! I've a notion she had; a kind of waiting woman to Madam Starkey."

"Please your worship," said humbled Dickon, "Mistress Bridget had a daughter—one Mistress Mary—who went abroad, and has never been heard on since; and folk do say that has crazed her mother."

Mr Gisborne shaded his eyes with his hand.

"I could wish she had not cursed me," he muttered. "She may have power—no one else could." After a while, he said aloud, no one understanding rightly what he meant, "Tush! it is impossible!"—and called for claret; and he and the other gentlemen set-to to a drinking-bout.

CHAPTER II

I now come to the time in which I myself was mixed up with the people that I have been writing about. And to make you understand how I became connected with them, I must give you some little account of myself. My father was the younger son of a Devonshire gentleman of moderate property; my eldest uncle succeeded to the estate of his forefathers, my second became an eminent attorney in London, and my father took orders. Like most poor clergymen, he had a large family; and I have no doubt was glad enough when my London uncle, who was a bachelor, offered to take charge of me, and bring me up to be his successor in business.

In this way I came to live in London, in my uncle's house, not far from Gray's Inn, and to be treated and esteemed as his son, and to labour with him in his office. I was very fond of the old gentleman. He was the confidential agent of many country squires, and had attained to his present position as much by knowledge of human nature as by knowledge of law; though he was learned enough in the latter. He used to say his business was law, his pleasure heraldry. From his intimate acquaintance with family history, and all the tragic courses of life therein involved, to hear him talk, at leisure times, about any coat of arms that came across his path was as good as a play or a romance. Many cases of disputed property, dependent on a love of genealogy, were brought to him, as to a great authority on such points. If the lawyer who came to consult him was young, he would take no fee, only give him a long lecture on the importance of attending to heraldry; if the lawyer was of mature age and good standing, he would mulct him pretty well, and abuse him to me afterwards as negligent of one great branch of the profession. His house was in a stately new street called

Ormond Street, and in it he had a handsome library; but all the books treated of things that were past; none of them planned or looked forward into the future. I worked away—partly for the sake of my family at home, partly because my uncle had really taught me to enjoy the kind of practice in which he himself took such delight. I suspect I worked too hard; at any rate, in seventeen hundred and eighteen I was far from well, and my good uncle was disturbed by my ill looks.

One day, he rang the bell twice into the clerk's room at the dingy office in Gray's Inn Lane. It was the summons for me, and I went into his private room just as a gentleman—whom I knew well enough by sight as an Irish lawyer of more reputation than he deserved—was leaving.

My uncle was slowly rubbing his hands together and considering. I was there two or three minutes before he spoke. Then he told me that I must pack up my portmanteau that very afternoon, and start that night by post-horse for West Chester. I should get there, if all went well, at the end of five days' time, and must then wait for a packet to cross over to Dublin; from thence I must proceed to a certain town named Kildoon, and in that neighbourhood I was to remain, making certain inquiries as to the existence of any descendants of the younger branch of a family to whom some valuable estates had descended in the female line. The Irish lawyer whom I had seen was weary of the case, and would willingly have given up the property, without further ado, to a man who appeared to claim them; but on laying his tables and trees before my uncle, the latter had foreseen so many possible prior claimants, that the lawyer had begged him to undertake the management of the whole business. In his youth, my uncle would have liked nothing better than going over to Ireland himself, and ferreting out every scrap of paper or parchment, and every word of tradition respecting the family. As it was, old and gouty, he deputed me.

Accordingly, I went to Kildoon. I suspect I had something of my uncle's delight in following up a genealogical scent, for I very soon found out, when on the spot, that Mr Rooney, the Irish lawyer, would have got both himself and the first claimant into a terrible scrape, if he had pronounced his opinion that the estates ought to be given up to him. There were three poor Irish fellows, each nearer of kin to the last possessor; but, a generation before, there was a still nearer relation, who had never been accounted for, nor his existence ever discovered by the lawyers, I venture to think, till I routed him out from the memory of some of the old dependants of the family. What had become of him? I travelled backwards and forwards; I crossed over to France, and came back again with a slight clue, which ended in my discovering that, wild and dissipated himself, he had left one child, a son, of yet worse character than his father; that this same Hugh Fitzgerald had married a very beautiful serving-woman of the Byrnes—a person below him in hereditary rank, but above him in character; that he had died soon after his marriage, leaving one child, whether a boy or a girl I could not learn, and that the mother had returned to live in the family of the Byrnes. Now, the chief of this latter family was serving in the Duke of Berwick's regiment, and it was long before I could hear from him; it was more than a year before I got a short, haughty letter—I fancy he had a soldier's contempt for a civilian, an Irishman's hatred for an Englishman, an exiled Jacobite's jealousy of one who prospered and lived tranquilly under the government he looked upon as an usurpation. "Bridget Fitzgerald," he said, "had been faithful to the fortunes of his sister—had followed her abroad, and to England when Mrs Starkey had thought fit to return.

Both his sister and her husband were dead; he knew nothing of Bridget Fitzgerald at the present time; probably Sir Philip Tempest, his nephew's guardian, might be able to give me some information." I have not given the little contemptuous terms; the way in which faithful service was meant to imply more than it said—all that has nothing to do with my story. Sir Philip, when applied to, told me that he paid an annuity regularly to an old woman named Fitzgerald, living at Coldholme (the village near Starkey Manor-house). Whether she had any descendants he could not say.

One bleak March evening, I came in sight of the places described at the beginning of my story. I could hardly understand the rude dialect in which the direction to old Bridget's house was given.

"Yo' see yon furleets," all run together, gave me no idea that I was to guide myself by the distant lights that shone in the windows of the Hall, occupied for the time by a farmer who held the post of steward, while the Squire, now four or five and twenty, was making the grand tour. However, at last, I reached Bridget's cottage—a low, moss-grown place; the palings that had once surrounded it were broken and gone; and the underwood of the forest came up to the walls, and must have darkened the windows. It was about seven o'clock—not late to my London notions—but, after knocking for some time at the door and receiving no reply, I was driven to conjecture that the occupant of the house was gone to bed. So I betook myself to the nearest church I had seen, three miles back on the road I had come, sure that close to that I should find an inn of some kind; and early the next morning I set off back to Coldholme, by a field-path which my host assured me I should find a shorter cut than the road I had taken the night before. It was a cold, sharp morning; my feet left prints in the sprinkling of hoar-frost that covered the ground; nevertheless, I saw an old woman, whom I instinctively suspected to be the object of my search, in a sheltered covert on one side of my path. I lingered and watched her. She must have been considerably above the middle size in her prime, for when she raised herself from the stooping position in which I first saw her, there was something fine and commanding in the erectness of her figure. She drooped again in a minute or two, and seemed looking for something on the ground, as, with bent head, she turned off from the spot where I gazed upon her, and was lost to my sight. I fancy I missed my way, and made a round in spite of the landlord's directions; for by the time I had reached Bridget's cottage she was there, with no semblance of hurried walk or discomposure of any kind. The door was slightly ajar. I knocked, and the majestic figure stood before me, silently awaiting the explanation of my errand. Her teeth were all gone, so the nose and chin were brought near together; the grey eyebrows were straight, and almost hung over her deep, cavernous eyes, and the thick white hair lay in silvery masses over the low, wide, wrinkled forehead. For a moment, I stood uncertain how to shape my answer to the solemn questioning of her silence.

"Your name is Bridget Fitzgerald, I believe?"

She bowed her head in assent.

"I have something to say to you. May I come in? I am unwilling to keep you standing."

"You cannot tire me," she said, and at first she seemed inclined to deny me the shelter of her roof. But the next moment—she had searched the very soul in me with her eyes during that instant—she led me in, and dropped the shadowing hood of her grey, draping cloak, which had previously hit part of the character of her countenance. The cottage was rude and bare enough. But before the picture of the Virgin, of which I have made mention, there stood a little cup filled with fresh primroses. While she paid her reverence to the Madonna, I understood why she had been out seeking through the clumps of green in the sheltered copse. Then she turned round, and bade me be seated. The expression of her face, which all this time I was studying, was not bad, as the stories of my last night's landlord had led me to expect; it was a wild, stern, fierce, indomitable countenance, seamed and scarred by agonies of solitary weeping; but it was neither cunning nor malignant.

"My name is Bridget Fitzgerald," said she, by way of opening our conversation.

"And your husband was Hugh Fitzgerald, of Knock-Mahon, near Kildoon, in Ireland?"

A faint light came into the dark gloom of her eyes.

"He was."

"May I ask if you had any children by him?"

The light in her eyes grew quick and red. She tried to speak, I could see; but something rose in her throat, and choked her, and until she could speak calmly, she would fain not speak at all before a stranger. In a minute or so she said—

"I had a daughter—one Mary Fitzgerald,"—then her strong nature mastered her strong will, and she cried out, with a trembling wailing cry: "Oh, man! what of her?—what of her?"

She rose from her seat, and came and clutched at my arm, and looked in my eyes. There she read, as I suppose, my utter ignorance of what had become of her child; for she went blindly back to her chair, and sat rocking herself and softly moaning, as if I were not there; I not daring to speak to the lone and awful woman. After a little pause, she knelt down before the picture of Our Lady of the

Holy Heart, and spoke to her by all the fanciful and poetic names of the Litany.

"O Rose of Sharon! O Tower of David! O Star of the Sea! have ye no comfort for my sore heart? Am I for ever to hope? Grant me at least despair!"—and so on she went, heedless of my presence. Her prayers grew wilder and wilder, till they seemed to me to touch on the borders of madness and blasphemy. Almost involuntarily, I spoke as if to stop her.

"Have you any reason to think that your daughter is dead?"

She rose from her knees, and came and stood before me.

"Mary Fitzgerald is dead," said she. "I shall never see her again in the flesh. No tongue ever told me; but I know she is dead. I have yearned so to see her, and my heart's will is fearful and strong: it would have drawn her to me before now, if she had been a wanderer on the other side of the world. I wonder often it has not drawn her out of the grave to come and stand before me, and hear me tell her how I loved her. For, sir, we parted unfriends."

I knew nothing but the dry particulars needed for my lawyer's quest, but I could not help feeling for the desolate woman; and she must have read the unusual sympathy with her wistful eyes.

"Yes, sir, we did. She never knew how I loved her; and we parted unfriends; and I fear me that I wished her voyage might not turn out well, only meaning,—O, blessed Virgin! you know I only meant that she should come home to her mother's arms as to the happiest place on earth; but my wishes are terrible—their power goes beyond my thought—and there is no hope for me, if my words brought Mary harm."

"But," I said, "you do not know that she is dead. Even now, you hoped she might be alive. Listen to me," and I told her the tale I have already told you, giving it all in the driest manner, for

I wanted to recall the clear sense that I felt almost sure she had possessed in her younger days, and by keeping up her attention to details, restrain the vague wildness of her grief.

She listened with deep attention, putting from time to time such questions as convinced me I had to do with no common intelligence, however dimmed and shorn by solitude and mysterious sorrow. Then she took up her tale; and in few brief words, told me of her wanderings abroad in vain search after her daughter; sometimes in the wake of armies, sometimes in camp, sometimes in city. The lady, whose waiting-woman Mary had gone to be, had died soon after the date of her last letter home; her husband, the foreign officer, had been serving in Hungary, whither Bridget had followed him, but too late to find him. Vague rumours reached her that Mary had made a great marriage: and this sting of doubt was added,—whether the mother might not be close to her child under her new name, and even hearing of her every day, and yet never recognising the lost one under the appellation she then bore. At length the thought took possession of her, that it was possible that all this time Mary might be at home at Coldholme, in the Trough of Bolland, in Lancashire, in England; and home came Bridget, in that vain hope, to her desolate hearth, and empty cottage. Here she had thought it safest to remain; if Mary was in life, it was here she would seek for her mother.

I noted down one or two particulars out of Bridget's narrative that I thought might be of use to me: for I was stimulated to further search in a strange and extraordinary manner. It seemed as if it were impressed upon me, that I must take up the quest where Bridget had laid it down; and this for no reason that had previously influenced me (such as my uncle's anxiety on the subject, my own reputation as a lawyer and so on), but from some strange power which had taken possession of my will only that very morning, and which forced it in the direction it chose.

"I will go," said I. "I will spare nothing in the search. Trust to me. I will learn all that can be learnt. You shall know all that money, or pains, or wit can discover. It is true she may be long dead: but she may have left a child."

"A child!" she cried, as if for the first time this idea had struck her mind. "Hear him, Blessed Virgin! he says she may have left a child. And you have never told me, though I have prayed so for a sign, waking or sleeping!"

"Nay," said I, "I know nothing but what you tell me. You say you heard of her marriage."

But she caught nothing of what I said. She was praying to the Virgin in a kind of ecstasy, which seemed to render her unconscious of my very presence.

From Coldholme I went to Sir Philip Tempest's. The wife of the foreign officer had been a cousin of his father's, and from him I thought I might gain some particulars as to the existence of the Count de la Tour d'Auvergne, and where I could find him; for I knew questions *de vive voix* aid the flagging recollection, and I was determined to lose no chance for want of trouble. But Sir Philip had gone abroad, and it would be some time before I could receive an answer. So I followed my uncle's advice, to whom I had mentioned how wearied I felt, both in body and mind, by my will-o'-the-wisp search. He immediately told me to go to Harrogate, there to await Sir Philip's reply. I should be near to one of the places connected with my search, Coldholme; not far from Sir Philip Tempest, in case he returned, and I wished to ask him any further questions; and, in conclusion, my uncle bade me try to forget all about my business for a time.

This was far easier said than done. I have seen a child on a common blown along by a high wind, without power of standing still and resisting the tempestuous force. I was somewhat in the same predicament as regarded my mental state. Something resistless seemed to urge my thoughts on, through every possible course by which there was a chance of attaining to my object. I did not see the sweeping moors when I walked out: when I held a book in my hand, and read the words, their sense did not penetrate to my brain. If I slept, I went on with the same ideas, always flowing in the same direction. This could not last long without having a bad effect on the body. I had an illness, which, although I was racked with pain, was a positive relief to me, as it compelled me to live in the present suffering, and not in the visionary researches I had been continually making before. My kind uncle came to nurse me; and after the immediate danger was over, my life seemed to slip away in delicious languor for two or three months. I did not ask—so much did I dread falling into the old channel of thought—whether any reply had been received to my letter to Sir Philip. I turned my whole imagination right away from all that subject. My uncle remained with me until nigh midsummer, and then returned to his business in London; leaving me perfectly well, although not completely strong. I was to follow him in a fortnight; when, as he said, "we would look over letters, and talk about several things". I knew what this little speech alluded to, and shrank from the train of thought it suggested, which was so intimately connected with my first feelings of illness. However, I had a fortnight more to roam on those invigorating Yorkshire moors.

In those days, there was one large, rambling inn, at Harrogate, close to the Medicinal Spring; but it was already becoming too small for the accommodation of the influx of visitors, and many lodged round about, in the farm-houses of the district. It was so early in the season, that I had the inn pretty much to myself; and, indeed, felt rather like a visitor in a private house, so intimate had the landlord and landlady become with me during my long illness. She would chide me for being out so late on the moors, or for having been too long without food, quite in a motherly way; while he consulted me about vintages and wines, and taught me many a Yorkshire wrinkle about horses. In my walks I met other strangers from time to time. Even before my uncle had left me, I had noticed, with half-torpid curiosity, a young lady of very striking appearance, who went about always accompanied by an elderly companion,—hardly a gentlewoman, but with something in her look that prepossessed me in her favour. The younger lady always put her veil down when any one approached; so it had been only once or twice, when I had come upon her at a sudden turn in the path, that I had even had a glimpse at her face. I am not sure if it was beautiful, though in after-life I grew to think it so. But it was at this time overshadowed by a sadness that never varied: a pale, quiet, resigned look of intense suffering, that irresistibly attracted me,—not with love, but with a sense of infinite compassion for one so young yet so hopelessly unhappy. The companion wore something of the same look: quiet melancholy, hopeless, yet resigned. I asked my landlord who they were. He said they were called Clarke, and wished to be considered as mother and daughter; but that, for his part, he did not believe that to be their right name, or that there was any such relationship between them. They had been in the neighbourhood of Harrogate for some time, lodging in a remote farm-house. The people there would tell nothing about them; saying that they paid handsomely, and never did any harm; so why should they be speaking of any strange things that might happen? That, as the landlord shrewdly observed, showed there was something out of the common way: he had heard that the elderly woman was a cousin of the farmer's where they lodged, and so the regard existing between relations might help to keep them quiet.

"What did he think, then, was the reason for their extreme seclusion?" asked I.

"Nay, he could not tell,—not he. He had heard that the young lady, for all as quiet as she seemed, played strange pranks at times." He shook his head when I asked him for more particulars, and refused to give them, which made me doubt if he knew any, for he was in general a talkative and communicative man. In default of other interests, after my uncle left, I set myself to watch these two people. I hovered about their walks drawn towards them with a strange fascination, which was not diminished by their evident annoyance at so frequently meeting me. One day, I had the sudden good fortune to be at hand when they were alarmed by the attack of a bull, which, in those unenclosed grazing districts, was a particularly dangerous occurrence. I have other and more important things to relate, than to tell of the accident which gave me an opportunity of rescuing them; it is enough to say, that this event was the beginning of an acquaintance, reluctantly acquiesced in by them, but eagerly prosecuted by me. I can hardly tell when intense curiosity became merged in love, but in less than ten days after my uncle's departure I was passionately enamoured of Mistress Lucy, as her attendant called her; carefully—for this I noted well—avoiding any address which appeared as if there was an equality of station between them. I noticed also that Mrs Clarke, the elderly woman, after her first reluctance to allow me to pay them any attentions had been overcome, was cheered by my evident attachment to the young girl; it seemed to lighten her heavy burden of care, and she evidently favoured my visits to the farm-house where they lodged. It was not so with Lucy. A more attractive person I never saw, in spite of her depression of manner, and shrinking avoidance of me. I felt sure at once, that whatever was the source of her grief, it rose from no fault of her own. It was difficult to draw her into conversation; but when at times, for a moment or two, I beguiled her into talk, I could see a rare intelligence in her face, and a grave, trusting look in the soft, grey eyes that were raised for a minute to mine. I made every excuse I possibly could for going there. I sought wild flowers for Lucy's sake; I planned walks for Lucy's sake; I watched the heavens by night, in hopes that some unusual beauty of sky would justify me in tempting Mrs Clarke and Lucy forth upon the moors, to gaze at the great purple dome above.

It seemed to me that Lucy was aware of my love; but that, for some motive which I could not guess, she would fain have repelled me; but then again I saw, or fancied I saw, that her heart spoke in my favour, and that there was a struggle going on in her mind, which at times (I loved so dearly) I could have begged her to spare herself, even though the happiness of my whole life should have been the sacrifice; for her complexion grew paler, her aspect of sorrow more hopeless, her delicate frame yet slighter. During this period I had written, I should say, to my uncle, to beg to be allowed to prolong my stay at Harrogate, not giving any reason; but such was his tenderness towards me, that in a few days I heard from him, giving me a willing permission, and only charging me to take care of myself, and not use too much exertion during the hot weather.

One sultry evening I drew near the farm. The windows of their parlour were open, and I heard voices when I turned the corner of the house, as I passed the first window (there were two windows in their little ground-floor room). I saw Lucy distinctly; but when I had knocked at their door—the house-door stood always ajar—she was gone, and I saw only Mrs Clarke, turning over the work-things lying on the table, in a nervous and purposeless manner. I felt by instinct that a conversation of some importance was coming on, in which I should be expected to say what was my object in paying these frequent visits. I was glad of the opportunity. My uncle had several times alluded to the pleasant possibility of my bringing home a young wife, to cheer and adorn the old house in Ormond Street. He was rich, and I was to succeed him, and had, as I knew, a fair reputation for so young a lawyer. So on my side I saw no obstacle. It was true that Lucy was shrouded in mystery; her name (I was convinced it was not Clarke), birth, parentage and previous life were unknown to me. But I was sure of her goodness and sweet innocence, and although I knew that there must be something painful to be told, to account for her mournful sadness, yet I was willing to bear my share in her grief, whatever it might be.

Mrs Clarke began, as if it was a relief to her to plunge into the subject.

"We have thought, sir—at least I have thought—that you knew very little of us, nor we of you, indeed; not enough to warrant the intimate acquaintance we have fallen into. I beg your pardon, sir," she went on, nervously; "I am but a plain kind of woman, and I mean to use no rudeness; but I must say straight out that I—we—think it would be better for you not to come so often to see us. She is very unprotected, and—"

"Why should I not come to see you, dear madam?" asked I, eagerly, glad of the opportunity of explaining myself. "I come, I own, because I have learnt to love Mistress Lucy, and wish to teach her to love me."

Mistress Clarke shook her head, and sighed.

"Don't, sir—neither love her, nor, for the sake of all you hold sacred, teach her to love you! If I am too late, and you love her already, forget her,—forget these last few weeks. O! I should never have allowed you to come!" she went on passionately; "but what am I to do? We are forsaken by all, except the great God, and even He permits a strange and evil power to afflict us—what am I to do! Where is it to end?" She wrung her hands in her distress; then she turned to me: "Go away, sir! go away, before you learn to care any more for her. I ask it for your own sake—I implore! You have been good and kind to us, and we shall always recollect you with gratitude; but go away now, and never come back to cross our fatal path!"

"Indeed, madam," said I, "I shall do no such thing. You urge it for my own sake. I have no fear, so urged—nor wish, except to hear more—all. I cannot have seen Mistress Lucy in all the intimacy of this last fortnight, without acknowledging her goodness and innocence; and without seeing—pardon me, madam—that for some reason you are two very lonely women, in some mysterious sorrow and distress. Now, though I am not powerful myself, yet I have friends who are so wise and kind that they may be said to possess power. Tell me some particulars. Why are you in grief—what is your secret—why are you here? I declare solemnly that nothing you have said has daunted me in my wish to become Lucy's husband; nor will I shrink from any difficulty that, as such an aspirant, I may have to encounter. You say you are friendless—why cast away an honest friend? I will tell you of people to whom you may write, and who will answer any questions as to my character and prospects. I do not shun inquiry."

She shook her head again. "You had better go away, sir. You know nothing about us."

"I know your names," said I, "and I have heard you allude to the part of the country from which you came, which I happen to know as a wild and lonely place. There are so few people living in it that, if I chose to go there, I could easily ascertain all about you; but I would rather hear it from yourself." You see I wanted to pique her into telling me something definite.

"You do not know our true names, sir," said she, hastily.

"Well, I may have conjectured as much. But tell me, then, I conjure you. Give me your reasons for distrusting my willingness to stand by what I have said with regard to Mistress Lucy."

"Oh, what can I do?" exclaimed she. "If I am turning away a true friend, as he says?—Stay!" coming to a sudden decision—"I will tell you something—I cannot tell you all—you would not believe it. But, perhaps, I can tell you enough to prevent your going on in your hopeless attachment. I am not Lucy's mother."

"So I conjectured," I said. "Go on."

"I do not even know whether she is the legitimate or illegitimate child of her father. But he is cruelly turned against her; and her mother is long dead; and for a terrible reason, she has no other creature to keep constant to her but me. She—only two years ago—such a darling and such a pride in her father's house! Why, sir, there is a mystery that might happen in connection with her any moment; and then you would go away like all the rest; and, when you next heard her name, you would loathe her. Others, who have loved her longer, have done so before now. My poor child! whom neither God nor man has mercy upon—or, surely, she would die!"

The good woman was stopped by her crying. I confess, I was a little stunned by her last words; but only for a moment. At any rate, till I knew definitely what was this mysterious stain upon one so simple and pure, as Lucy seemed, I would not desert her, and so I said; and she made me answer:—

"If you are daring in your heart to think harm of my child, sir, after knowing her as you have done, you are no good man yourself; but I am so foolish and helpless in my great sorrow, that I would fain hope to find a friend in you. I cannot help trusting that, although you may no longer feel toward her as a lover, you will have pity upon us; and perhaps, by your learning you can tell us where to go for aid."

"I implore you to tell me what this mystery is," I cried, almost maddened by this suspense.

"I cannot," said she, solemnly. "I am under a deep vow of secrecy. If you are to be told, it must be by her." She left the room, and I remained to ponder over this strange interview. I mechanically turned over the few books, and with eyes that saw nothing at the time, examined the tokens of Lucy's frequent presence in that room.

When I got home at night, I remembered how all these trifles spoke of a pure and tender heart and innocent life. Mistress Clarke returned; she had been crying sadly.

"Yes," said she, "it is as I feared: she loves you so much that she is willing to run the fearful risk of telling you all herself—she acknowledges it is but a poor chance; but your sympathy will be a balm, if you give it. To-morrow, come here at ten in the morning; and, as you hope for pity in your hour of agony, repress all show of fear or repugnance you may feel towards one so grievously afflicted."

I half smiled. "Have no fear," I said. It seemed too absurd to imagine my feeling dislike to Lucy.

"Her father loved her well," said she, gravely, "yet he drove her out like some monstrous thing."

Just at this moment came a peal of ringing laughter from the garden. It was Lucy's voice; it sounded as if she were standing just on one side of the open casement—and as though she were suddenly stirred to merriment—merriment verging on boisterousness, by the doings or sayings of some other person. I can scarcely say why, but the sound jarred on me inexpressibly. She knew the subject of our conversation, and must have been at least aware of the state of agitation her friend was in; she herself usually so gentle and quiet. I half rose to go to the window, and satisfy my instinctive curiosity as to what had provoked this burst of ill-timed laughter; but Mrs Clarke threw her whole weight and power upon the hand with which she pressed and kept me down.

"For God's sake!" she said, white and trembling all over, "sit still; be quiet. Oh! be patient. To-morrow you will know all. Leave us, for we are all sorely afflicted. Do not seek to know more about us."

Again that laugh—so musical in sound, yet so discordant to my heart. She held me tight—tighter; without positive violence I could not have risen. I was sitting with my back to the window, but I felt a shadow pass between the sun's warmth and me, and a strange shudder ran through my frame. In a minute or two she released me.

"Go," repeated she. "Be warned, I ask you once more. I do not think you can stand this knowledge that you seek. If I had had my own way, Lucy should never have yielded, and promised to tell you all. Who knows what may come of it?"

"I am firm in my wish to know all. I return at ten to-morrow morning, and then expect to see Mistress Lucy herself."

I turned away; having my own suspicions, I confess, as to Mistress Clarke's sanity.

Conjectures as to the meaning of her hints, and uncomfortable thoughts connected with that strange laughter, filled my mind. I could hardly sleep. I rose early; and long before the hour I had appointed, I was on the path over the common that led to the old farm-house where they lodged. I suppose that Lucy had passed no better a night than I; for there she was also, slowly pacing with her even step, her eyes bent down, her whole look most saintly and pure. She started when I came close to her, and grew paler as I reminded her of my appointment, and spoke with something of the impatience of obstacles that, seeing her once more, had called up afresh in my mind. All strange and terrible hints, and giddy merriment were forgotten. My heart gave forth words of fire, and my tongue uttered them. Her colour went and came, as she listened; but, when I had ended my passionate speeches, she lifted her soft eyes to me, and said—

"But you know that you have something to learn about me yet. I only want to say this: I shall not think less of you—less well of you, I mean—if you, too, fall away from me when you know all. Stop!" said she, as if fearing another burst of mad words. "Listen to me. My father is a man of great wealth. I never knew my mother; she must have died when I was very young. When first I remember anything, I was living in a great, lonely house, with my dear and faithful Mistress Clarke. My father, even, was not there; he was—he is—a soldier, and his duties lie abroad. But he came from time to time, and every time I think he loved me more and more. He brought me rarities from foreign lands, which prove to me now how much he must have thought of me during his absences. I can sit down and measure the depth of his lost love now, by such standards as these. I never thought whether he loved me or not, then; it was so natural, that it was like the air I breathed. Yet he was an angry man at times, even then; but never with me. He was very reckless, too; and, once or twice, I heard a whisper among the servants that a doom was over him, and that he knew it, and tried to drown his knowledge in wild activity, and even sometimes, sir, in wine. So I grew up in this grand mansion, in that lonely place. Everything around me seemed at my disposal, and I think every one loved me; I am sure I loved them. Till about two years ago—I remember it well—my father had come to England, to us; and he seemed so proud and so pleased with me and all I had done. And one day his tongue seemed loosened with wine, and he told me much that I had not known till then,—how dearly he had loved my mother, yet how his wilful usage had caused her death; and then he went on to say how he loved me better than any creature on earth, and how, some day, he hoped to take me to foreign places, for that he could hardly bear these long absences from his only child. Then he seemed to change suddenly, and said, in a strange, wild way, that I was not to believe what he said; that there was many a thing he loved better—his horse—his dog—I know not what.

"And 'twas only the next morning that, when I came into his room to ask his blessing as was my wont, he received me with fierce and angry words. 'Why had I,' so he asked, 'been delighting myself in such wanton mischief—dancing over the tender plants in the flower-beds, all set with the famous Dutch bulbs he had brought from Holland?' I had never been out of doors that morning, sir, and I could not conceive what he meant, and so I said; and then he swore at me for a liar, and said I was of no true blood, for he had seen me doing all that mischief himself—with his own eyes. What could I say? He would not listen to me, and even my tears seemed only to irritate him. That day was the beginning of my great sorrows. Not long after, he reproached me for my undue familiarity—all unbecoming a gentlewoman—with his grooms. I had been in the stable-yard, laughing and talking, he said. Now, sir, I am something of a coward by nature, and I had always dreaded horses; besides that, my father's servants—those whom he brought with him from foreign parts—were wild fellows, whom I had always avoided, and to whom I had never spoken, except as a lady must needs from time to time speak to her father's people. Yet my father called me by names of which I hardly know the meaning, but my heart told me they were such as shame any modest woman; and from that day he turned quite against me;—nay, sir, not many weeks after that, he came in with a riding-whip in his hand; and, accusing me harshly of evil doings, of which I knew no more than you, sir, he was about to strike me, and I, all in bewildering tears, was ready to take his stripes as great kindness compared to his harder words, when suddenly he stopped his arm mid-way, gasped and staggered, crying out, 'The curse—the curse!' I looked up in terror. In the great mirror opposite I saw myself, and right behind, another wicked, fearful self, so like me that my soul seemed to quiver within me, as though not knowing to which similitude of body it belonged. My father saw my double at the same moment, either in its dreadful reality, whatever that might be, or in the scarcely less terrible reflection in the mirror; but what came of it at that moment I cannot say, for I suddenly swooned away; and when I came to myself I was lying in my bed, and my faithful Clarke sitting by me. I was in my bed for days; and even while I lay there my double was seen by all, flitting about the house and gardens, always about some mischievous or detestable work. What wonder that every one shrank from me in dread—that my father drove me forth at length, when the disgrace of which I was the cause was past his patience to bear. Mistress Clarke came with me; and here we try to live such a life of piety and prayer as may in time set me free from the curse."

All the time she had been speaking, I had been weighing her story in my mind. I had hitherto put cases of witchcraft on one side, as mere superstitions; and my uncle and I had had many an argument, he supporting himself by the opinion of his good friend Sir Matthew Hale. Yet this sounded like the tale of one bewitched; or was it merely the effect of a life of extreme seclusion telling on the nerves of a sensitive girl? My scepticism inclined me to the latter belief, and when she paused I said:

"I fancy that some physician could have disabused your father in his belief in visions—"

Just at that instant, standing as I was opposite to her in the full and perfect morning light, I saw behind her another figure—a ghastly resemblance, complete in likeness, so far as form and feature and minutest touch of dress could go, but with a loathsome demon soul looking out of the grey eyes, that were in turns mocking and voluptuous. My heart stood still within me; every hair rose up erect; my flesh crept with horror. I could not see the grave and tender Lucy—my eyes were fascinated by the creature beyond. I know not why, but I put out my hand to clutch it; I grasped nothing but empty air, and my whole blood curdled to ice. For a moment I could not see; then my sight came back, and I saw Lucy standing before me, alone, deathly pale, and, I could have fancied, almost, shrunk in size.

"IT has been near me?" she said, as if asking a question.

The sound seemed taken out of her voice; it was husky as the notes on an old harpsichord when the strings have ceased to vibrate. She read her answer in my face, I suppose, for I could not speak. Her look was one of intense fear, but that died away into an aspect of most humble patience. At length she seemed to force herself to face behind and around her: she saw the purple moors, the blue distant hills, quivering in the sunlight, but nothing else.

"Will you take me home?" she said, meekly.

I took her by the hand, and led her silently through the budding heather—we dared not speak; for we could not tell but that the dread creature was listening, although unseen,—but that IT might appear and push us asunder. I never loved her more fondly than now when—and that was the unspeakable misery—the idea of her was becoming so inextricably blended with the shuddering thought of IT. She seemed to understand what I must be feeling. She let go my hand, which she had kept clasped until then, when we reached the garden gate, and went forwards to meet her anxious friend, who was standing by the window looking for her. I could not enter the house: I needed silence, society, leisure, change—I knew not what—to shake off the sensation of that creature's presence. Yet I lingered about the garden—I hardly know why; I partly suppose, because I feared to encounter the resemblance again on the solitary common, where it had vanished, and partly from a feeling of inexpressible compassion for Lucy. In a few minutes Mistress Clarke came forth and joined me. We walked some paces in silence.

"You know all now," said she, solemnly.

"I saw IT," said I, below my breath.

"And you shrink from us, now," she said, with a hopelessness which stirred up all that was brave or good in me.

"Not a whit," said I. "Human flesh shrinks from encounter with the powers of darkness; and, for some reason unknown to me, the pure and holy Lucy is their victim."

"The sins of the fathers shall be visited upon the children," she said.

"Who is her father?" asked I. "Knowing as much as I do, I may surely know more—know all. Tell me, I entreat you, madam, all that you can conjecture respecting this demoniac persecution of one so good."

"I will; but not now. I must go to Lucy now. Come this afternoon, I will see you alone; and oh, sir! I will trust that you may yet find some way to help us in our sore trouble!"

I was miserably exhausted by the swooning affright which had taken possession of me. When I reached the inn, I staggered in like one overcome by wine. I went to my own private room. It was some time before I saw that the weekly post had come in, and brought me my letters. There was one from my uncle, one from my home in Devonshire and one, re-directed over the first address, sealed with a great coat of arms. It was from Sir Philip Tempest: my letter of inquiry respecting Mary Fitzgerald had reached him at Liége, where it so happened that the Count de la Tour d'Auvergne was quartered at the very time. He remembered his wife's beautiful attendant; she had had high words with the deceased countess, respecting her intercourse with an English gentleman of good standing, who was also in the foreign service. The countess augured evil of his intentions; while Mary, proud and vehement, asserted that he would soon marry her, and resented her mistress's warnings as an insult. The consequence was, that she had left Madam de la Tour d'Auvergne's service, and, as the Count believed, had gone to live with the Englishman; whether he had married her, or not, he could not say. "But," added Sir Philip Tempest, "you may easily hear what particulars you wish to know respecting Mary Fitzgerald from the Englishman himself, if, as I suspect, he is no other than my neighbour and former acquaintance, Mr Gisborne, of Skipford Hall, in the West Riding. I am led to the belief that he is no other, by several small particulars, none of which are in themselves conclusive, but which, taken together, furnish a mass of presumptive evidence. As far as I could make out from the Count's foreign pronunciation, Gisborne was the name of the

Englishman: I know that Gisborne of Skipford was abroad and in the foreign service at that time—he was a likely fellow enough for such an exploit, and, above all, certain expressions recur to my mind which he used in reference to old Bridget Fitzgerald, of Coldholme, whom he once encountered while staying with me at Starkey Manor-house. I remember that the meeting seemed to have produced some extraordinary effect upon his mind, as though he had suddenly discovered some connection which she might have had with his previous life. I beg you to let me know if I can be of any further service to you. Your uncle once rendered me a good turn, and I will gladly repay it, so far as in me lies, to his nephew."

I was now apparently close on the discovery which I had striven so many months to attain. But success had lost its zest. I put my letters down, and seemed to forget them all in thinking of the morning I had passed that very day. Nothing was real but the unreal presence, which had come like an evil blast across my bodily eyes, and burnt itself down upon my brain. Dinner came, and went away untouched. Early in the afternoon I walked to the farm-house. I found Mistress Clarke alone, and I was glad and relieved. She was evidently prepared to tell me all I might wish to hear.

"You asked me for Mistress Lucy's true name; it is Gisborne," she began.

"Not Gisborne of Skipford?" I exclaimed, breathless with anticipation.

"The same," said she, quietly, not regarding my manner. "Her father is a man of note; although, being a Roman Catholic, he cannot take that rank in this country to which his station entitles him. The consequence is that he lives much abroad—has been a soldier, I am told."

"And Lucy's mother?" I asked.

She shook her head. "I never knew her," said she. "Lucy was about three years old when I was engaged to take charge of her. Her mother was dead."

"But you know her name?—you can tell if it was Mary Fitzgerald?"

She looked astonished. "That was her name. But, sir, how came you to be so well acquainted with it? It was a mystery to the whole household at Skipford Court. She was some beautiful young woman whom he lured away from her protectors while he was abroad. I have heard said he practised some terrible deceit upon her, and when she came to know it, she was neither to have nor to hold, but rushed off from his very arms, and threw herself into a rapid stream and was drowned. It stung him deep with remorse, but I used to think the remembrance of the mother's cruel death made him love the child yet dearer."

I told her, as briefly as might be, of my researches after the descendant and heir of the Fitzgeralds of Kildoon, and added— something of my old lawyer spirit returning into me for the moment—that I had no doubt but that we should prove Lucy to be by right possessed of large estates in Ireland.

No flush came over her grey face; no light into her eyes. "And what is all the wealth in the whole world to that poor girl?" she said. "It will not free her from the ghastly bewitchment which persecutes her. As for money, what a pitiful thing it is! it cannot touch her."

"No more can the Evil Creature harm her," I said. "Her holy nature dwells apart, and cannot be defiled or stained by all the devilish arts in the whole world."

"True! but it is a cruel fate to know that all shrink from her, sooner or later, as from one possessed—accursed."

"How came it to pass?" I asked.

"Nay, I know not. Old rumours there are, that were bruited through the household at Skipford."

"Tell me," I demanded.

"They came from servants, who would fain account for everything. They say that, many years ago, Mr Gisborne killed a dog belonging to an old witch at Coldholme; that she cursed, with a dreadful and mysterious curse, the creature, whatever it might be, that he should love best; and that it struck so deeply into his heart that for years he kept himself aloof from any temptation to love aught. But who could help loving Lucy?"

"You never heard the witch's name?" I gasped.

"Yes—they called her Bridget: they said he would never go near the spot again for terror. Yet he was a brave man!"

"Listen," said I, taking hold of her arm, the better to arrest her full attention; "if what I suspect holds true, that man stole Bridget's only child—the very Mary Fitzgerald who was Lucy's mother; if so, Bridget cursed him in ignorance of the deeper wrong he had done her. To this hour she yearns after her lost child, and questions the saints whether she be living or not. The roots of that curse lie deeper than she knows: she unwittingly banned him for a deeper guilt than that of killing a dumb beast. The sins of the fathers are indeed visited upon the children."

"But," said Mistress Clarke, eagerly, "she would never let evil rest on her own grandchild? Surely, sir, if what you say be true, there are hopes for Lucy. Let us go—go at once, and tell this fearful woman all that you suspect, and beseech her to take off the spell she has put upon her innocent grandchild."

It seemed to me, indeed, that something like this was the best course we could pursue. But first it was necessary to ascertain more than what mere rumour or careless hearsay could tell. My thoughts turned to my uncle—he could advise me wisely—he ought to know all. I resolved to go to him without delay; but I did not choose to tell Mistress Clarke of all the visionary plans that flitted through my mind. I simply declared my intention of proceeding straight to London on Lucy's affairs. I bade her believe that my interest on the young lady's behalf was greater than ever, and that my whole time should be given up to her cause. I saw that Mistress Clarke distrusted me, because my mind was too full of thoughts for my words to flow freely. She sighed and shook her head, and said, "Well, it is all right!" in such a tone that it was an implied reproach. But I was firm and constant in my heart, and I took confidence from that.

I rode to London. I rode long days drawn out into the lovely summer nights: I could not rest. I reached London. I told my uncle all, though in the stir of the great city the horror had faded away, and I could hardly imagine that he would believe the account I gave him of the fearful double of Lucy which I had seen on the lonely moor-side. But my uncle had lived many years, and learnt many things; and, in the deep secrets of family history that had been confided to him, he had heard of cases of innocent people bewitched and taken possession of by evil spirits yet more fearful than Lucy's. For, as he said, to judge from all I told him, that resemblance had no power over her—she was too pure and good to be tainted by its evil, haunting presence. It had, in all probability, so my uncle conceived, tried to suggest wicked thoughts and to tempt to wicked actions; but she, in her saintly maidenhood, had passed on undefiled by evil thought or deed. It could not touch her soul: but true, it set her apart from all sweet love or common human intercourse. My uncle threw himself with an energy more like six-and-twenty than sixty into the consideration of the whole case. He undertook the proving Lucy's descent, and volunteered to go and find out Mr Gisborne, and obtain, firstly, the legal proofs of her descent from the Fitzgeralds of Kildoon, and, secondly, to try and hear all that he could respecting the working of the curse, and whether any and what means had been taken to exorcise that terrible appearance. For he told me of instances where, by prayers and long fasting, the evil possessor had been driven forth with howling and many cries from the body which it had come to inhabit; he spoke of those strange New England cases which had happened not so long before; of Mr Defoe, who had written a book, wherein he had named many modes of subduing apparitions, and sending them back whence they came; and, lastly, he spoke low of dreadful ways of compelling witches to undo their witchcraft. But I could not endure to hear of those tortures and burnings. I said that Bridget was rather a wild and savage woman than a malignant witch; and, above all, that Lucy was of her kith and kin; and that, in putting her to the trial, by water or by fire, we should be torturing—it might be to the death—the ancestress of her we sought to redeem.

My uncle thought awhile, and then said, that in this last matter I was right—at any rate, it should not be tried, with his consent, till all other modes of remedy had failed; and he assented to my proposal that I should go myself and see Bridget, and tell her all.

In accordance with this, I went down once more to the wayside inn near Coldholme. It was late at night when I arrived there; and, while I supped, I inquired of the landlord more particulars as to Bridget's ways. Solitary and savage had been her life for many years. Wild and despotic were her words and manner to those few people who came across her path. The country-folk did her imperious bidding, because they feared to disobey. If they pleased her, they prospered; if, on the contrary, they neglected or traversed her behests, misfortune, small or great, fell on them and theirs. It was not detestation so much as an indefinable terror that she excited.

In the morning I went to see her. She was standing on the green outside her cottage, and received me with the sullen grandeur of a throneless queen. I read in her face that she recognised me, and that I was not unwelcome; but she stood silent till I had opened my errand.

"I have news of your daughter," said I, resolved to speak straight to all that I knew she felt of love, and not to spare her. "She is dead!"

The stern figure scarcely trembled, but her hand sought the support of the door-post.

"I knew that she was dead," said she, deep and low, and then was silent for an instant. "My tears that should have flowed for her were burnt up long years ago. Young man, tell me about her."

"Not yet," said I, having a strange power given me of confronting one, whom, nevertheless, in my secret soul I dreaded.

"You had once a little dog," I continued. The words called out in her more show of emotion than the intelligence of her daughter's death. She broke in upon my speech:—

"I had! It was hers—the last thing I had of hers—and it was shot for wantonness! It died in my arms. The man who killed that dog rues it to this day. For that dumb beast's blood, his best-beloved stands accursed."

Her eyes distended, as if she were in a trance and saw the working of her curse. Again I spoke:—

"O, woman!" I said, "that best-beloved, standing accursed before men, is your dead daughter's child."

The life, the energy, the passion, came back to the eyes with which she pierced through me, to see if I spoke truth; then, without another question or word, she threw herself on the ground with fearful vehemence, and clutched at the innocent daisies with convulsed hands.

"Bone of my bone! flesh of my flesh! have I cursed thee—and art thou accursed?"

So she moaned, as she lay prostrate in her great agony. I stood aghast at my own work. She did not hear my broken sentences; she asked no more, but the dumb confirmation which my sad looks had given that one fact, that her curse rested on her own daughter's child. The fear grew on me lest she should die in her strife of body and soul; and then might not Lucy remain under the spell as long as she lived?

Even at this moment, I saw Lucy coming through the woodland path that led to Bridget's cottage; Mistress Clarke was with her: I felt at my heart that it was she, by the balmy peace which the look of her sent over me, as she slowly advanced, a glad surprise shining out of her soft quiet eyes. That was as her gaze met mine. As her looks fell on the woman lying stiff, convulsed on the earth, they became full of tender pity; and she came forward to try and lift her up. Seating herself on the turf, she took Bridget's head into her lap; and, with gentle touches, she arranged the dishevelled grey hair streaming thick and wild from beneath her mutch.

"God help her!" murmured Lucy. "How she suffers!"

At her desire we sought for water; but when we returned, Bridget had recovered her wandering senses, and was kneeling with clasped hands before Lucy, gazing at that sweet sad face as though her troubled nature drank in health and peace from every moment's contemplation. A faint tinge on Lucy's pale cheeks showed me that she was aware of our return; otherwise it appeared as if she was conscious of her influence for good over the passionate and troubled woman kneeling before her, and would not willingly avert her grave and loving eyes from that wrinkled and careworn countenance.

Suddenly—in the twinkling of an eye—the creature appeared, there, behind Lucy; fearfully the same as to outward semblance, but kneeling exactly as Bridget knelt, and clasping her hands in jesting mimicry as Bridget clasped hers in her ecstasy that was deepening into a prayer. Mistress Clarke cried out—Bridget arose slowly, her gaze fixed on the creature beyond: drawing her breath with a hissing sound, never moving her terrible eyes, that were steady as stone, she made a dart at the phantom, and caught, as I had done, a mere handful of empty air. We saw no more of the creature—it vanished as suddenly as it came, but Bridget looked slowly on, as if watching some receding form. Lucy sat still, white, trembling, drooping—I think she would have swooned if I had not been there to uphold her. While I was attending to her, Bridget passed us, without a word to any one, and, entering her cottage, she barred herself in, and left us without.

All our endeavours were now directed to get Lucy back to the house where she had tarried the night before. Mistress Clarke told me that, not hearing from me (some letter must have miscarried), she had grown impatient and despairing, and had urged Lucy to the enterprise of coming to seek her grandmother; not telling her, indeed, of the dread reputation she possessed, or how we suspected her of having so fearfully blighted that innocent girl; but, at the same time, hoping much from the mysterious stirring of blood, which Mistress Clarke trusted in for the removal of the curse. They had come, by a different route from that which I had taken, to a village inn not far from Coldholme, only the night before. This was the first interview between ancestress and descendant.

All through the sultry noon I wandered along the tangled wood-paths of the old neglected forest; thinking where to turn for remedy in a matter so complicated and mysterious. Meeting a countryman, I asked my way to the nearest clergyman, and went, hoping to obtain some counsel from him. But he proved to be a coarse and common-minded man, giving no time or attention to the intricacies of a case, but dashing out a strong opinion involving immediate action. For instance, as soon as I named Bridget Fitzgerald, he exclaimed:—

"The Coldholme witch! the Irish papist! I'd have had her ducked long since but for that other papist, Sir Philip Tempest. He has had to threaten honest folk about here over and over again, or they'd have had her up before the justices for her black doings. And it's the law of the land that witches should be burnt! Ay, and of Scripture, too, sir! Yet you see a papist, if he's a rich squire, can overrule both law and Scripture. I'd carry a faggot myself to rid the country of her!"

Such a one could give me no help. I rather drew back what I had already said; and tried to make the parson forget it, by treating him to several pots of beer, in the village inn, to which we had adjourned for our conference at his suggestion. I left him as soon as I could, and returned to Coldholme, shaping my way past deserted Starkey Manor-house, and coming upon it by the back. At that side were the oblong remains of the old moat, the waters of which lay placid and motionless under the crimson rays of the setting sun; with the forest-trees lying straight along each side, and their deep-green foliage mirrored to blackness in the burnished surface of the moat below—and the broken sun-dial at the end nearest the hall—and the heron, standing on one leg at the water's edge, lazily looking down for fish—the lonely and desolate house scarce needed the broken windows, the weeds on the door-sill, the broken shutter softly flapping to and fro in the twilight breeze, to fill up the picture of desertion and decay. I lingered about the place until the growing darkness warned me on. And then I passed along the path, cut by the orders of the last lady of Starkey Manor-house, that led me to Bridget's cottage. I resolved at once to see her; and, in spite of closed doors—it might be of resolved will—she should see me. So I knocked at her door, gently, loudly, fiercely. I shook it so vehemently that at length the old hinges gave way, and with a crash it fell inwards, leaving me suddenly face to face with Bridget—I, red, heated, agitated with my so long baffled efforts—she, stiff as any stone, standing right facing me, her eyes dilated with terror, her ashen lips trembling, but her body motion-less. In her hands she held her crucifix, as if by that holy symbol she sought to oppose my entrance. At sight of me, her whole frame relaxed, and she sank back upon a chair. Some mighty tension had given way. Still her eyes looked fearfully into the gloom of the outer air, made more opaque by the glimmer of the lamp inside, which she had placed before the picture of the Virgin.

"Is she there?" asked Bridget, hoarsely.

"No! Who? I am alone. You remember me."

"Yes," replied she, still terror stricken. "But she—that crea-ture—has been looking in upon me through that window all day long. I closed it up with my shawl; and then I saw her feet below the door, as long as it was light, and I knew she heard my very breathing—nay, worse, my very prayers; and I could not pray, for her listening choked the words ere they rose to my lips. Tell me, who is she?—what means that double girl I saw this morning? One had a look of my dead Mary; but the other curdled my blood, and yet it was the same!"

She had taken hold of my arm, as if to secure herself some human companionship. She shook all over with the slight, never-ceasing tremor of intense terror. I told her my tale as I have told it you, sparing none of the details.

How Mistress Clarke had informed me that the resemblance had driven Lucy forth from her father's house—how I had disbelieved, until, with mine own eyes, I had seen another Lucy standing behind my Lucy, the same in form and feature, but with the demon-soul looking out of the eyes. I told her all, I say, believing that she—whose curse was working so upon the life of her innocent grandchild—was the only person who could find the remedy and the redemption. When I had done, she sat silent for many minutes.

"You love Mary's child?" she asked.

"I do, in spite of the fearful working of the curse—I love her. Yet I shrink from her ever since that day on the moor-side. And men must shrink from one so accompanied; friends and lovers must stand afar off. Oh, Bridget Fitzgerald! loosen the curse! Set her free!"

"Where is she?"

I eagerly caught at the idea that her presence was needed, in order that, by some strange prayer or exorcism, the spell might be reversed.

"I will go and bring her to you," I exclaimed. But Bridget tightened her hold upon my arm.

"Not so," said she, in a low, hoarse voice. "It would kill me to see her again as I saw her this morning. And I must live till I have worked my work. Leave me!" said she, suddenly, and again taking up the cross. "I defy the demon I have called up. Leave me to wrestle with it!"

She stood up, as if in an ecstasy of inspiration, from which all fear was banished. I lingered—why I can hardly tell—until once more she bade me begone. As I went along the forest way, I looked back, and saw her planting the cross in the empty threshold, where the door had been.

The next morning Lucy and I went to seek her, to bid her join her prayers with ours. The cottage stood open and wide to our gaze. No human being was there: the cross remained on the threshold, but Bridget was gone.

CHAPTER III

What was to be done next? was the question that I asked myself. As for Lucy, she would fain have submitted to the doom that lay upon her. Her gentleness and piety, under the pressure of so horrible a life, seemed over-passive to me. She never complained. Mrs Clarke complained more than ever. As for me, I was more in love with the real Lucy than ever; but I shrunk from the false similitude with an intensity proportioned to my love. I found out by instinct that Mrs Clarke had occasional temptations to leave Lucy. The good lady's nerves were shaken, and, from what she said, I could almost have concluded that the object of the Double was to drive away from Lucy this last, and almost earliest friend. At times, I could scarcely bear to own it, but I myself felt inclined to turn recreant; and I would accuse Lucy of being too patient—too resigned. One after another, she won the little children of Coldholme. (Mrs Clarke and she had resolved to stay there, for was it not as good a place as any other, to such as they? and did not all our faint hopes rest on Bridget—never seen or heard of now, but still we trusted to come back, or give some token?) So, as I say, one after another, the little children came about my Lucy, won by her soft tones, and her gentle smiles, and kind actions. Alas! one after another they fell away, and shrunk from her path with blanching terror; and we too surely guessed the reason why. It was the last drop. I could bear it no longer. I resolved no more to linger around the spot, but to go back to my uncle, and among the learned divines of the city of London, seek for some power whereby to annul the curse.

My uncle, meanwhile, had obtained all the requisite testimonials relating to Lucy's descent and birth, from the Irish lawyers, and from Mr Gisborne. The latter gentleman had written from abroad (he was again serving in the Austrian army), a letter alternately passionately self-reproachful and stoically repellent. It was evident that when he thought of Mary—her short life—how he had wronged her, and of her violent death, he could hardly find words severe enough for his own conduct; and from this point of view, the curse that Bridget had laid upon him and his, was regarded by him as a prophetic doom, to the utterance of which she was moved by a Higher Power, working for the fulfilment of a deeper vengeance than for the death of the poor dog. But then, again, when he came to speak of his daughter, the repugnance which the conduct of the demoniac creature had produced in his mind, was but ill-disguised under a show of profound indifference as to Lucy's fate. One almost felt as if he would have been as content to put her out of existence, as he would have been to destroy some disgusting reptile that had invaded his chamber or his couch.

The great Fitzgerald property was Lucy's; and that was all—was nothing.

My uncle and I sat in the gloom of a London November evening, in our house in Ormond Street. I was out of health, and felt as if I were in an inextricable coil of misery. Lucy and I wrote to each other, but that was little; and we dared not see each other for dread of the fearful Third, who had more than once taken her place at our meetings. My uncle had, on the day I speak of, bidden prayers to be put up on the ensuing Sabbath in many a church and meeting-house in London, for one grievously tormented by an evil spirit. He had faith in prayers—I had none; I was fast losing faith in all things. So we sat, he trying to interest me in the old talk of other days, I oppressed by one thought—when our old servant, Anthony, opened the door, and, without speaking, showed in a very gentlemanly and prepossessing man, who had something remarkable about his dress, betraying his profession to be that of the Roman Catholic priesthood. He glanced at my uncle first, then at me. It was to me he bowed.

"I did not give my name," said he, "because you would hardly have recognised it; unless, sir, when, in the north, you heard of Father Bernard, the chaplain at Stoney Hurst?"

I remembered afterwards that I had heard of him, but at the time I had utterly forgotten it; so I professed myself a complete stranger to him; while my ever-hospitable uncle, although hating a papist as much as it was in his nature to hate anything, placed a chair for the visitor, and bade Anthony bring glasses, and a fresh jug of claret.

Father Bernard received this courtesy with the graceful ease and pleasant acknowledgement which belongs to a man of the world. Then he turned to scan me with his keen glance. After some slight conversation, entered into on his part, I am certain, with an intention of discovering on what terms of confidence I stood with my uncle, he paused, and said gravely—

"I am sent here with a message to you, sir, from a woman to whom you have shown kindness, and who is one of my penitents, in Antwerp—one Bridget Fitzgerald."

"Bridget Fitzgerald!" exclaimed I. "In Antwerp? Tell me, sir, all that you can about her."

"There is much to be said," he replied. "But may I inquire if this gentleman—if your uncle is acquainted with the particulars of which you and I stand informed?"

"All that I know, he knows," said I, eagerly laying my hand on my uncle's arm, as he made a motion as if to quit the room.

"Then I have to speak before two gentlemen who, however they may differ from me in faith, are yet fully impressed with the fact that there are evil powers going about continually to take cognisance of our evil thoughts; and, if their Master gives them power, to bring them into overt action. Such is my theory of the nature of that sin, which I dare not disbelieve—as some sceptics would have us do—the sin of witchcraft. Of this deadly sin, you and I are aware, Bridget Fitzgerald has been guilty. Since you saw her last, many prayers have been offered in our churches, many masses sung, many penances undergone, in order that, if God and the holy saints so willed it, her sin might be blotted out. But it has not been so willed."

"Explain to me," said I, "who you are, and how you come connected with Bridget. Why is she at Antwerp? I pray you, sir, tell me more. If I am impatient, excuse me; I am ill and feverish, and in consequence bewildered."

There was something to me inexpressibly soothing in the tone of voice with which he began to narrate, as it were from the beginning, his acquaintance with Bridget.

"I had known Mr and Mrs Starkey during their residence abroad, and so it fell out naturally that, when I came as chaplain to the Sherburnes at Stoney Hurst, our acquaintance was renewed; and thus I became the confessor of the whole family, isolated as they were from the offices of the Church, Sherburne being their nearest neighbour who professed the true faith. Of course, you are aware that facts revealed in confession are sealed as in the grave; but I learnt enough of Bridget's character to be convinced that I had to do with no common woman; one powerful for good as for evil. I believe that I was able to give her spiritual assistance from time to time, and that she looked upon me as a servant of that Holy Church, which has such wonderful power of moving men's hearts, and relieving them of the burden of their sins. I have known her cross the moors on the wildest nights of storm, to confess and be absolved; and then she would return, calmed and subdued, to her daily work about her mistress, no one witting where she had been during the hours that most passed in sleep upon their beds. After her daughter's departure—after Mary's mysterious disappearance—I had to impose many a long penance, in order to wash away the sin of impatient repining that was fast leading her into the deeper guilt of blasphemy. She set out on that long journey of which you have possibly heard—that fruitless journey in search of Mary—and during her absence, my superiors ordered my return to my former duties at Antwerp, and for many years I heard no more of Bridget.

"Not many months ago, as I was passing homewards in the evening, along one of the streets near St Jacques, leading into the Meer Straet, I saw a woman sitting crouched up under the shrine of the Holy Mother of Sorrows. Her hood was drawn over her head, so that the shadow caused by the light of the lamp above fell deep over her face; her hands were clasped round her knees. It was evident that she was some one in hopeless trouble, and as such it was my duty to stop and speak. I naturally addressed her first in Flemish, believing her to be one of the lower class of inhabitants.

She shook her head, but did not look up. Then I tried French, and she replied in that language, but speaking it so indifferently, that I was sure she was either English or Irish, and consequently spoke to her in my own native tongue. She recognised my voice; and, starting up, caught at my robes, dragging me before the blessed shrine, and throwing herself down, and forcing me, as much by her evident desire as by her action, to kneel beside her, she exclaimed:

"'O Holy Virgin! you will never hearken to me again, but hear him; for you know him of old, that he does your bidding, and strives to heal broken hearts. Hear him!'

"She turned to me.

"'She will hear you, if you will only pray. She never hears me: she and all the saints in heaven cannot hear my prayers, for the Evil One carries them off, as he carried that first away. O, Father Bernard, pray for me!'

"I prayed for one in sore distress, of what nature I could not say; but the Holy Virgin would know. Bridget held me fast, gasping with eagerness at the sound of my words. When I had ended, I rose, and, making the sign of the Cross over her, I was going to bless her in the name of the Holy Church, when she shrank away like some terrified creature, and said—

"'I am guilty of deadly sin, and am not shriven.'

"'Arise, my daughter,' said I, 'and come with me.' And I led the way into one of the confessionals of St Jacques.

"She knelt; I listened. No words came. The evil powers had stricken her dumb, as I heard afterwards they had many a time before, when she approached confession.

"She was too poor to pay for the necessary forms of exorcism; and hitherto those priests to whom she had addressed herself were either so ignorant of the meaning of her broken French, or her

Irish-English, or else esteemed her to be one crazed—as, indeed, her wild and excited manner might easily have led any one to think—that they had neglected the sole means of loosening her tongue, so that she might confess her deadly sin, and, after due penance, obtain absolution. But I knew Bridget of old, and felt that she was a penitent sent to me. I went through those holy offices appointed by our Church for the relief of such a case. I was the more bound to do this, as I found that she had come to Antwerp for the sole purpose of discovering me, and making confession to me. Of the nature of that fearful confession I am forbidden to speak. Much of it you know; possibly all.

"It now remains for her to free herself from mortal guilt, and to set others free from the consequences thereof. No prayers, no masses, will ever do it, although they may strengthen her with that strength by which alone acts of deepest love and purest self-devotion may be performed. Her words of passion, and cries for revenge—her unholy prayers could never reach the ears of the holy saints! Other powers intercepted them, and wrought so that the curses thrown up to heaven have fallen on her own flesh and blood; and so, through her very strength of love, have bruised and crushed her heart. Henceforward her former self must be buried,—yea, buried quick, if need be,—but never more to make sign, or utter cry on earth! She has become a Poor Clare, in order that, by perpetual penance and constant service of others, she may at length so act as to obtain final absolution and rest for her soul. Until then, the innocent must suffer. It is to plead for the innocent that I come to you; not in the name of the witch, Bridget Fitzgerald, but of the penitent and servant of all men, the Poor Clare, Sister Magdalen."

"Sir," said I, "I listen to your request with respect; only I may tell you it is not needed to urge me to do all that I can on behalf of one, love for whom is part of my very life. If for a time I have absented myself from her, it is to think and work for her redemption. I, a member of the English Church—my uncle, a Puritan—pray morning and night for her by name: the congregations of London, on the next Sabbath, will pray for one unknown, that she may be set free from the Powers of Darkness. Moreover, I must tell you, sir, that those evil ones touch not the great calm of her soul. She lives her own pure and loving life, unharmed and untainted, though all men fall off from her. I would I could have her faith!"

My uncle now spoke.

"Nephew," said he, "it seems to me that this gentleman, although professing what I consider an erroneous creed, has touched upon the right point in exhorting Bridget to acts of love and mercy, whereby to wipe out her sin of hate and vengeance. Let us strive after our fashion, by almsgiving and visiting of the needy and fatherless, to make our prayers acceptable. Meanwhile, I myself will go down into the north, and take charge of the maiden. I am too old to be daunted by man or demon. I will bring her to this house as to a home; and let the Double come if it will! A company of godly divines shall give it the meeting, and we will try issue."

The kindly, brave old man! But Father Bernard sat on musing.

"All hate," said he, "cannot be quenched in her heart; all Christian forgiveness cannot have entered into her soul, or the demon would have lost its power. You said, I think, that her grandchild was still tormented?"

"Still tormented!" I replied, sadly, thinking of Mistress Clarke's last letter—

He rose to go. We afterwards heard that the occasion of his coming to London was a secret political mission on behalf of the Jacobites. Nevertheless, he was a good and a wise man.

Months and months passed away without any change. Lucy entreated my uncle to leave her where she was—dreading, as I learnt, lest if she came, with her fearful companion, to dwell in the same house with me, that my love could not stand the repeated shocks to which I should be doomed. And this she thought from no distrust of the strength of my affection, but from a kind of pitying sympathy for the terror to the nerves which she clearly observed that the demoniac visitation caused in all.

I was restless and miserable. I devoted myself to good works; but I performed them from no spirit of love, but solely from the hope of reward and payment, and so the reward was never granted. At length, I asked my uncle's leave to travel; and I went forth, a wanderer, with no distincter end than that of many another wanderer—to get away from myself. A strange impulse led me to Antwerp, in spite of the wars and commotions then raging in the Low Countries—or rather, perhaps, the very craving to become interested in something external, led me into the thick of the struggle then going on with the Austrians. The cities of Flanders were all full at that time of civil disturbances and rebellions, only kept down by force, and the presence of an Austrian garrison in every place.

I arrived in Antwerp, and made inquiry for Father Bernard. He was away in the country for a day or two. Then I asked my way to the Convent of Poor Clares; but, being healthy and prosperous, I could only see the dim, pent-up, grey walls, shut closely in by narrow streets, in the lowest part of the town. My landlord told me, that had I been stricken by some loathsome disease, or in desperate case of any kind, the Poor Clares would have taken me, and tended me. He spoke of them as an order of mercy of the strictest kind, dressing scantily in the coarsest materials, going barefoot, living on what the inhabitants of Antwerp chose to bestow and sharing even those fragments and crumbs with the poor and helpless that swarmed all around; receiving no letters or communication with the outer world; utterly dead to everything but the alleviation of suffering. He smiled at my inquiring whether I could get speech of one of them; and told me that they were even forbidden to speak for the purposes of begging their daily food; while yet they lived, and fed others upon what was given in charity.

"But," exclaimed I, "supposing all men forgot them! Would they quietly lie down and die, without making sign of their extremity?"

"If such were the rule, the Poor Clares would willingly do it; but their founder appointed a remedy for such extreme cases as you suggest. They have a bell—'tis but a small one, as I have heard, and has yet never been rung in the memory of man: when the Poor Clares have been without food for twenty-four hours, they may ring this bell, and then trust to our good people of Antwerp for rushing to the rescue of the Poor Clares, who have taken such blessed care of us in all our straits."

It seemed to me that such rescue would be late in the day; but I did not say what I thought. I rather turned the conversation, by asking my landlord if he knew, or had ever heard, anything of a certain Sister Magdalen.

"Yes," said he, rather under his breath, "news will creep out, even from a convent of Poor Clares. Sister Magdalen is either a great sinner or a great saint. She does more, as I have heard, than all the other nuns put together; yet, when last month they would fain have made her mother-superior, she begged rather that they would place her below all the rest, and make her the meanest servant of all."

"You never saw her?" asked I.

"Never," he replied.

I was weary of waiting for Father Bernard, and yet I lingered in Antwerp. The political state of things became worse than ever, increased to its height by the scarcity of food consequent on many deficient harvests. I saw groups of fierce, squalid men, at every corner of the street, glaring out with wolfish eyes at my sleek skin and handsome clothes.

At last Father Bernard returned. We had a long conversation, in which he told me that, curiously enough, Mr Gisborne, Lucy's father, was serving in one of the Austrian regiments, then in garrison at Antwerp. I asked Father Bernard if he would make us acquainted; which he consented to do. But, a day or two afterwards, he told me that, on hearing my name, Mr Gisborne had declined responding to any advances on my part, saying he had adjured his country, and hated his countrymen.

Probably he recollected my name in connection with that of his daughter Lucy. Anyhow, it was clear enough that I had no chance of making his acquaintance. Father Bernard confirmed me in my suspicions of the hidden fermentation, for some coming evil, working among the "blouses" of Antwerp, and he would fain have had me depart from out the city; but I rather craved the excitement of danger, and stubbornly refused to leave.

One day, when I was walking with him in the Place Verte, he bowed to an Austrian officer, who was crossing towards the cathedral.

"That is Mr Gisborne," said he, as soon as the gentleman was past.

I turned to look at the tall, slight figure of the officer. He carried himself in a stately manner, although he was past middle age, and from his years might have had some excuse for a slight stoop. As I looked at the man, he turned round, his eyes met mine and I saw his face. Deeply lined, sallow and scathed was that countenance; scarred by passion as well as by the fortunes of war. 'Twas but a moment our eyes met. We each turned round, and went on our separate way.

But his whole appearance was not one to be easily forgotten; the thorough appointment of the dress, and evident thought bestowed on it, made but an incongruous whole with the dark, gloomy expression of his countenance. Because he was Lucy's father, I sought instinctively to meet him everywhere. At last he must have become aware of my pertinacity, for he gave me a haughty scowl whenever I passed him. In one of these encounters, however, I chanced to be of some service to him. He was turning the corner of a street, and came suddenly on one of the groups of discontented Flemings of whom I have spoken. Some words were exchanged, when my gentleman out with his sword, and with a slight but skilful cut drew blood from one of those who had insulted him, as he fancied, though I was too far off to hear the words. They would all have fallen upon him had I not rushed forwards and raised the cry, then well known in Antwerp, of rally, to the Austrian soldiers who were perpetually patrolling the streets, and who came in numbers to the rescue. I think that neither Mr Gisborne nor the mutinous group of plebeians owed me much gratitude for my interference. He had planted himself against a wall, in a skilful attitude of fence, ready with his bright glancing rapier to do battle with all the heavy, fierce, unarmed men, some six or seven in number. But when his own soldiers came up, he sheathed his sword; and, giving some careless word of command, sent them away again, and continued his saunter all alone down the street, the workmen snarling in his rear, and more than half-inclined to fall on me for my cry for rescue. I cared not if they did, my life seemed so dreary a burden just then; and, perhaps, it was this daring loitering among them that prevented their attacking me. Instead, they suffered me to fall into conversation with them; and I heard some of their grievances. Sore and heavy to be borne were they, and no wonder the sufferers were savage and desperate.

The man whom Gisborne had wounded across his face would fain have got out of me the name of his aggressor, but I refused to tell it. Another of the group heard his inquiry, and made answer—

"I know the man. He is one Gisborne, aide-de-camp to the General-Commandant. I know him well."

He began to tell some story in connection with Gisborne in a low and muttering voice; and while he was relating a tale, which I saw excited their evil blood, and which they evidently wished me not to hear, I sauntered away and back to my lodgings.

That night Antwerp was in open revolt. The inhabitants rose in rebellion against their Austrian masters. The Austrians, holding the gates of the city, remained at first pretty quiet in the citadel; only, from time to time, the boom of the great cannon swept sullenly over the town. But if they expected the disturbance to die away, and spend itself in a few hours' fury, they were mistaken. In a day or two, the rioters held possession of the principal municipal buildings. Then the Austrians poured forth in bright flaming array, calm and smiling, as they marched to the posts assigned, as if the fierce mob were no more to them than the swarms of buzzing summer flies. Their practised manoeuvres, their well-aimed shot, told with terrible effect; but in the place of one slain rioter, three sprang up of his blood to avenge his loss. But a deadly foe, a ghastly ally of the Austrians, was at work. Food, scarce and dear for months, was now hardly to be obtained at any price. Desperate efforts were being made to bring provisions into the city, for the rioters had friends without. Close to the city port, nearest to the Scheldt, a great struggle took place. I was there, helping the rioters, whose cause I had adopted. We had a savage encounter with the Austrians. Numbers fell on both sides; I saw them lie bleeding for a moment; then a volley of smoke obscured them; and when it cleared away, they were dead—trampled, upon or smothered, pressed down and hidden by the freshly-wounded whom those last guns had brought low. And then a grey-robed and grey-veiled figure came right across the flashing guns and stooped over some one, whose life-blood was ebbing away; sometimes it was to give him drink from cans which they carried slung at their sides; sometimes I saw the cross held above a dying man, and rapid prayers were being uttered, unheard by men in that hellish din and clangour, but listened to by One above. I saw all this as in a dream: the reality of that stern time was battle and carnage. But I knew that these grey figures, their bare feet all wet with blood, and their faces hidden by their veils, were the Poor Clares—sent forth now because dire agony was abroad and imminent danger at hand. Therefore, they left their cloistered shelter, and came into that thick and evil mêlée.

Close to me—driven past me by the struggle of many fighters—came the Antwerp burgess with the scarce-healed scar upon his face; and in an instant more, he was thrown by the press upon the Austrian officer Gisborne, and ere either had recovered the shock, the burgess had recognised his opponent.

"Ha! the Englishman Gisborne!" he cried, and threw himself upon him with redoubled fury. He had struck him hard—the Englishman was down; when out of the smoke came a dark-grey figure, and threw herself right under the uplifted flashing sword.

The burgess's arm stood arrested. Neither Austrians nor Anversois willingly harmed the Poor Clares.

"Leave him to me!" said a low stern voice. "He is mine enemy—mine for many years."

Those words were the last I heard. I myself was struck down by a bullet. I remember nothing more for days. When I came to myself, I was at the extremity of weakness, and was craving for food to recruit my strength. My landlord sat watching me. He, too, looked pinched and shrunken; he had heard of my wounded state, and sought me out. Yes! the struggle still continued, but the famine was sore: and some, he had heard, had died for lack of food. The tears stood in his eyes as he spoke. But soon he shook off his weakness, and his natural cheerfulness returned. Father Bernard had been to see me—no one else. (Who should indeed?) Father Bernard would come back that afternoon—he had promised. But Father Bernard never came, although I was up and dressed, and looking eagerly for him.

My landlord brought me a meal which he had cooked himself: of what it was composed he would not say, but it was most excellent, and with every mouthful I seemed to gain strength. The good man sat looking at my evident enjoyment with a happy smile of sympathy; but, as my appetite became satisfied, I began to detect a certain wistfulness in his eyes, as if craving for the food I had so nearly devoured—for, indeed, at that time I was hardly aware of the extent of the famine. Suddenly, there was a sound of many rushing feet past our window. My landlord opened one of the sides of it, the better to learn what was going on. Then we heard a faint, cracked, tinkling bell, coming shrill upon the air, clear and distinct from all other sounds. "Holy Mother!" exclaimed my landlord, "the Poor Clares!"

He snatched up the fragments of my meal, and crammed them into my hands, bidding me follow. Down stairs he ran, clutching at more food, as the women of his house eagerly held it out to him; and in a moment we were in the street, moving along with the great current, all tending towards the Convent of the Poor Clares. And still, as if piercing our ears with its inarticulate cry, came the shrill tinkle of the bell. In that strange crowd were old men trembling and sobbing, as they carried their little pittance of food; women with tears running down their cheeks, who had snatched up what provisions they had in the vessels in which they stood, so that the burden of these was in many cases much greater than that which they contained; children, with flushed faces, grasping tight the morsel of bitten cake or bread, in their eagerness to carry it safe to the help of the Poor Clares; strong men—yea, both Anversois and Austrians—pressing onward with set teeth, and no word spoken; and over all, and through all, came that sharp tinkle—that cry for help in extremity.

We met the first torrent of people returning with blanched and piteous faces: they were issuing out of the convent to make way for the offerings of others. "Haste, haste!" said they. "A Poor Clare is dying! A Poor Clare is dead for hunger! God forgive us and our city!"

We pressed on. The stream bore us along where it would. We were carried through refectories, bare and crumbless; into cells over whose doors the conventual name of the occupant was written. Thus it was that I, with others, was forced into Sister Magdalen's cell. On her couch lay Gisborne, pale unto death, but not dead. By his side was a cup of water, and a small morsel of mouldy bread, which he had pushed out of his reach, and could not move to obtain. Over against his bed were these words, copied in the

English version: "Therefore, if thine enemy hunger, feed him; if he thirst, give him drink."

Some of us gave him of our food, and left him eating greedily, like some famished wild animal. For now it was no longer the sharp tinkle, but that one solemn toll, which in all Christian countries tells of the passing of the spirit out of earthly life into eternity; and again a murmur gathered and grew, as of many people speaking with awed breath, "A Poor Clare is dying! a Poor Clare is dead!"

Borne along once more by the motion of the crowd, we were carried into the chapel belonging to the Poor Clares. On a bier before the high altar, lay a woman—lay Sister Magdalen—lay Bridget Fitzgerald. By her side stood Father Bernard, in his robes of office, and holding the crucifix on high while he pronounced the solemn absolution of the Church, as to one who had newly confessed herself of deadly sin. I pushed on with passionate force, till I stood close to the dying woman, as she received extreme unction amid the breathless and awed hush of the multitude around. Her eyes were glazing, her limbs were stiffening; but when the rite was over and finished, she raised her gaunt figure slowly up, and her eyes brightened to a strange intensity of joy, as, with the gesture of her finger and the trance-like gleam of her eye, she seemed like one who watched the disappearance of some loathed and fearful creature.

"She is freed from the curse!" said she, as she fell back dead.

A STORY TOLD IN A CHURCH

Ada Buisson

Ada Buisson (1839–1866) is one of the less frequently discussed writers to appear in this anthology. *Put to the Test* (1865) is the only novel Buisson published during her tragically short life. Other known work includes a second novel, *A Terrible Wrong* (1867), and six ghost stories: "My Aunt's Pearl Ring" (1867), "A Story Told in a Church" (1867), "The Ghost's Summons" (1868), "The Baron's Coffin" (1869), "My Sister Caroline" (1870) and "The Sins of the Fathers" (1870). Each piece of short fiction appeared posthumously in *Belgravia*, a periodical edited by Mary Elizabeth Braddon, the long-term partner of John Maxwell who published *Put to the Test*.

Buisson's authorial identity was nearly lost when Montague Summers claimed that her signature was a pseudonym for M. E. Braddon. Summers's mistake, published in the *Times Literary Supplement* on 30 September 1944, was corrected three weeks later by Buisson's nephew, F. B. Evans.

First published in Braddon's *Belgravia Annual* for Christmas 1867, "A Story Told in a Church" relays the tale of historic sins and the impact they have had on those who survived.

"**W**hat shall we do? We are absolutely locked in! Every door is firmly closed, and I believe it is the doing of those dreadful boys, who have been trying to frighten us out of our wits all the afternoon with their ghost-stories." And Katie Bernard came laughing back to the spot where we were all standing and saying farewell words, after going through the pleasant labour of decking our little church with holly-wreaths and shining laurel.

Katie was blessed with excellent nerves and a constitution that defied winter snows and summer heats, and I verily believe that she could have curled herself up in one of the great pews and slept the long night away as soundly as in her own white bed in the parsonage. But there were others amongst us (and I confess I was one of them) who already longed for the warmth of a fire, and who moreover began to find the glimmering of the white monuments and strange sculptured faces round about weird and a little ghostly.

"The dusk is falling. This is certainly most annoying," exclaimed Miss Montem, Ella Willis's governess, under whose charge we all were.

She turned a little pale as she spoke,—a rare thing for her; for a more self-possessed person than that handsome Miss Montem I never saw.

"What! are you, too, afraid of ghosts, Miss Montem?" laughed Katie. "Those boys will be delighted, then, at the success of their trick."

The governess turned almost scornfully. "I do not understand how one can fear that in which one does not believe," she said; "but I confess I have a particular dislike to remain in a church after dusk; it recalls to my mind the most painful story I ever heard." And then, turning hastily away, Miss Montem herself went and examined every door, even tried the vestry window.

Those "dreadful boys," however, had taken infinite care to bar every mode of exit; and even Dora Montem was obliged to admit that nothing could be done, but patiently to submit to imprisonment until our absence should cause anxiety at our various homes, and someone should be sent after us.

Meanwhile the twilight was momentarily deepening, and to my mind, at least, those half-wreathed pillars, those white faces peeping out from between the dark laurel, those stone figures on the two ancient tombs of Sir Guy and Sir Geoffrey Willis, lying with their legs crossed, began to look very eerie indeed.

We grouped ourselves about the seats in the chancel, and for a time talked and even laughed; but somehow, first one voice grew silent and then another, and at last those grim knights lying beside us were not more silent than we.

"Well, I must say this is a dismal way of spending Christmas-eve," at length sighed Kate Bernard. "We ought to be round the fire now, roasting chestnuts and telling stories."

"Telling stories! ah, what a good idea! Why not amuse ourselves by that now?" exclaimed another voice. "Come, Ella, you have travelled; tell us some of your adventures."

"I? I never told a story in my life. No, ask Miss Montem; she has a gift for it."

The governess had been sitting a little apart from us, closer to the tombs than we cared to go; but as Ella spoke she raised her face, which she had been leaning on her hands, and even in the fading light I saw that she was deadly pale.

"I could not tell a story here," she murmured, "unless—would you like to hear the one of which I just now spoke? It is a terribly painful one, an awful one, but—"

There was a universal interruption of "Never mind. Yes, yes. Tell us that, Miss Montem."

We all knew the strange power the usually silent governess possessed for story-telling. It was the only time indeed she unbent or seemed like other human beings; but when she did condescend to indulge us, she possessed a fascination which none of us could resist; and we all knew that whilst listening to her we should care very little for the cold or darkness.

This was the story she told us:

Ten years ago I was seventeen, and serving my first year as governess-pupil at Mrs Morris's school near Chichester.

No, Ella, you need not look pityingly at me, for I was very happy. Mrs Morris treated me kindly and fairly; and amongst the girls I had friends whom I loved dearly. Besides, Mount Silver, as the place was called, was conducted on the home principle, and there was not one of us who regarded our existence whilst there but as intensely satisfactory and enjoyable.

You may imagine that Mrs Morris could not have been a very rigid schoolmistress when I tell you that we even received the news that we should be obliged to spend Christmas-day under her roof with no greater regret than one naturally feels when one finds the pleasure of seeing dear friends suddenly deferred.

The Christmas of ten years ago was the snowiest I remember. Roads were blocked up; even railways were subject to constant stoppages; and it happened that in our part of the country a small river had been so swelled by the snow as to have laid the surrounding ways under water. So, what with one thing and another, Mount Silver lay separated from Chichester, with almost as many difficulties to be overcome in a distance of twenty miles as if a hemisphere was between them.

Most of us were London girls, and the railway being unreachable, our fate was quickly settled. The only two who remained voluntary prisoners were Millicent Power and her cousin Irena Dupont.

Milly Power was the niece of the lady of the manor, Lady Jane Power, who, it was believed, intended to make her her heiress; and her home lay but a couple of miles from Mount Silver. But Christmas or any other "mass" was so dull with Lady Jane, who passed her time nursing her cat, knitting, and physicking her various imaginary ailments, that both Milly and Irena no sooner heard that the rest of us would be forced to spend part of the holiday at school, than they begged Mrs Morris to allow them to do the same.

I think we were all glad that they did not desert us, though, perhaps, had—but I must not anticipate. They were our head girls, our leaders—Milly Power by right of age and rank, Irena Dupont by right of her daring spirit and rich beauty. Ah, heavens! how beautiful that girl was! I see her before me now, with her dark glowing eyes, her oval face, the rich Southern blood mantling her cheek with every emotion; so fresh; so eager in her enjoyment of her young life and splendid health.

She was cousin to Millicent by the mother's side; but, though daughters of two sisters, there was not a shadow of resemblance either in character or feature between them.

Millicent was fair, cold, haughty, proud of her ancient family—a little proud, I sometimes thought, of having money always at her command, and being the heiress of her aunt. But *I* ought not to make her any reproach, for she was a kind friend to me, and it was thanks to Milly's purse that my poor wardrobe could boast anything beyond the very humblest attire.

How it was that Irena Dupont lived also under the protection of Lady Jane I never rightly understood. She was not a penniless orphan, I knew, for she often alluded to her father and his vineyards down in the south of France; but yet she appeared to be in a great measure dependent on Lady Jane, and once or twice I noticed that she gave way to Millicent, proudly, but in a manner that betrayed she had a reason for so doing.

Were they fond of each other, those two cousins? Ah, that was a question which none of us could satisfactorily answer *then*—not even I, who was Milly's bosom friend.

They sang together sweetly, rode together; but never by any chance were they known to talk together beyond joining in ordinary conversation, and never did I see Irena give Milly one of those gushing kisses which she bestowed so liberally and gracefully on those she loved amongst us.

It was not, however, till the Christmas I am speaking of that I knew the great obstacle between them to be Milly's jealousy of her cousin's beauty.

We were sitting in the schoolroom after tea, as merry a party as could be, in spite of our imprisonment, when Mrs Morris entered rather abruptly, and with not an altogether satisfied expression of countenance.

"Millicent, my dear, I want you in the drawing-room," she said, slowly shutting the door. "Your cousin, Arthur Power, has ridden over perfectly desperate at finding the Manor House only presided over by Lady Jane; and he declares that the cold is so intense he really can't face it again to-night, and give him shelter I must. Most improper of him to come to a school for young ladies, I am sure!"

Millicent's fair face flushed, and a peculiar half-vexed smile curved her lips.

"Just like Arthur—he is *so* inconsiderate," she exclaimed, rising with her work in her hand.

"He wanted to come down here, but I would not allow that."

"Of course not," said Milly, walking rather hastily towards the door.

"Ah, Irena, you may as well come too. I—"

But Millicent turned almost abruptly, and with a strange forgetfulness of the respect she usually paid Mrs Morris, exclaimed: "What for? Arthur is my cousin, not Irena's. She does not know him even."

Irena had risen, and was following, but at those words she dropped back into her corner by the fire, and a smile, half angry, half scornful, passed over her beautiful face. "True," she said quietly.

Mrs Morris looked a little puzzled, but even she sometimes gave way to Miss Power; and so, without further remark, she linked her arm in Milly's, and they left the schoolroom.

We were not so discreet as our governess, however; and no sooner had the door closed than there was a general exclamation against Millicent, for Irena was the idol of the school; and then the French girl for an instant seemed to forget the restraint she had always imposed on herself, and lifting up her flushed face, with its rich, angry, glowing eyes, she exclaimed: "Nonsense! You forget

Millicent is almost engaged to her cousin Arthur. It was natural she should wish to see him alone."

"Or natural, you mean, that she should not wish him to see *you*," exclaimed someone.

But if that was Millicent's wish, she was cruelly disappointed. Mrs Morris, anxious to make up in some measure for our disappointment, had invited the doctor's and lawyer's families, living in the village close by, with the vicar's nieces, to come and celebrate Christmas-eve in the good old-fashioned manner; and no sooner did Arthur hear of the "party," than he invited himself to remain for it; and not all Mrs Morris's hints at impropriety and inconvenience could induce the handsome young officer to dislodge himself.

To the excellent lady's intense relief, Mr Power was a fashionably late riser, and she contrived to despatch us all the next morning to the church which we were to assist in decorating before he made his appearance; and I firmly believe, as she watched us all pass out of the garden gate, she thought she had manœuvred skilfully past all danger until at least the evening.

School-girls of seventeen and eighteen are apt to talk a good deal on those subjects which good Mrs Morris dreaded so; but I don't think my mind was ever much given that way, and Arthur Power certainly never crossed my thoughts when once I found myself in that ancient church, with holly and laurel wreaths, waiting to do justice to all the artistic taste we could muster among us.

We were soon scattered over the church, which was a singularly beautiful one, though centuries old, it having belonged to a wealthy monastery; and as usual Milly and I worked together.

She was not in a talkative humour, and so we spoke little except about the work; and when she suddenly left me, saying she must have a little exercise to warm her, I scarcely missed her.

Alas, that she ever took that ramble!

She was not gone long, and when she returned she was out of breath. "What do you think, Dora, I have found," she began; and then suddenly she paused and looked sharply round, for a man's laugh sounded from the chancel. "That's Arthur; let us go and see," she exclaimed.

And we did go, and what we saw was beautiful—Irena mounted on a chair, twining a holly wreath round a cherub's head; and there beside her, gazing up and handing sprays of shining green, stood Arthur Power. Two other girls were near, but it was Irena Dupont on whom those handsome blue eyes were fixed so earnestly that even our approach was unnoticed.

"So you have found us out, Arthur, in spite of Mrs Morris," Milly exclaimed, with a smile on her lips, but O, such wildly angry eyes!

He turned immediately and held out his hand.

"Of course; you know I always manage for myself."

"So it seems, even your introductions."

"As to that, Miss Dupont is a kind of cousin, you know, and therefore an introduction was unnecessary; besides, I am making myself so decidedly useful, that even if I have offended against the *convenances*, I ought to be forgiven."

"And so you shall be if you will mount and finish this for me," interrupted Irena; and before even he could reply, she had jumped lightly down from the chair and joined another group of workers at the other end of the church.

Arthur turned and looked after her rather dolefully, and Milly's eyes flashed.

*

Ah, Heaven! how well I remember that Christmas-eve! How joyously it began! how gay we were! I know I can say for myself that never since have I laughed with such freehearted joy as I did that night. There was little ceremony, no elaborate toilettes; we all knew each other, and the female element considerably preponderated; but the dancing was no less delightful, the smiles no less radiant, the enjoyment no less intense.

In the early part of the evening perhaps there might have been a little jealousy regarding the attentions of Arthur Power; but he soon showed such evident preference for Irena Dupont, that the rest retired from the contest.

And who could wonder that she should be preferred? Simply dressed in white muslin, with a sash of scarlet silk round her waist, Irena seemed to float amongst us like some goddess amongst her attendant nymphs. She never seemed to try to be dignified, and yet she always walked like a young queen, always stood amongst us with her tall graceful form as superior to the rest of us as Diana amongst her nymphs.

It was no use Millicent Power looking cold and haughty; Arthur cared not: he saw only those sweet dark eyes of her French cousin, heard only that rich merry laugh, cared only to wind his arm round that pliant waist.

Even in the games which relieved the dance, Arthur contrived always to be near Irena; and though now and then he paid attention to his cousin Milly, even she saw that it was because he felt it a duty rather than because he wished to do so.

I thought I knew Millicent Power well; I thought I understood her reserved character; but that night she puzzled me. She was too ladylike to show temper or even jealousy at Arthur's sudden desertion but now and then she glanced at that part of the room where he was with such wild pained eyes, now passionately angry, now sorrowful, that even I wondered she could so betray herself to him.

Still she did not keep herself away from the rest; she joined in all the dances and games, and talked and laughed as excitedly as any of us. More so almost; and I recollect that it was Millicent's voice which was the first to accept the challenge that led to so much sorrow.

Our party was too large to be accommodated, even at the large school table, all at the same time, so we younger ones had taken our supper first and then returned to the dancing-room, leaving Mrs Morris to entertain the elders; and so it happened that we had no wise friend near to prevent the commencement of as foolish a freak as ever wild young creatures planned.

How it was that the subject of ghosts was started I know not; but I remember that instead of returning to our games we stood grouped together listening to a wild story Arthur Power was telling; and though all laughed and declared their disbelief in it, there were few voices that responded to his challenge at the conclusion. "I would wager this," and he held up a small gold locket, "that not one person here would venture now to cross the churchyard alone, enter the church, and pass through and bring me a piece of the cypress waving over the broken tomb on the other side."

"What, make the tour of the churchyard in this cold! No, thank you," said one sensibly.

"O, you may put on goloshes and a warm cloak; besides, it's a splendid night, the snow is hard as iron. Ha! ha! I see, ladies and gentlemen, it is the white feather, not the cold."

"I should not be afraid," exclaimed Millicent. "As you say, it is a splendid night: I will go."

"And so will I," I exclaimed.

"And so will I," said Irena.

No sooner said than done.

Upstairs we three adventurous ones crept to don warm cloaks; and then, cautiously opening the front-door (for we knew if Mrs Morris heard aught of such a proceeding she would quickly stop it), not five minutes later, I, with the key of the church in my hand, started at a quick pace over the hard snowy walk.

It was agreed that ten minutes after I had started, Millicent should follow, and at an equal period after Irena was to come; for, argued Arthur, the elders would probably have finished supper soon; and it would not be safe to wait for the return of each before the other started.

Ah, how well I remember that mad midnight walk! It was a brilliant night, but the cold was so intense that I had not reached the gate of the churchyard, close as it was, before I repented of my folly. However, I went in.

I was not of a timid nature; and that walk across the snowy churchyard was not in the least fearful to me. The silence of the decorated ancient church, about which I had heard legends enough to terrify anyone, affected me more; and I confess, as the door grated slowly on its hinges, I felt sorely tempted to turn and flee.

I did walk very quickly along the stone aisle; and it was with a gasp of intense relief that I stepped out into the snow and moon-light again through the little chancel-door, close to which stood the broken tomb and its dark cypress.

My hand trembled so, that I could scarcely pluck the bough; and then I fairly ran along the side-path which led to the other gate opening into the back garden of Mount Silver.

"By St George, you have only been a quarter of an hour!" exclaimed Arthur Power. "I wonder how fast Milly will run. You look rather white, though, Miss Montem."

"The cold is intense," I answered rather crossly; "and it was a foolish thing to do."

"Did you meet the ghost of the monk?"

"Never mind whom I met; there is the cypress bough."

Arthur shrugged his shoulders and turned away, still watch in hand.

"Twenty minutes; no, twenty-five minutes. Milly must be having quite a gossip with the monk," he said presently, not quite so pleasantly though.

"Twenty-seven—ah, there she is!"

Yes, there was Milly, ghostly white and shivering.

Arthur approached her almost anxiously; and though he made some joking remark about her having met a legion of ghosts, I observed that he took her hand and began rubbing it, and then muttered something in a low tone, which, however, only turned Milly's shivering into a convulsive shudder.

"Give her something hot to drink," I exclaimed from my corner, where I was also still shivering. "The cold—no one knows what the cold of that church is."

And then Milly lifted up her eyes with a look. Heaven, how that look haunted me afterwards! And she managed to mutter with her sweet lips, "Yes; the awful cold."

"I wish to goodness Irena would come now, before Mrs Morris returns," said someone. "She will be so angry about this;" and then Arthur Power looked at his watch again, but this time said nothing.

A silence fell upon us all; not a word was spoken; no one moved even; everyone listened—listened for that light step which should announce the approach for which somehow we all so longed.

The clock struck one; and again Arthur looked at his watch, and then again that silence continued unbroken; and there, motionless, we all remained waiting for her—for her who was *never to come to us!*

No use our listening; no use watching those slow-moving hands of the great clock—never, never more were we to hear the fall of those quick light feet. Time might come and time might go, but Irena Dupont would not return with it.

O, that miserable night! how the memory of it has haunted me! Those sad, horror-stricken faces, which not two hours ago had been so happy; the frightened whispering; the coming to and fro of anxious searchers waving their lurid torchlight over the snow; the sobs, the tears, the wild hopes, and at length the blank despair—how I remember it all, as some dreadful confusion, which, strive as I would, I could not comprehend.

A mystery indeed had fallen upon us that Christmas night— a mystery which none could solve. All we knew was that Irena Dupont had gone out fresh and living into the snow and darkness, and that she never came back. The path from the house to the church was direct enough—it was perfectly safe; there were no bad characters about; so far as our human ken could reach it, all of us could declare to its perfect safety; and evidence of any struggle or accident there was none.

Search was not spared; and for weeks every means of discovering what had become of the lost girl was freely tried. But that solemn Christmas night refused to give up its secret; and the mystery of the beautiful French girl's fate remained still darkly hidden.

*

But, in spite of those great sorrows which come to disturb the current of life, commonplace daily realities must be thought of and faced. I had learnt that lesson in the year of hard struggling I went through on quitting Mrs Morris's pleasant roof to take the place of junior teacher in a German school; and yet I confess I felt almost horrified at the contents of a letter I received one June morning from my old friend, Millicent Power.

She was going to be married to Arthur, she wrote, and she hoped I would come and act as bridesmaid. What! had she forgotten so soon that horrible Christmas story? I thought. With her usual forethought, she had enclosed a banknote for my travelling expenses; and she made her request in terms which a lonely orphan like myself was not likely to resist.

Lady Jane was dead, leaving Millicent sole heiress to her property; but Milly told me she could not endure the solitude of Power Place, and still lived with Mrs Morris, from whose house she was to be married. I was to go to her there, and I should find more than one familiar face to welcome me.

It is only those who are homeless who can sympathise with me in the intense affection I bore to that dear old house and all its occupants, and the eagerness with which, in spite of my weariness, I leaned forward in the coach to catch the first glimpse of the tall, ivy-covered chimneys.

I knew the horn announcing the entrance of the coach into the village would be heard at Mount Silver, and I quite expected to see Milly's fair face at the garden-gate waiting for me. There was one figure standing there between the rose-bushes; but it was Mrs Morris's, not Millicent's.

"No, my dear, I would not allow Milly out so late, though the evening is mild," she answered, after the first embraces were over: "her health is very delicate, and I sent her to bed."

Though Mrs Morris spoke drily, and almost indifferently, I could detect anxiety in her eyes, and I knew that before long I should hear something of the reason; for I was a favourite of hers, and she had always treated me as a friend rather than a pupil.

I found that I was to sup in private with my former instructress; and I was scarcely surprised when, as soon as the first hospitable cares were over, she began abruptly, "Do you know, Dora, I am very uneasy about Milly? I am not at all sure that this marriage ought to take place."

I started.

"I mean, of course, on account of her health. Ever since that night when—when—you remember—Milly has been altering in a manner that perhaps others may not have observed, but which I have. There is a family malady hereditary to the Powers, you probably know—"

"Consumption! Ah, I have heard that."

"I wish it were only that," sternly replied Mrs Morris, as if forcing herself to utter the words. "It is something more awful—insanity. Milly's nerves never seem to have recovered the shock of that dreadful night."

I was literally too horrified to say a word, and I knew scarcely whether to be glad or not when Mrs Morris suddenly rose and proposed going to Millicent.

I was accustomed to her abrupt ways. Still, when she paused at Milly's door, and said in a sharp whisper, "There is a week still to the wedding—we must *both* watch and do our duty, Dora"—I shrank back in alarm.

143

And though that first interview relieved my mind, I had not been twenty-four hours constantly in Milly's company before I saw that Mrs Morris's observations were correct: Milly was altered. She would suddenly break off in the middle of a sentence, even about Arthur, and fall into a stony kind of quietude, which was too strange to be the result of mere weakness. Sometimes, too, she was restless, and the anxiety for her wedding-day to arrive was incomprehensible and almost painful.

She could not endure solitude, either; and if by any chance she awoke from one of her frequent dozings and found herself alone, she would ring her bell with a fury which more than once broke the wire. Still she never permitted anyone to sleep in her room at night; and I was quite surprised when, the day before the wedding, she asked me if I would mind sleeping on the sofa at the foot of her bed.

Ah, that Sunday night was to be another of those which terror scorched into my memory!

It was an exceedingly hot night. The room was a large one, on the ground floor, and the open window looked into the garden. I could not sleep. Milly, too, tossed restlessly from side to side, and, though she slept, moaned piteously. Time seemed as if it would never move on, and hours seemed to elapse between the striking of each quarter. I suppose, however, I must have dozed, for suddenly I started up with the impression that someone had passed by me, and hastily looking towards Millicent's bed, I saw that it was empty!

Why, instead of rushing to the door, I flung on a cloak, and, barefooted as I was, darted through the French window into the garden, I know not—it must have been some fate that guided me, for there, dimly visible passing through the little gate into the church-yard, was a white figure. I flew along, but Millicent went faster than I, and with a strength and steadiness she never displayed in the day.

On she went—up the little side-paths, never pausing, but going on swiftly, steadily, towards the chancel-door.

Surely now she must pause, unless by some chance the preparations for the marriage had caused the door to be left unlocked.

She passed in!

Ah, how I flew then, though why, except fearing some horrible catastrophe, I know not; and at length a second time I stood within that ancient church in the dead of night.

Even as I entered, a low piteous moan directed me to where I should follow my unfortunate friend; and there in one of the grim side-aisles, where the stone pavement still bore Latin inscriptions to departed monks, I saw that white figure kneeling and moaning and bruising her soft fingers against the hard stone.

"There—I know it is there," she muttered. "I lifted it then so easily, it must come up again. Don't shriek so, Irena—O, O, don't shriek so!"

And then, lifting up her white agonised face, she desisted from her awful scratching at the stone, and put her hands to her ears, as if to shut out some dismal sounds.

I stood transfixed with horror, not daring to approach, for I saw that though she had her eyes open she was asleep; but at that moment the chancel-door slammed. With an awful cry the sleeper started up, gazed wildly round, and then I saw her fall prone on the stone floor, the life-blood flowing from her lips.

There was no wedding the next day in that ancient church. Millicent Power lay gasping away her life, and murmuring only two words, "God forgive! God forgive!" But there was a horrified group standing round that stone and watching for the return of the explorer of the unknown ancient vault which was found under that cracked pavement. There was no need to make much inquiry as to whose remains those were which then were brought to the light of day—the long dark hair, a small ring, told all that was necessary to be told—Irena Dupont was found again!

But beyond those words which in her miserable sleep Millicent Power uttered, no light was shed on the mystery which enveloped her fate. I, who knew all that had passed, and had seen the wild agony of her face as she knelt and tore at the stones, felt that, unless insanity could be alleged in her excuse, Millicent Power's soul was loaded with an awful crime; and as I remembered how she had been walking in that aisle when she left me and returned uttering that exclamation which was never finished, I joined fervently in that dying prayer of hers, "God forgive."

That stone was broken in such a way that a chance glance would more likely have noticed that it could be raised easily than one accustomed to pass it day by day.

Probably she had raised it and discovered the vault, and leaving it open had forgotten it until that mad midnight visit. I had passed through the centre aisle; but Irena might easily have taken the side one, and—but enough of this—it is too dreadful, and—God forgive us all!

We were all huddled together as Miss Montem's voice dropped; and if there was a word murmured before we were silenced by the sound of steps without, it was only an echo of the prayer with which Dora Montem closed her story.

IN THE CONFESSIONAL

Amelia B. Edwards

Now most frequently discussed in relation to her work as an Egyptologist, Amelia Ann Blanford Edwards (1831–1892) was a woman of many talents. Educated at home, she spent her childhood writing fiction and poetry, illustrating her work as her artistic talents developed. After time spent working as a Church organist, Edwards left a musical career to focus on forming a professional life as a writer. Writing across genres, Edwards produced short stories, poetry anthologies and non-fiction books with an historical or archaeological focus. She also produced numerous novels, the most successful being *Barbara's History* (1864) and *Lord Brackenbury* (1880). Edwards was also a seasoned traveller who wrote several accounts of her time abroad. Noticeable early travelogues include *Untrodden Peaks and Unfrequented Valleys* (1873), the account of a trip through the Dolomites with her friend, Lucy Renshawe and *A Thousand Miles up the Nile* (1877), a text which centres on time Edwards and Renshawe spent in Egypt.

"In the Confessional" is one of several spectral stories penned by Edwards, the most anthologised of which is perhaps "The Phantom Coach" (1864). Initially published in the 1871 Christmas number of *All the Year Round*, "In the Confessional" was later reprinted in *Monsieur Maurice and Other Stories* (1873). Like "A Story Told in a Church", the phantasmal presence in this tale imprints human wickedness onto a holy site.

The things of which I write befell—let me see, some fifteen or eighteen years ago. I was not young then; I am not old now. Perhaps I was about thirty-two; but I do not know my age very exactly, and I cannot be certain to a year or two one way or the other.

My manner of life at that time was desultory and unsettled. I had a sorrow—no matter of what kind—and I took to rambling about Europe; not certainly in the hope of forgetting it, for I had no wish to forget, but because of the restlessness that made one place after another *triste* and intolerable to me.

It was change of place, however, and not excitement, that I sought. I kept almost entirely aloof from great cities, Spas, and beaten tracks, and preferred for the most part to explore districts where travellers and foreigners rarely penetrated.

Such a district at that time was the Upper Rhine. I was traversing it that particular Summer for the first time, and on foot; and I had set myself to trace the course of the river from its source in the great Rhine glacier to its fall at Schaffhausen. Having done this, however, I was unwilling to part company with the noble river; so I decided to follow it yet a few miles farther—perhaps as far as Mayence, but at all events as far as Basle.

And now began, if not the finest, certainly not the least charming part of my journey. Here, it is true, were neither Alps, nor glaciers, nor ruined castles perched on inaccessible crags; but my way lay through a smiling country, studded with picturesque hamlets, and beside a bright river, hurrying along over swirling rapids, and under the dark arches of antique covered bridges, and between hill-sides garlanded with vines.

It was towards the middle of a long day's walk among such scenes as these that I came to Rheinfelden, a small place on the left bank of the river, about fourteen miles above Basle.

As I came down the white road in the blinding sunshine, with the vines on either hand, I saw the town lying low on the opposite bank of the Rhine. It was an old walled town, enclosed on the land side and open to the river, the houses going sheer down to the water's edge, with flights of slimy steps worn smooth by the wash of the current, and overhanging eaves, and little built-out rooms with pent-house roofs, supported from below by jutting piles black with age and tapestried with water-weeds. The stunted towers of a couple of churches stood up from amid the brown and tawny roofs within the walls.

Beyond the town, height above height, stretched a distance of wooded hills. The old covered bridge, divided by a bit of rocky island in the middle of the stream, led from bank to bank—from Germany to Switzerland. The town was in Switzerland; I, looking towards it from the road, stood on Baden territory; the river ran sparkling and foaming between.

I crossed, and found the place all alive in anticipation of a Kermess, or fair, that was to be held there the next day but one. The townsfolk were all out in the streets or standing about their doors; and there were carpenters hard at work knocking up rows of wooden stands and stalls the whole length of the principal thoroughfare. Shop-signs in open-work of wrought iron hung over the doors. A runlet of sparkling water babbled down a stone channel in the middle of the street. At almost every other house (to judge by the rows of tarnished watches hanging in the dingy parlour windows), there lived a watchmaker; and presently I came to a fountain—a regular Swiss fountain, spouting water from four ornamental pipes, and surmounted by the usual armed knight in old grey stone.

As I rambled on thus (looking for an inn, but seeing none), I suddenly found that I had reached the end of the street, and with it the limit of the town on this side. Before me rose a lofty, picturesque old gate-tower, with a tiled roof and a little window over the archway; and there was a peep of green grass and golden sunshine beyond. The town walls (sixty or seventy feet in height, and curiously roofed with a sort of projecting shed on the inner side) curved away to right and left, unchanged since the Middle Ages. A rude wain, laden with clover and drawn by mild-eyed, cream-coloured oxen, stood close by in the shade.

I passed out through the gloom of the archway into the sunny space beyond. The moat outside the walls was bridged over and filled in—a green ravine of grasses and wild-flowers. A stork had built its nest on the roof of the gate-tower. The cicalas shrilled in the grass. The shadows lay sleeping under the trees, and a family of cocks and hens went plodding inquisitively to and fro among the cabbages in the adjacent field. Just beyond the moat, with only this field between, stood a little solitary church—a church with a wooden porch, and a quaint, bright-red steeple, and a churchyard like a rose-garden, full of colour and perfume, and scattered over with iron crosses wreathed with immortelles.

The churchyard gate and the church door stood open. I went in. All was clean, and simple, and very poor. The walls were whitewashed; the floor was laid with red bricks; the roof raftered. A tiny confessional like a sentry-box stood in one corner; the font was covered with a lid like a wooden steeple; and over the altar, upon which stood a pair of battered brass candlesticks and two vases of artificial flowers, hung a daub of the Holy Family, in oils.

All here was so cool, so quiet, that I sat down for a few moments and rested. Presently an old peasant woman trudged up the church-path with a basket of vegetables on her head. Having set this down in the porch, she came in, knelt before the altar, said her simple prayers, and went her way.

Was it not time for me also to go my way? I looked at my watch. It was past four o'clock, and I had not yet found a lodging for the night.

I got up, somewhat unwillingly; but, attracted by a tablet near the altar, crossed over to look at it before leaving the church. It was a very small slab, and bore a very brief German inscription to this effect:—

TO THE SACRED MEMORY

OF

THE REVEREND PÈRE CHESSEZ,
For twenty years the beloved Pastor of this Parish.
Died April 16th, 1825. Aged 44.
HE LIVED A SAINT; HE DIED A MARTYR.

I read it over twice, wondering idly what story was wrapped up in the concluding line. Then, prompted by a childish curiosity, I went up to examine the confessional.

It was, as I have said, about the size of a sentry-box, and was painted to imitate old dark oak. On the one side was a narrow door with a black handle, on the other a little opening like a ticket-taker's window, closed on the inside by a faded green curtain.

I know not what foolish fancy possessed me, but, almost without considering what I was doing, I turned the handle and opened the door. Opened it—peeped in—found the priest sitting in his place—started back as if I had been shot—and stammered an unintelligible apology.

"I—I beg a thousand pardons," I exclaimed. "I had no idea—seeing the church empty—"

He was sitting with averted face, and clasped hands lying idly in his lap—a tall, gaunt man, dressed in a black soutane. When I paused, and not till then, he slowly, very slowly, turned his head, and looked me in the face.

The light inside the confessional was so dim that I could not see his features very plainly. I only observed that his eyes were large, and bright, and wild looking, like the eyes of some fierce animal, and that his face, with the reflection of the green curtain upon it, looked lividly pale.

For a moment we remained thus, gazing at each other, as if fascinated. Then, finding that he made no reply, but only stared at me with those strange eyes, I stepped hastily back, shut the door without another word, and hurried out of the church.

I was very much disturbed by this little incident; more disturbed, in truth, than seemed reasonable, for my nerves for the moment were shaken. Never, I told myself, never while I lived could I forget that fixed attitude and stony face, or the glare of those terrible eyes. What was the man's history? Of what secret despair, of what life-long remorse, of what wild unsatisfied longings was he the victim? I felt I could not rest till I had learned something of his past life.

Full of these thoughts, I went on quickly into the town, half running across the field, and never looking back. Once past the gateway and inside the walls, I breathed more freely. The wain was still standing in the shade, but the oxen were gone now, and two men were busy forking out the clover into a little yard close by. Having inquired of one of these regarding an inn, and being directed to the Krone, "over against the Frauenkirche," I made my way to the upper part of the town, and there, at one corner of a forlorn, weed-grown market-place, I found my hostelry.

The landlord, a sedate, bald man in spectacles, who, as I presently discovered, was not only an innkeeper but a clock-maker, came out from an inner room to receive me. His wife, a plump, pleasant body, took my orders for dinner. His pretty daughter showed me to my room. It was a large, low, whitewashed room, with two lattice windows overlooking the market-place, two little beds, covered with puffy red eiderdowns at the farther end, and an army of clocks and ornamental timepieces arranged along every shelf, table, and chest of drawers in the room. Being left here to my meditations, I sat down and counted these companions of my solitude.

Taking little and big together, Dutch clocks, cuckoo clocks, *châlet* clocks, skeleton clocks, and *pendules* in ormolu, bronze, marble, ebony, and alabaster cases, there were exactly thirty-two. Twenty-eight were going merrily. As no two among them were of the same opinion as regarded the time, and as several struck the quarters as well as the hours, the consequence was that one or other gave tongue about every five minutes. Now, for a light and nervous sleeper such as I was at that time, here was a lively prospect for the night!

Going downstairs presently with the hope of getting my land-lady to assign me a quieter room, I passed two eight-day clocks on the landing, and a third at the foot of the stairs. The public room was equally well-stocked. It literally bristled with clocks, one of which played a spasmodic version of "Gentle Zitella" with variations every quarter of an hour. Here I found a little table prepared by the open window, and a dish of trout and a flask of country wine awaiting me. The pretty daughter waited upon me; her mother bustled to and fro with the dishes; the landlord stood by, and beamed upon me through his spectacles.

"The trout were caught this morning, about two miles from here," he said, complacently.

"They are excellent," I replied, filling him out a glass of wine, and helping myself to another. "Your health, Herr Wirth."

"Thanks, mein Herr—yours."

Just at this moment two clocks struck at opposite ends of the room—one twelve, and the other seven. I ventured to suggest that mine host was tolerably well reminded of the flight of time; whereupon he explained that his work lay chiefly in the repairing and regulating line, and that at that present moment he had no less than one hundred and eighteen clocks of various sorts and sizes on the premises.

"Perhaps the Herr Engländer is a light sleeper," said his quick-witted wife, detecting my dismay. "If so, we can get him a bedroom elsewhere. Not, perhaps, in the town, for I know no place where he would be as comfortable as with ourselves; but just outside the Friedrich's Thor, not five minutes' walk from our door."

I accepted the offer gratefully.

"So long," I said, "as I ensure cleanliness and quiet, I do not care how homely my lodgings may be."

"Ah, you'll have both, mein Herr, if you go where my wife is thinking of," said the landlord. "It is at the house of our pastor—the Père Chessez."

"The Père Chessez!" I exclaimed. "What, the pastor of the little church out yonder?"

"The same, mein Herr."

"But—but surely the Père Chessez is dead! I saw a tablet to his memory in the chancel."

"Nay, that was our pastor's elder brother," replied the landlord, looking grave. "He has been gone these thirty years and more. His was a tragical ending."

But I was thinking too much of the younger brother just then to feel any curiosity about the elder; and I told myself that I would put up with the companionship of any number of clocks, rather than sleep under the same roof with that terrible face and those unearthly eyes.

"I saw your pastor just now in the church," I said, with apparent indifference. "He is a singular-looking man."

"He is too good for this world," said the landlady.

"He is a saint upon earth!" added the pretty Fräulein.

"He is one of the best of men," said, more soberly, the husband and father. "I only wish he was less of a saint. He fasts, and prays, and works beyond his strength. A little more beef and a little less devotion would be all the better for him."

"I should like to hear something more about the life of so good a man," said I, having by this time come to the end of my simple dinner. "Come, Herr Wirth, let us have a bottle of your best, and then sit down and tell me your pastor's history!"

The landlord sent his daughter for a bottle of the "green seal," and, taking a chair, said:—

"Ach Himmel! mein Herr, there is no history to tell. The good father has lived here all his life. He is one of us. His father, Johann Chessez, was a native of Rheinfelden and kept this very inn. He was a wealthy farmer and vine grower. He had only those two sons—Nicholas, who took to the church and became pastor of Feldkirche; and this one, Matthias, who was intended to inherit the business; but who also entered religion after the death of his elder brother, and is now pastor of the same parish."

"But why did he 'enter religion?'" I asked. "Was he in any way to blame for the accident (if it was an accident) that caused the death of his elder brother?"

"Ah Heavens! no!" exclaimed the landlady, leaning on the back of her husband's chair. "It was the shock—the shock that told so terribly upon his poor nerves! He was but a lad at that time, and as sensitive as a girl—but the Herr Engländer does not know the story. Go on, my husband."

So the landlord, after a sip of the "green seal," continued:—

"At the time my wife alludes to, mein Herr, Johann Chessez was still living. Nicholas, the elder son, was in holy orders and established in the parish of Feldkirche, outside the walls; and Matthias, the younger, was a lad of about fourteen years old, and lived with his father. He was an amiable good boy—pious and thoughtful—fonder of his books than of the business. The neighbour-folk used to say even then that Matthias was cut out for a priest, like his elder brother. As for Nicholas, he was neither more nor less than a saint. Well, mein Herr, at this time there lived on the other side of Rheinfelden, about a mile beyond the Basel Thor, a farmer named Caspar Rufenacht and his wife Margaret. Now Caspar Rufenacht was a jealous, quarrelsome fellow; and the Frau Margaret was pretty; and he led her a devil of a life. It was said that he used to beat her when he had been drinking, and that sometimes, when he went to fair or market, he would lock her up for the whole day in a room at the top of the house. Well, this poor, ill-used Frau Margaret—"

"Tut, tut, my man," interrupted the landlady. "The Frau Margaret was a light one!"

"Peace, wife! Shall we speak hard words of the dead? The Frau Margaret was young and pretty, and a flirt; and she had a bad husband, who left her too much alone."

The landlady pursed up her lips and shook her head, as the best of women will do when the character of another woman is under discussion. The innkeeper went on.

"Well, mein Herr, to cut a long story short, after having been jealous first of one and then of another, Caspar Rufenacht became furious about a certain German, a Badener named Schmidt, living on the opposite bank of the Rhine. I remember the man quite well—a handsome, merry fellow, and no saint; just the sort to make mischief between man and wife. Well, Caspar Rufenacht swore a great oath that, cost what it might, he would come at the truth about his wife and Schmidt; so he laid all manner of plots to surprise them—waylaid the Frau Margaret in her walks; followed her at a distance when she went to church; came home at unexpected hours; and played the spy as if he had been brought up to the trade. But his spying was all in vain. Either the Frau Margaret was too clever for him, or there was really nothing to discover; but still he was not satisfied. So he cast about for some way to attain his end, and, by the help of the Evil One, he found it."

Here the innkeeper's wife and daughter, who had doubtless heard the story a hundred times over, drew near and listened breathlessly.

"What, think you," continued the landlord, "does this black-souled Caspar do? Does he punish the poor woman within an inch of her life, till she confesses? No. Does he charge Schmidt with having tempted her from her duty, and fight it out with him like a man? No. What else then? I will tell you. He waits till the vigil of St Margaret—her saint's day—when he knows the poor sinful soul is going to confession; and he marches straight to the house of the Père Chessez—the very house where our own Père Chessez is now living—and he finds the good priest at his devotions in his little study, and he says to him:

"'Father Chessez, my wife is coming to the church this afternoon to make her confession to you.'

"'She is,' replies the priest.

"'I want you to tell me all she tells you,' says Caspar; and I will wait here till you come back from the church, that I may hear it. Will you do so?'

"'Certainly not,' replies the Père Chessez. 'You must surely know, Caspar, that we priests are forbidden to reveal the secrets of the confessional.'

"'That is nothing to me,' says Caspar, with an oath. 'I am resolved to know whether my wife is guilty or innocent; and know it I will, by fair means or foul.'

"'You shall never know it from me, Caspar,' says the Père Chessez, very quietly.

"'Then, by Heavens!' says Caspar, 'I'll learn it for myself.' And with that he pulls out a heavy horse-pistol from his pocket, and with the butt-end of it deals the Père Chessez a tremendous blow upon the head, and then another, and another, till the poor young man lay senseless at his feet. Then Caspar, thinking he had quite killed him, dressed himself in the priest's own soutane and hat; locked the door; put the key in his pocket; and stealing round the back way into the church, shut himself up in the confessional."

"Then the priest died!" I exclaimed, remembering the epitaph upon the tablet.

"Ay, mein Herr—the Père Chessez died; but not before he had told the story of his assassination, and identified his murderer."

"And Caspar Rufenacht, I hope, was hanged?"

"Wait a bit, mein Herr, we have not come to that yet. We left Caspar in the confessional, waiting for his wife."

"And she came?"

"Yes, poor soul! she came."

"And made her confession?"

"And made her confession, mein Herr."

"What did she confess?"

The innkeeper shook his head.

"That no one ever knew, save the good God and her murderer."

"Her murderer!" I exclaimed.

"Ay, just that. Whatever it was that she confessed, she paid for it with her life. He heard her out, at all events, without discovering himself, and let her go home believing that she had received absolution for her sins. Those who met her that afternoon said she seemed unusually bright and happy. As she passed through the town, she went into the shop in the Mongarten Strasse, and bought some ribbons. About half an hour later, my own father met her outside the Basel Thor, walking briskly homewards. He was the last who saw her alive.

"That evening (it was in October, and the days were short), some travellers coming that way into the town heard shrill cries, as of a woman screaming, in the direction of Caspar's farm. But the night was very dark, and the house lay back a little way from the road; so they told themselves it was only some drunken peasant quarrelling with his wife, and passed on. Next morning Caspar Rufenacht came to Rheinfelden, walked very quietly into the Polizei, and gave himself up to justice.

"'I have killed my wife,' said he. 'I have killed the Père Chessez. And I have committed sacrilege.'

"And so, indeed, it was. As for the Frau Margaret, they found her body in an upper chamber, well-nigh hacked to pieces, and the hatchet with which the murder was committed lying beside her on the floor. He had pursued her, apparently, from room to room; for there were pools of blood and handfuls of long light hair, and marks of bloody hands along the walls, all the way from the kitchen to the spot where she lay dead."

"And so he was hanged?" said I, coming back to my original question.

"Yes, yes," replied the innkeeper and his womankind in chorus. "He was hanged—of course he was hanged."

"And it was the shock of this double tragedy that drove the younger Chessez into the church?"

"Just so, mein Herr."

"Well, he carries it in his face. He looks like a most unhappy man."

"Nay, he is not that, mein Herr!" exclaimed the landlady. "He is melancholy, but not unhappy."

"Well, then, austere."

"Nor is he austere, except towards himself."

"True, wife," said the innkeeper; "but, as I said, he carries that sort of thing too far. You understand, mein Herr," he added, touching his forehead with his forefinger, "the good pastor has let his mind dwell too much upon the past. He is nervous—too nervous, and too low."

I saw it all now. That terrible light in his eyes was the light of insanity. That stony look in his face was the fixed, hopeless melancholy of a mind diseased.

"Does he know that he is mad?" I asked, as the landlord rose to go.

He shrugged his shoulders and looked doubtful.

"I have not said that the Père Chessez is *mad*, mein Herr," he replied. "He has strange fancies sometimes, and takes his fancies for facts—that is all. But I am quite sure that he does not believe himself to be less sane than his neighbours."

So the innkeeper left me, and I (my head full of the story I had just heard) put on my hat, went out into the market-place, asked my way to the Basel Thor, and set off to explore the scene of the Frau Margaret's murder.

I found it without difficulty—a long, low-fronted, beetle-browed farm-house, lying back a meadow's length from the road. There were children playing upon the threshold, a flock of turkeys gobbling about the barn-door, and a big dog sleeping outside his kennel close by. The chimneys, too, were smoking merrily. Seeing these signs of life and cheerfulness, I abandoned all idea of asking to go over the house. I felt that I had no right to carry my morbid curiosity into this peaceful home; so I turned away, and retraced my steps towards Rheinfelden.

It was not yet seven, and the sun had still an hour's course to run. I re-entered the town, strolled back through the street, and presently came again to the Friedrich's Thor and the path leading to the church. An irresistible impulse seemed to drag me back to the place.

Shudderingly, and with a sort of dread that was half longing, I pushed open the churchyard gate and went in. The doors were closed; a goat was browsing among the graves; and the rushing of the Rhine, some three hundred yards away, was distinctly audible in the silence. I looked round for the priest's house—the scene of the first murder; but from this side, at all events, no house was visible. Going round, however, to the back of the church, I saw a gate, a box-bordered path, and, peeping through some trees, a chimney and the roof of a little brown-tiled house.

This, then, was the path along which Caspar Rufenacht, with the priest's blood upon his hands and the priest's gown upon his shoulders, had taken his guilty way to the confessional! How quiet it all looked in the golden evening light! How like the church-path of an English parsonage!

I wished I could have seen something more of the house than that bit of roof and that one chimney. There must, I told myself, be some other entrance—some way round by the road! Musing and lingering thus, I was startled by a quiet voice close against my shoulder, saying:—

"A pleasant evening, mein Herr!"

I turned, and found the priest at my elbow. He had come noiselessly across the grass, and was standing between me and the sunset, like a shadow.

"I—I beg your pardon," I stammered, moving away from the gate. "I was looking—"

I stopped in some surprise, and indeed with some sense of relief, for it was not the same priest that I had seen in the morning. No two, indeed, could well be more unlike, for this man was small, white-haired, gentle-looking, with a soft, sad smile inexpressibly sweet and winning.

"You were looking at my arbutus?" he said.

I had scarcely observed the arbutus till now, but I bowed and said something to the effect that it was an unusually fine tree.

"Yes," he replied; "but I have a rhododendron round at the front that is still finer. Will you come in and see it?"

I said I should be pleased to do so. He led the way, and I followed.

"I hope you like this part of our Rhine-country?" he said, as we took the path through the shrubbery.

"I like it so well," I replied, "that if I were to live anywhere on the banks of the Rhine, I should certainly choose some spot on the Upper Rhine between Schaffhausen and Basle."

"And you would be right," he said. "Nowhere is the river so beautiful. Nearer the glaciers it is milky and turbid—beyond Basle it soon becomes muddy. Here we have it blue as the sky—sparkling as champagne. Here is my rhododendron. It stands twelve feet high, and measures as many in diameter. I had more than two hundred blooms upon it last Spring."

When I had duly admired this giant shrub, he took me to a little arbour on a bit of steep green bank overlooking the river, where he invited me to sit down and rest. From hence I could see the porch and part of the front of his little house; but it was all so closely planted round with trees and shrubs that no clear view of it seemed obtainable in any direction. Here we sat for some time chatting about the weather, the approaching vintage, and so forth, and watching the sunset. Then I rose to take my leave.

"I heard of you this evening at the Krone, mein Herr," he said. "You were out, or I should have called upon you. I am glad that chance has made us acquainted. Do you remain over to-morrow?"

"No; I must go on to-morrow to Basle," I answered. And then, hesitating a little, I added:—"you heard of me, also, I fear, in the church."

"In the church?" he repeated.

"Seeing the door open, I went in—from curiosity—as a traveller; just to look round for a moment and rest."

"Naturally."

"I—I had no idea, however, that I was not alone there. I would not for the world have intruded—"

"I do not understand," he said, seeing me hesitate. "The church stands open all day long. It is free to every one."

"Ah! I see he has not told you!"

The priest smiled but looked puzzled.

"He? Whom do you mean?"

"The other priest, mon père—your colleague. I regret to have broken in upon his meditations; but I had been so long in the church, and it was all so still and quiet, that it never occurred to me that there might be some one in the confessional."

The priest looked at me in a strange, startled way.

"In the confessional!" he repeated, with a catching of his breath. "You saw some one—in the confessional?"

"I am ashamed to say that, having thoughtlessly opened the door—"

"You saw—what did you see?"

"A priest, mon père."

"A priest! Can you describe him? Should you know him again? Was he pale, and tall, and gaunt, with long black hair?"

"The same, undoubtedly."

"And his eyes—did you observe anything particular about his eyes?"

"Yes; they were large, wild-looking, dark eyes, with a look in them—a look I cannot describe."

"A look of terror!" cried the pastor, now greatly agitated. "A look of terror—of remorse—of despair!"

"Yes, it was a look that might mean all that," I replied, my astonishment increasing at every word. "You seem troubled. Who is he?"

"But instead of answering my question, the pastor took off his hat, looked up with a radiant, awe-struck face, and said:—

"All-merciful God, I thank Thee! I thank Thee that I am not mad, and that Thou hast sent this stranger to be my assurance and my comfort!"

Having said these words, he bowed his head, and his lips moved in silent prayer. When he looked up again, his eyes were full of tears.

"My son," he said, laying his trembling hand upon my arm, "I owe you an explanation; but I cannot give it to you now. It must wait till I can speak more calmly—till to-morrow, when I must see you again. It involves a terrible story—a story peculiarly painful to myself—enough now if I tell you that I have seen the Thing you describe—seen It many times; and yet, because It has been visible to my eyes alone, I have doubted the evidence of my senses. The good people here believe that much sorrow and meditation have touched my brain. I have half believed it myself till now. But you—you have proved to me that I am the victim of no illusion."

"But in Heaven's name," I exclaimed, "what do you suppose I saw in the confessional?"

"You saw the likeness of one who, guilty also of a double murder, committed the deadly sin of sacrilege in that very spot, more than thirty years ago," replied the Père Chessez, solemnly.

"Caspar Rufenacht!"

"Ah! you have heard the story? Then I am spared the pain of telling it to you. That is well."

I bent my head in silence. We walked together without another word to the wicket, and thence round to the churchyard gate. It was now twilight, and the first stars were out.

"Good night, my son," said the pastor, giving me his hand. "Peace be with you."

As he spoke the words, his grasp tightened—his eyes dilated—his whole countenance became rigid.

"Look!" he whispered. "Look where it goes!"

I followed the direction of his eyes, and there, with a freezing horror which I have no words to describe, I saw—distinctly saw through the deepening gloom—a tall, dark figure in a priest's soutane and broad-brimmed hat, moving slowly across the path leading from the parsonage to the church. For a moment it seemed to pause—then passed on to the deeper shade, and disappeared.

"You saw it?" said the pastor.

"Yes—plainly."

He drew a deep breath; crossed himself devoutly; and leaned upon the gate, as if exhausted.

"This is the third time I have seen it this year," he said. "Again I thank God for the certainty that I see a visible thing, and that His great gift of reason is mine unimpaired. But I would that He were graciously pleased to release me from the sight—the horror of it is sometimes more than I know how to bear. Good night."

With this he again touched my hand; and so, seeing that he wished to be alone, I silently left him. At the Friedrich's Thor I turned and looked back. He was still standing by the churchyard gate, just visible through the gloom of the fast deepening twilight.

*

167

I never saw the Père Chessez again. Save his own old servant, I was the last who spoke with him in this world. He died that night—died in his bed, where he was found next morning with his hands crossed upon his breast, and with a placid smile upon his lips, as if he had fallen asleep in the act of prayer.

As the news spread from house to house, the whole town rang with lamentations. The church-bells tolled; the carpenters left their work in the streets; the children, dismissed from school, went home weeping.

"'Twill be the saddest Kermess in Rheinfelden to-morrow, mein Herr!" said my good host of the Krone, as I shook hands with him at parting. "We have lost the best of pastors and of friends. He was a saint. If you had come but one day later, you would not have seen him!"

And with this he brushed his sleeve across his eyes, and turned away.

Every shutter was up, every blind down, every door closed, as I passed along the Friedrich's Strasse about midday on my way to Basle; and the few townsfolk I met looked grave and downcast. Then I crossed the bridge and, having shown my passport to the German sentry on the Baden side, I took one long, last farewell look at the little walled town as it lay sleeping in the sunshine by the river—knowing that I should see it no more.

MAN-SIZE IN MARBLE

E. Nesbit

Edith Nesbit (1858–1924) is a well-known author of children's literature, perhaps most frequently discussed in relation to *The Railway Children* (1905) and *Five Children and It* (1902). However, Nesbit was also a prolific poet, praised by A. C. Swinburne and included in Alfred Miles's eight volume *Poets and Poetry of the Century* (1892) alongside Oscar Wilde, Rudyard Kipling and Edmund Gosse. In addition, Nesbit wrote numerous short stories and novels for adults, publishing in both her own name and under the pseudonym Fabian Bland. This chosen pen name reflects Nesbit's political activism, an aspect of her life often overlooked. A committed socialist, she was a founding member of the Fabian Society and close friends with other left-leaning intellectuals, including George Bernard Shaw, Sydney and Beatrice Webb.

Originally published in *Home Chimes*, a London-based monthly magazine, "Man-Size in Marble" was later reprinted in a collection of horror stories entitled *Grim Tales* (1893). Other supernatural fiction appeared in *Something Wrong* (1893), *Man and Maid* (1906) and *Fear* (1910). Set in Brenzett, Kent, the Norman church visited by the narrator and his wife may be based on St Eanswith's, an Anglican church which, like its fictional counterpart, is set amidst trees and houses a tomb topped with life-sized marble effigies.

Although every word of this story is as true as despair, I do not expect people to believe it. Nowadays a "rational explanation" is required before belief is possible. Let me then, at once, offer the "rational explanation" which finds most favour among those who have heard the tale of my life's tragedy. It is held that we were "under a delusion," Laura and I, on that 31st of October; and that this supposition places the whole matter on a satisfactory and believable basis. The reader can judge, when he, too, has heard my story, how far this is an "explanation," and in what sense it is "rational." There were three who took part in this: Laura and I and another man. The other man still lives, and can speak to the truth of the least credible part of my story.

I never in my life knew what it was to have as much money as I required to supply the most ordinary needs—good colours, books and cab-fares—and when we were married we knew quite well that we should only be able to live at all by "strict punctuality and attention to business." I used to paint in those days, and Laura used to write, and we felt sure we could keep the pot at least simmering. Living in town was out of the question, so we went to look for a cottage in the country, which should be at once sanitary and picturesque. So rarely do these two qualities meet in one cottage that our search was for some time quite fruitless. We tried advertisements, but most of the desirable rural residences which we did look at proved to be lacking in both essentials, and when a cottage chanced to have drains it always had stucco as well and was shaped like a tea-caddy. And if we found a vine or rose-covered porch, corruption invariably lurked within. Our minds got so befogged by the eloquence of house-agents and the rival disadvantages of the fever-traps and outrages to beauty which we had seen and scorned, that I very much doubt whether either of us, on our wedding morning, knew the difference between a house and a haystack. But when we got away from friends and house-agents, on our honeymoon, our wits grew clear again, and we knew a pretty cottage when at last we saw one. It was at Brenzett—a little village set on a hill over against the southern marshes. We had gone there, from the seaside village where we were staying, to see the church, and two fields from the church we found this cottage. It stood quite by itself, about two miles from the village. It was a long, low building, with rooms sticking out in unexpected places. There was a bit of stone-work—ivy-covered and moss-grown, just two old rooms, all that was left of a big house that had once stood there—and round this stone-work the house had grown up. Stripped of its roses and jasmine it would have been hideous. As it stood it was charming, and after a brief examination we took it. It was absurdly cheap. The rest of our honeymoon we spent in grubbing about in second-hand shops in the county town, picking up bits of old oak and Chippendale chairs for our furnishing. We wound up with a run up to town and a visit to Liberty's, and soon the low oak-beamed lattice-windowed rooms began to be home. There was a jolly old-fashioned garden, with grass paths, and no end of hollyhocks and sunflowers, and big lilies. From the window you could see the marsh-pastures, and beyond them the blue, thin line of the sea. We were as happy as the summer was glorious, and settled down into work sooner than we ourselves expected. I was never tired of sketching the view and the wonderful cloud effects from the open lattice, and Laura would sit at the table and write verses about them, in which I mostly played the part of foreground.

We got a tall old peasant woman to do for us. Her face and figure were good, though her cooking was of the homeliest; but she understood all about gardening, and told us all the old names of the coppices and cornfields, and the stories of the smugglers and highwaymen, and, better still, of the "things that walked," and of the "sights" which met one in lonely glens of a starlight night. She was a great comfort to us, because Laura hated housekeeping as much as I loved folklore, and we soon came to leave all the domestic business to Mrs Dorman, and to use her legends in little magazine stories which brought in the jingling guinea.

We had three months of married happiness, and did not have a single quarrel. One October evening I had been down to smoke a pipe with the doctor—our only neighbour—a pleasant young Irishman. Laura had stayed at home to finish a comic sketch of a village episode for the *Monthly Marplot*. I left her laughing over her own jokes, and came in to find her a crumpled heap of pale muslin weeping on the window seat.

"Good heavens, my darling, what's the matter?" I cried, taking her in my arms. She leaned her little dark head against my shoulder and went on crying. I had never seen her cry before—we had always been so happy, you see—and I felt sure some frightful misfortune had happened.

"What *is* the matter? Do speak."

"It's Mrs Dorman," she sobbed.

"What has she done?" I inquired, immensely relieved.

"She says she must go before the end of the month, and she says her niece is ill; she's gone down to see her now, but I don't believe that's the reason, because her niece is always ill. I believe some one has been setting her against us. Her manner was so queer—"

"Never mind, Pussy," I said; "whatever you do, don't cry, or I shall have to cry too, to keep you in countenance, and then you'll never respect your man again!"

She dried her eyes obediently on my handkerchief, and even smiled faintly.

"But you see," she went on, "it is really serious, because these village people are so sheepy, and if one won't do a thing you may be quite sure none of the others will. And I shall have to cook the dinners, and wash up the hateful greasy plates; and you'll have to carry cans of water about, and clean the boots and knives—and we shall never have any time for work, or earn any money, or anything. We shall have to work all day, and only be able to rest when we are waiting for the kettle to boil!"

I represented to her that even if we had to perform these duties, the day would still present some margin for other toils and recreations. But she refused to see the matter in any but the greyest light. She was very unreasonable, my Laura, but I could not have loved her any more if she had been as reasonable as Whately.

"I'll speak to Mrs Dorman when she comes back, and see if I can't come to terms with her," I said. "Perhaps she wants a rise in her screw. It will be all right. Let's walk up to the church."

The church was a large and lonely one, and we loved to go there, especially upon bright nights. The path skirted a wood, cut through it once, and ran along the crest of the hill through two meadows, and round the churchyard wall, over which the old yews loomed in black masses of shadow. This path, which was partly paved, was called "the bier-balk," for it had long been the way by which the corpses had been carried to burial. The churchyard was richly treed, and was shaded by great elms which stood just outside and stretched their majestic arms in benediction over the happy dead. A large, low porch let one into the building by a Norman doorway and a heavy oak door studded with iron. Inside, the arches rose into darkness, and between them the reticulated windows, which stood out white in the moonlight. In the chancel, the windows were of rich glass, which showed in faint light their noble colouring, and made the black oak of the choir pews hardly more solid than the shadows. But on each side of the altar lay a grey marble figure of a knight in full plate armour lying upon a low slab, with hands held up in everlasting prayer, and these figures, oddly enough, were always to be seen if there was any glimmer of light in the church. Their names were lost, but the peasants told of them that they had been fierce and wicked men, marauders by land and sea, who had been the scourge of their time, and had been guilty of deeds so foul that the house they had lived in—the big house, by the way, that had stood on the site of our cottage—had been stricken by lightning and the vengeance of Heaven. But for all that, the gold of their heirs had bought them a place in the church. Looking at the bad hard faces reproduced in the marble, this story was easily believed.

The church looked at its best and weirdest on that night, for the shadows of the yew trees fell through the windows upon the floor of the nave and touched the pillars with tattered shade. We sat down together without speaking, and watched the solemn beauty of the old church, with some of that awe which inspired its early builders. We walked to the chancel and looked at the sleeping warriors. Then we rested some time on the stone seat in the porch, looking out over the stretch of quiet moonlit meadows feeling in every fibre of our being the peace of the night and of our happy love; and came away at last with a sense that even scrubbing and blackleading were but small troubles at their worst.

Mrs Dorman had come back from the village, and I at once invited her to a *tête-à-tête*.

"Now, Mrs Dorman," I said, when I had got her into my painting room, "what's all this about your not staying with us?"

"I should be glad to get away, sir, before the end of the month," she answered, with her usual placid dignity.

"Have you any fault to find, Mrs Dorman?"

"None at all, sir; you and your lady have always been most kind, I'm sure—"

"Well, what is it? Are your wages not high enough?"

"No, sir, I gets quite enough."

"Then why not stay?"

"I'd rather not"—with some hesitation—"my niece is ill."

"But your niece has been ill ever since we came."

No answer. There was a long and awkward silence. I broke it.

"Can't you stay for another month?" I asked.

"No, sir. I'm bound to go by Thursday."

And this was Monday!

"Well, I must say, I think you might have let us know before. There's no time now to get any one else, and your mistress is not fit to do heavy housework. Can't you stay till next week?"

"I might be able to come back next week."

I was now convinced that all she wanted was a brief holiday, which we should have been willing enough to let her have, as soon as we could get a substitute.

"But why must you go this week?" I persisted. "Come, out with it."

Mrs Dorman drew the little shawl, which she always wore, tightly across her bosom, as though she were cold. Then she said, with a sort of effort—

"They say, sir, as this was a big house in Catholic times, and there was a many deeds done here."

The nature of the "deeds" might be vaguely inferred from the inflection of Mrs Dorman's voice—which was enough to make one's blood run cold. I was glad that Laura was not in the room. She was always nervous, as highly-strung natures are, and I felt that these tales about our house, told by this old peasant woman, with her impressive manner and contagious credulity, might have made our home less dear to my wife.

"Tell me all about it, Mrs Dorman," I said; "you needn't mind about telling me. I'm not like the young people who make fun of such things."

Which was partly true.

"Well, sir"—she sank her voice—"you may have seen in the church, beside the altar, two shapes."

"You mean the effigies of the knights in armour," I said cheerfully.

"I mean them two bodies, drawed out man-size in marble," she returned, and I had to admit that her description was a thousand times more graphic than mine, to say nothing of a certain weird force and uncanniness about the phrase "drawed out man-size in marble."

"They do say, as on All Saints' Eve them two bodies sits up on their slabs, and gets off of them, and then walks down the aisle, *in their marble*"—(another good phrase, Mrs Dorman)—"and as the church clock strikes eleven they walks out of the church door, and over the graves, and along the bier-balk, and if it's a wet night there's the marks of their feet in the morning."

"And where do they go?" I asked, rather fascinated.

"They comes back here to their home, sir and if any one meets them—"

"Well, what then?" I asked.

But no—not another word could I get from her, save that her niece was ill and she must go. After what I had heard I scorned to discuss the niece, and tried to get from Mrs Dorman more details of the legend. I could get nothing but warnings.

"Whatever you do, sir, lock the door early on All Saints' Eve, and make the cross-sign over the doorstep and on the windows."

"But has any one ever seen these things?" I persisted.

"That's not for me to say. I know what I know, sir."

"Well, who was here last year?"

"No one, sir; the lady as owned the house only stayed here in summer, and she always went to London a full month afore *the* night. And I'm sorry to inconvenience you and your lady, but my niece is ill and I must go on Thursday."

I could have shaken her for her absurd reiteration of that obvious fiction, after she had told me her real reasons.

She was determined to go, nor could our united entreaties move her in the least.

I did not tell Laura the legend of the shapes that "walked in their marble," partly because a legend concerning our house might perhaps trouble my wife, and partly, I think, from some more occult reason. This was not quite the same to me as any other story, and I did not want to talk about it till the day was over. I had very soon ceased to think of the legend, however. I was painting a portrait of Laura, against the lattice window, and I could not think of much else. I had got a splendid background of yellow and grey sunset, and was working away with enthusiasm at her face. On Thursday Mrs Dorman went. She relented, at parting, so far as to say—

"Don't you put yourself about too much, ma'am, and if there's any little thing I can do next week, I'm sure I shan't mind."

From which I inferred that she wished to come back to us after Halloween. Up to the last she adhered to the fiction of the niece with touching fidelity.

Thursday passed off pretty well. Laura showed marked ability in the matter of steak and potatoes, and I confess that my knives, and the plates, which I insisted upon washing, were better done than I had dared to expect.

Friday came. It is about what happened on that Friday that this is written. I wonder if I should have believed it, if any one had told it to me. I will write the story of it as quickly and plainly as I can. Everything that happened on that day is burnt into my brain. I shall not forget anything, nor leave anything out.

I got up early, I remember, and lighted the kitchen fire, and had just achieved a smoky success, when my little wife came running down, as sunny and sweet as the clear October morning itself. We prepared breakfast together, and found it very good fun. The housework was soon done, and when brushes and brooms and pails were quiet again, the house was still indeed. It is wonderful what a difference one makes in a house. We really missed Mrs Dorman, quite apart from considerations concerning pots and pans. We spent the day in dusting our books and putting them straight, and dined gaily on cold steak and coffee. Laura was, if possible, brighter and gayer and sweeter than usual, and I began to think that a little domestic toil was really good for her. We had never been so merry since we were married, and the walk we had that afternoon was, I think, the happiest time of all my life. When we had watched the deep scarlet clouds slowly pale into leaden grey against a pale-green sky, and saw the white mists curl up along the hedgerows in the distant marsh, we came back to the house, silently, hand in hand.

"You are sad, my darling," I said, half-jestingly, as we sat down together in our little parlour. I expected a disclaimer, for my own silence had been the silence of complete happiness. To my surprise she said—

"Yes. I think I am sad, or rather I am uneasy. I don't think I'm very well, I have shivered three or four times since we came in, and it is not cold, is it?"

"No," I said, and hoped it was not a chill caught from the treacherous mists that roll up from the marshes in the dying light. No—she said, she did not think so. Then, after a silence, she spoke suddenly—

"Do you ever have presentiments of evil?"

"No," I said, smiling, "and I shouldn't believe in them if I had."

"I do," she went on; "the night my father died I knew it, though he was right away in the north of Scotland." I did not answer in words.

She sat looking at the fire for some time in silence, gently stroking my hand. At last she sprang up, came behind me, and, drawing my head back, kissed me.

"There, it's over now," she said. "What a baby I am! Come, light the candles, and we'll have some of these new Rubinstein duets."

And we spent a happy hour or two at the piano.

At about half-past ten I began to long for the good-night pipe, but Laura looked so white that I felt it would be brutal of me to fill our sitting-room with the fumes of strong cavendish.

"I'll take my pipe outside," I said.

"Let me come, too."

"No, sweetheart, not to-night; you're much too tired. I shan't be long. Get to bed, or I shall have an invalid to nurse to-morrow as well as the boots to clean."

I kissed her and was turning to go, when she flung her arms round my neck, and held me as if she would never let me go again. I stroked her hair.

"Come, Pussy, you're over-tired. The housework has been too much for you."

She loosened her clasp a little and drew a deep breath.

"No. We've been very happy to-day, Jack, haven't we? Don't stay out too long."

"I won't, my dearie."

I strolled out of the front door, leaving it unlatched. What a night it was! The jagged masses of heavy dark cloud were rolling at intervals from horizon to horizon, and thin white wreaths covered the stars. Through all the rush of the cloud river, the moon swam, breasting the waves and disappearing again in the darkness. When now and again her light reached the woodlands they seemed to be slowly and noiselessly waving in time to the swing of the clouds above them. There was a strange grey light over all the earth; the fields had that shadowy bloom over them which only comes from the marriage of dew and moonshine, or frost and starlight.

I walked up and down, drinking in the beauty of the quiet earth and the changing sky. The night was absolutely silent. Nothing seemed to be abroad. There was no skurrying of rabbits, or twitter of the half-asleep birds. And though the clouds went sailing across the sky, the wind that drove them never came low enough to rustle the dead leaves in the woodland paths. Across the meadows I could see the church tower standing out black and grey against the sky. I walked there thinking over our three months of happiness—and of my wife, her dear eyes, her loving ways. Oh, my little girl! my own little girl; what a vision came then of a long, glad life for you and me together!

I heard a bell-beat from the church. Eleven already! I turned to go in, but the night held me. I could not go back into our little warm rooms yet. I would go up to the church. I felt vaguely that it would be good to carry my love and thankfulness to the sanctuary whither so many loads of sorrow and gladness had been borne by the men and women of the dead years.

I looked in at the low window as I went by. Laura was half lying on her chair in front of the fire. I could not see her face, only her little head showed dark against the pale blue wall. She was quite still. Asleep, no doubt. My heart reached out to her, as I went on. There must be a God, I thought, and a God who was good. How otherwise could anything so sweet and dear as she have ever been imagined?

I walked slowly along the edge of the wood. A sound broke the stillness of the night, it was a rustling in the wood. I stopped and listened. The sound stopped too. I went on, and now distinctly heard another step than mine answer mine like an echo. It was a poacher or a wood-stealer, most likely, for these were not unknown in our Arcadian neighbourhood. But whoever it was, he was a fool not to step more lightly. I turned into the wood, and now the footstep seemed to come from the path I had just left. It must be an echo, I thought. The wood looked perfect in the moonlight. The large dying ferns and the brushwood showed where through thinning foliage the pale light came down. The tree trunks stood up like Gothic columns all around me. They reminded me of the church, and I turned into the bier-balk, and passed through the corpse-gate between the graves to the low porch. I paused for a moment on the stone seat where Laura and I had watched the fading landscape. Then I noticed that the door of the church was open, and I blamed myself for having left it unlatched the other night. We were the only people who ever cared to come to the church except on Sundays, and I was vexed to think that through our carelessness the damp autumn airs had had a chance of getting in and injuring the old fabric. I went in. It will seem strange, perhaps, that I should have gone halfway up the aisle before I remembered—with a sudden chill, followed by as sudden a rush of self-contempt—that this was the very day and hour when, according to tradition, the "shapes drawed out man-size in marble" began to walk.

Having thus remembered the legend, and remembered it with a shiver, of which I was ashamed, I could not do otherwise than walk up towards the altar, just to look at the figures—as I said to myself; really what I wanted was to assure myself, first, that I did not believe the legend, and, secondly, that it was not true. I was rather glad that I had come. I thought now I could tell Mrs Dorman how vain her fancies were, and how peacefully the marble figures slept on through the ghastly hour. With my hands in my pockets I passed up the aisle. In the grey dim light the eastern end of the church looked larger than usual, and the arches above the two tombs looked larger too. The moon came out and showed me the reason. I stopped short, my heart gave a leap that nearly choked me, and then sank sickeningly.

The "bodies drawed out man-size" *were gone*, and their marble slabs lay wide and bare in the vague moonlight that slanted through the east window.

Were they really gone? or was I mad? Clenching my nerves, I stooped and passed my hand over the smooth slabs, and felt their flat unbroken surface. Had some one taken the things away? Was it some vile practical joke? I would make sure, anyway. In an instant I had made a torch of a newspaper, which happened to be in my pocket, and lighting it held it high above my head. Its yellow glare illuminated the dark arches and those slabs. The figures *were* gone. And I was alone in the church; or was I alone?

And then a horror seized me, a horror indefinable and indescribable—an overwhelming certainty of supreme and accomplished calamity. I flung down the torch and tore along the aisle and out through the porch, biting my lips as I ran to keep myself from shrieking aloud. Oh, was I mad—or what was this that possessed me? I leaped the churchyard wall and took the straight cut across the fields, led by the light from our windows. Just as I got over the first stile, a dark figure seemed to spring out of the ground. Mad still with that certainty of misfortune, I made for the thing that stood in my path, shouting, "Get out of the way, can't you!"

But my push met with a more vigorous resistance than I had expected. My arms were caught just above the elbow and held as in a vice, and the raw-boned Irish doctor actually shook me.

"Would ye?" he cried, in his own unmistakable accents—"would ye, then?"

"Let me go, you fool," I gasped. "The marble figures have gone from the church; I tell you they've gone."

He broke into a ringing laugh. "I'll have to give ye a draught to-morrow, I see. Ye've bin smoking too much and listening to old wives' tales."

"I tell you, I've seen the bare slabs."

"Well, come back with me. I'm going up to old Palmer's—his daughter's ill; we'll look in at the church and let me see the bare slabs."

"You go, if you like," I said, a little less frantic for his laughter; "I'm going home to my wife."

"Rubbish, man," said he; "d'ye think I'll permit of that? Are ye to go saying all yer life that ye've seen solid marble endowed with vitality, and me to go all me life saying ye were a coward? No, sir—ye shan't do ut."

The night air—a human voice—and I think also the physical contact with this six feet of solid common sense, brought me back a little to my ordinary self, and the word "coward" was a mental shower-bath.

"Come on, then," I said sullenly; "perhaps you're right."

He still held my arm tightly. We got over the stile and back to the church. All was still as death. The place smelt very damp and earthy. We walked up the aisle. I am not ashamed to confess that I shut my eyes: I knew the figures would not be there. I heard Kelly strike a match.

"Here they are, ye see, right enough; ye've been dreaming or drinking, asking yer pardon for the imputation."

I opened my eyes. By Kelly's expiring vesta I saw two shapes lying "in their marble" on their slabs. I drew a deep breath, and caught his hand.

"I'm awfully indebted to you," I said. "It must have been some trick of light, or I have been working rather hard, perhaps that's it. Do you know, I was quite convinced they were gone."

"I'm aware of that," he answered rather grimly; "ye'll have to be careful of that brain of yours, my friend, I assure ye."

He was leaning over and looking at the right-hand figure, whose stony face was the most villainous and deadly in expression.

"By Jove," he said, "something has been afoot here—this hand is broken."

And so it was. I was certain that it had been perfect the last time Laura and I had been there.

"Perhaps some one has *tried* to remove them," said the young doctor.

"That won't account for my impression," I objected.

"Too much painting and tobacco will account for that, well enough."

"Come along," I said, "or my wife will be getting anxious. You'll come in and have a drop of whisky and drink confusion to ghosts and better sense to me."

"I ought to go up to Palmer's, but it's so late now I'd best leave it till the morning," he replied. "I was kept late at the Union, and I've had to see a lot of people since. All right, I'll come back with ye."

I think he fancied I needed him more than did Palmer's girl, so, discussing how such an illusion could have been possible, and deducing from this experience large generalities concerning ghostly apparitions, we walked up to our cottage. We saw, as we walked up the garden-path, that bright light streamed out of the front door, and presently saw that the parlour door was open too. Had she gone out?

"Come in," I said, and Dr Kelly followed me into the parlour. It was all ablaze with candles, not only the wax ones, but at least a dozen guttering, glaring tallow dips, stuck in vases and ornaments in unlikely places. Light, I knew, was Laura's remedy for nervousness. Poor child! Why had I left her? Brute that I was.

We glanced round the room, and at first we did not see her. The window was open, and the draught set all the candles flaring one way. Her chair was empty and her handkerchief and book lay on the floor. I turned to the window. There, in the recess of the window, I saw her. Oh, my child, my love, had she gone to that window to watch for me? And what had come into the room behind her? To what had she turned with that look of frantic fear and horror? Oh, my little one, had she thought that it was I whose step she heard, and turned to meet—what?

She had fallen back across a table in the window, and her body lay half on it and half on the window-seat, and her head hung down over the table, the brown hair loosened and fallen to the carpet. Her lips were drawn back, and her eyes wide, wide open. They saw nothing now. What had they seen last?

The doctor moved towards her, but I pushed him aside and sprang to her; caught her in my arms and cried—

"It's all right, Laura! I've got you safe, wifie."

She fell into my arms in a heap. I clasped her and kissed her, and called her by all her pet names, but I think I knew all the time that she was dead. Her hands were tightly clenched. In one of them she held something fast. When I was quite sure that she was dead, and that nothing mattered at all any more, I let him open her hand to see what she held.

It was a grey marble finger.

THE FACE OF THE MONK

Robert Hichens

The eldest son of Reverend Frederick Harrison Hichens and his wife Abigail, Robert Hichens (1864–1950) was born at his father's Rectory in Speldhurst, Kent. Displaying musical talent from an early age, Hichens studied at the Royal College of Music and worked briefly as a lyricist before starting a writing career. After studying at the London School of Journalism, Hichens contributed to several popular periodicals and spent some time as the music critic at *The World*.

Today, Hichens is perhaps best remembered for *The Green Carnation* (1894), a satirical novel that attacks aestheticism and centres around characters largely based on Oscar Wilde and his lover, Lord Alfred Douglas. However, Hichens wrote widely, producing drama and travel narratives in addition to fiction. Some of his more popular novels were adapted for stage and screen, including *The Garden of Allah* (1904), *Bella Donna* (1909) and *The Paradine Case* (1933).

"The Face of the Monk" was published in *Byeways*, a collection of short fiction, in 1897. The narrator's encounters with the titular monk echo an event recounted in Hichens's autobiography, which recalls an encounter with a Mexican seer who proclaimed the presence of the author's monastic spirit guide[*]. In depicting

[*] Robert Hichens, *Yesterday: The Autobiography of Robert Hichens* (London: Cassell & Company, 1947), 78.

one man and his spiritual double, the tale juxtaposes good and evil, highlighting the internal battles that underpin the believer's search for eternal salvation.

"No, it will not hurt him to see you," the doctor said to me; "and I have no doubt he will recognise you. He is the quietest patient I have ever had under my care—gentle, kind, agreeable, perfect in conduct, and yet quite mad. You know him well?"

"He was my dearest friend," I said. "Before I went out to America three years ago we were inseparable. Doctor, I cannot believe that he is mad, he—Hubert Blair—one of the cleverest young writers in London, so brilliant, so acute! Wild, if you like, a libertine perhaps, a strange mixture of the intellectual and the sensual—but mad! I can't believe it!"

"Not when I tell you that he was brought to me suffering from acute religious mania?"

"Religious! Hubert Blair!"

"Yes. He tried to destroy himself, declaring that he was unfit to live, that he was a curse to some person unknown. He protested that each deed of his affected this unknown person, that his sins were counted as the sins of another, and that this other had haunted him—would haunt him for ever."

The doctor's words troubled me.

"Take me to him," I said at last. "Leave us together."

It was a strange, sad moment when I entered the room in which Hubert was sitting. I was painfully agitated. He knew me, and greeted me warmly. I sat down opposite to him.

*

There was a long silence. Hubert looked away into the fire. He saw, I think, traced in scarlet flames, the scenes he was going to describe to me; and I, gazing at him, wondered of what nature the change in my friend might be. That he had changed since we were together three years ago was evident, yet he did not look mad. His dark, clean-shaven young face was still passionate. The brown eyes were still lit with a certain devouring eagerness. The mouth had not lost its mingled sweetness and sensuality. But Hubert was curiously transformed. There was a dignity, almost an elevation, in his manner. His former gaiety had vanished. I knew, without words, that my friend was another man—very far away from me now. Yet once we had lived together as chums, and had no secrets the one from the other.

At last Hubert looked up and spoke.

"I see you are wondering about me," he said.

"Yes."

"I have altered, of course—completely altered."

"Yes," I said, awkwardly enough. "Why is that?"

I longed to probe this madness of his that I might convince myself of it, otherwise Hubert's situation must for ever appal me.

He answered quietly, "I will tell you—nobody else knows—and even you may—"

He hesitated, then he said:

"No, you will believe it."

"Yes, if you tell me it is true."

"It is absolutely true."

"Bernard, you know what I was when you left England for America—gay, frivolous in my pleasures, although earnest when I was working. You know how I lived to sound the depths of sensation, how I loved to stretch all my mental and physical capacities to the snapping-point, how I shrank from no sin that could add one jot or tittle to my knowledge of the mind of any man or woman who interested me. My life seemed a full life then. I moved in the midst of a thousand intrigues. I strung beads of all emotions upon my rosary, and told them until at times my health gave way. You remember my recurring periods of extraordinary and horrible mental depression—when life was a demon to me, and all my success in literature less than nothing; when I fancied myself hated, and could believe I heard phantom voices abusing me. Then those fits passed away, and once more I lived as ardently as ever, the most persistent worker, and the most persistent excitement-seeker in London.

"Well, after you went away I continued my career. As you know, my success increased. Through many sins I had succeeded in diving very deep into human hearts of men and women. Often I led people deliberately away from innocence in order that I might observe the gradual transformation of their natures. Often I spurred them on to follies that I might see the effect our deeds have upon our faces—the seal our actions set upon our souls. I was utterly unscrupulous, and yet I thought myself good-hearted. You remember that my servants always loved me, that I attracted people. I can say this to you. For some time my usual course was not stayed. Then—I recollect it was in the middle of the London season—one of my horrible fits of unreasonable melancholy swept over me. It stunned my soul like a heavy blow. It numbed me. I could not go about. I could not bear to see anybody. I could only shut myself up and try to reason myself back into my usual gaiety and excitement. My writing was put aside. My piano was locked. I tried to read, but even that solace was denied to me. My attention was utterly self-centred, riveted upon my own condition.

"Why, I said to myself, am I the victim of this despair, this despair without a cause? What is this oppression which weighs me down without reason? It attacks me abruptly, as if it were sent to me by some power, shot at me like an arrow by an enemy hidden in the dark. I am well—I am gay. Life is beautiful and wonderful to me. All that I do interests me. My soul is full of vitality. I know that I have troops of friends, that I am loved and thought of by many people. And then suddenly the arrow strikes me. My soul is wounded and sickens to death. Night falls over me, night so sinister that I shudder when its twilight comes. All my senses faint within me. Life is at once a hag, weary, degraded, with tears on her cheeks, and despair in her hollow eyes. I feel that I am deserted, that my friends despise me, that the world hates me, that I am less than all other men—less in powers, less in attraction—that I am the most crawling, the most grovelling of all the human species, and that there is no one who does not know it. Yet the doctors say I am not physically ill, and I know that I am not mad. Whence does this awful misery, this unmeaning, causeless horror of life and of myself come? Why am I thus afflicted?

"Of course I could find no answer to all these old questions, which I had asked many times before. But this time, Bernard, my depression was more lasting, more overwhelming than usual. I grew terribly afraid of it. I thought I might be driven to suicide. One day a crisis seemed to come. I dared no longer remain alone, so I put on my hat and coat, took my stick, and hurried out, without any definite intention. I walked along Piccadilly, avoiding the glances of those whom I met. I fancied they could all read the agony, the degradation of my soul. I turned into Bond Street, and suddenly I felt a strong inclination to stop before a certain door. I obeyed the impulse, and my eyes fell on a brass plate, upon which was engraved these words:

VANE.

Clairvoyant.

11 till 4 daily.

"I remember I read them several times over and even repeated them in a whisper to myself. Why? I don't know. Then I turned away, and was about to resume my walk. But I could not. Again I stopped and read the legend on the brass plate. On the right-hand side of the door was an electric bell. I put my finger on it and pressed the button inwards. The door opened, and I walked, like a man in a dream, I think, up a flight of narrow stairs. At the top of them was a second door, at which a maidservant was standing.

"'You want to see Mr Vane, sir?'

"'Yes. Can I?'

"'If you will come in, sir, I will see.'

"She showed me into a commonplace, barely-furnished little room, and, after a short period of waiting, summoned me to another, in which stood a tall, dark youth, dressed in a gown rather like college gown. He bowed to me, and I silently returned the salutation. The servant left us. Then he said:

"'You wish me to exert my powers for you?'

"'Yes.'

"'Will you sit here?'

"He motioned me to a seat beside a small round table, sat down opposite me, and took my hand. After examining it through a glass, and telling my character fairly correctly by the lines in it, he laid the glass down and regarded me narrowly.

"'You suffer terribly from depression,' he said.

"'That is true.'

"He continued to gaze upon me more and more fixedly. At length he said:

"'Do you know that everybody has a companion?'

"'How—a companion?'

"'Somebody incessantly with them, somebody they cannot see.'

"'You believe in the theory of guardian angels?'

"'I do not say these companions are always guardian angels. I see your companion now, as I look at you. His face is by your shoulder.'

"I started, and glanced hastily round; but, of course, could see nothing.

"'Shall I describe him?'

"'Yes,' I said.

"'His face is dark, like yours; shaven, like yours. He has brown eyes, just as brown as yours are. His mouth and his chin are firm and small, as firm and small as yours.'

"'He must be very like me.'

"'He is. But there is a difference between you.'

"'What is it?'

"'His hair is cut more closely than yours, and part of it is shaved off.'

"'He is a priest, then?'

"'He wears a cowl. He is a monk.'

"'A monk! But why does he come to me?'

"'I should say that he cannot help it, that he is your spirit in some former state. Yes'—and he stared at me till his eyes almost mesmerised me—'you must have been a monk once.'

"'I—a monk! Impossible! Even if I had lived on earth before, it could never have been as a monk.'

"'How do you know that?'

"'Because I am utterly without superstitions, utterly free from any lingering desire for an ascetic life. That existence of silence, of ignorance, of perpetual prayer, can never have been mine.'

"'You cannot tell,' was all his answer.

II

"When I left Bond Street that afternoon I was full of disbelief. However, I had paid my half-guinea and escaped from my own core of misery for a quarter of an hour. That was something. I didn't regret my visit to this man Vane, whom I regarded as an agreeable charlatan. For a moment he had interested me. For a moment he had helped me to forget my useless wretchedness. I ought to have been grateful to him. And, as always, my soul regained its composure at last. One morning I awoke and said to myself that I was happy. Why? I did not know. But I got up. I was able to write once more. I was able to play. I felt that I had friends who loved me and a career before me. I could again look people in the face without fear. I could even feel a certain delightful conceit of mind and body. Bernard, I was myself. So I thought, so I knew. And yet, as days went by, I caught myself often thinking of this invisible, tonsured, and cowled companion of mine, whom Vane had seen, whom I did not see. Was he indeed with me? And, if so, had he thoughts, had he the holy thoughts of a spirit that has renounced the world and all fleshly things? Did he still keep that cloistered nature which is at home with silence, which aspires, and prays, and lives for possible eternity, instead of for certain time? Did he still hold desolate vigils? Did he still scourge himself along the thorny paths of faith? And, if he did, how must he regard me?

"I remember one night especially how this last thought was with me in a dreary house, where I sinned, and where I dissected a heart.

"And I trembled as if an eye was upon me. And I went home.

"You will say that my imagination is keen, and that I gave way to it. But wait and hear the end.

"This definite act of mine—this, my first conscious renunciation—did not tend, as you might suppose, to the peace of my mind. On the contrary, I found myself angry, perturbed, as I analysed the cause of my warfare with self. I have naturally a supreme hatred of all control. Liberty is my fetish. And now I had offered a sacrifice to a prisoning unselfishness, to a false god that binds and gags its devotees. I was angry, and I violently resumed my former course. But now I began to be ceaselessly companioned by uneasiness, by a furtive cowardice that was desolating. I felt that I was watched, and by some one who suffered when I sinned, who shrank and shuddered when I followed where my desires led.

"It was the monk.

"Soon I gave to him a most definite personality. I endowed him with a mind and with moods. I imagined not only a heart for him, but a voice, deep with a certain ecclesiastical beauty, austere, with a note more apt for denunciation than for praise. His face was my own face, but with an expression not mine, elevated, almost fanatical, yet nobly beautiful; praying eyes—and mine were only observant; praying lips—and mine were but sensitively sensual. And he was haggard with abstinence, while I—was I not often haggard with indulgence? Yes, his face was mine, and not mine. It seemed the face of a great saint who might have been a great sinner. Bernard, that is the most attractive face in all the world. Accustoming myself thus to a thought-companion, I at length—for we men are so inevitably materialistic—embodied him, gave to him hands, feet, a figure, all—as before, mine, yet not mine, a sort of saintly replica of my sinfulness. For do not hands, feet, figure cry our deeds as the watchman cries the hour in the night?

"So, I had the man. There he stood in my vision as you are now.

"Yes, he was there; but only when I sinned.

"When I worked and yielded myself up to the clear assertion of my intellect, when I fought to give out the thoughts that lingered like reluctant fish far down in the deep pools of my mind, when I wrestled for beauty of diction and for nameless graces of expression, when I was the author, I could not see him.

"But when I was the man, and lived the fables that I was afterwards to write, then he was with me. And his face was as the face of one who is wasted with grey grief.

"He came to me when I sinned, as if by my sins I did him grave injury. And, allowing my imagination to range wildly, as you will say, I grew gradually to feel as if each sin did indeed strike a grievous blow upon his holy nature.

"This troubled me at last. I found myself continually brooding over the strange idea. I was aware that if my friends could know I entertained it, they would think me mad. And yet I often fancied that thought moved me in the direction of a sanity more perfect, more desirable than my sanity of self-indulgence. Sometimes even I said to myself that I would reorganise my life, that I would be different from what I had been. And then, again, I laughed at my folly of the imagination, and cursed that clairvoyant of Bond Street, who made a living by trading upon the latent imbecility of human nature. Yet, the desire of change, of soul-transformation, came and lingered, and the vision of the monk's worn young face was often with me. And whenever, in my waking dreams, I looked upon it, I felt that a time might come when I could pray and weep for the wild catalogue of my many sins.

"Bernard, at last the day came when I left England. I had long wished to travel. I had grown tired of the hum of literary cliques, and the jargon of that deadly parasite called 'modernity.' Praise fainted, and lay like a corpse before my mind. I was sick of gaiety. It seemed to me that London was stifling my powers, narrowing my outlook, barring out real life from me with its moods and its fashions, and its idols of the hour, and its heroes of a day, who are the traitors of the day's night.

"So I went away.

"And now I come to the part of my story that you may find it hard to believe. Yet it is true.

"One day, in my wanderings, I came to a monastery. I remember the day well. It was an afternoon of early winter, and I was *en route* to a warm climate. But to gain my climate, and snatch a vivid contrast such as I love, I toiled over a gaunt and dreary pass, presided over by heavy, beetling-browed mountains. I rode upon a mule, attended only by my manservant and by a taciturn guide who led a baggage-mule. Slowly we wound, by thin paths, among the desolate crags, which sprang to sight in crowds at each turn of the way, pressing upon us, like dead faces of Nature, the corpses of things we call inanimate, but which had surely once lived. For the earth is alive, and gives life. But these mountains were now utterly dead. These grey, petrified countenances of the hills subdued my soul. The pattering shuffle of the mules woke an occasional echo, and even an echo I hated. For the environing silence was immense and I wished to steep myself in it. As we still ascended, in the waste winter afternoon, towards the hour of twilight, snow—the first snow of the season—began to fall. I watched the white vision of the flakes against the grey vision of the crags, and I thought that this path, which I had chosen as my road to Summer, was like the path by which holy men slowly gain Paradise, treading difficult ways through life that they may attain at last those eternal roses which bloom beyond the granite and the snows. Up and up I rode, into the clouds and the night, into the veil of the world, into the icy winds of the heights. An eagle screamed above my head, poised like a black shadow in the opaque gloom. That flying life was the only life in this waste.

"And then my mule, edging ever to the precipice as a man to his fate, sidled round a promontory of rock and set its feet in snow. For we had passed the snow-line. And upon the snow lay thin spears of yellow light. They streamed from the lattices of the monastery which crowns the very summit of the pass.

III

"At this monastery I was to spend the night. The good monks entertain all travellers, and in summer-time their hospitalities are lavishly exercised. But in winter, wanderers are few, and these holy men are left almost undisturbed in their meditative solitudes. My mule paused upon a rocky plateau before the door of the narrow grey building. The guide struck upon the heavy wood. After a while we were admitted by a robed figure, who greeted us kindly and made us welcome. Within, the place was bare and poor enough, but scrupulously clean. I was led through long, broad, and bitterly cold corridors to a big chamber in which I was to pass the night. Here were ranged in a row four large beds with white curtains. I occupied one bed, my servant another. The rest were untenanted. The walls were lined with light wood. The wooden floor was uncarpeted. I threw open the narrow window. Dimly I could see a mountain of rocks, on which snow lay in patches, towering up into the clouds in front of me. And to the left there was a glimmer of water. On the morrow, by that water, I should ride down into the land of flowers to which I was bound. Till then I would allow my imagination to luxuriate in the bleak romance of this wild home of prayer. The pathos of the night, shivering in the snow, and of this brotherhood of aspiring souls, detached from the excitement of the world for ever, seeking restlessly their final salvation day by day, night by night, in clouds of mountain vapour and sanctified incense, entered into my soul. And I thought of that imagined companion of mine. If he were with me now, surely he would feel that he had led me to his home at length. Surely he would secretly long to remain here.

"I smiled, as I said to myself—'Monk, to-morrow, if, indeed, you are fated to be my eternal attendant, you must come with me from this cold station of the cross down into the sunshine, where the blood of men is hot, where passions sing among the vineyards, where the battle is not of souls but of flowers. To-morrow you must come with me. But to-night be at peace!'

"And I smiled to myself again as I fancied that my visionary companion was glad.

"Then I went down into the refectory.

"That night, before I retired to my room of the four beds, I asked if I might go into the chapel of the monastery. My request was granted. I shall never forget the curious sensation which overtook me as my guide led me down some steps past a dim, little, old, painted window set in the wall, to the chapel. That there should be a church here, that the deep tones of an organ should ever sound among these rocks and clouds, that the Host should be elevated and the censer swung, and litanies and masses be chanted amid these everlasting snows, all this was wonderful and quickening to me. When we reached the chapel, I begged my kind guide to leave me for a while. I longed to meditate alone. He left me, and instinctively I sank down upon my knees.

"I could just hear the keening of the wind outside. A dim light glimmered near the altar, and in one of the oaken stalls I saw a bent form praying. I knelt a long time. I did not pray. At first I scarcely thought definitely. Only, I received into my heart the strange, indelible impression of this wonderful place; and, as I knelt, my eyes were ever upon that dark praying figure near to me. By degrees I imagined that a wave of sympathy flowed from it to me, that in this monk's devotions my name was not forgotten.

"'What absurd tricks our imaginations can play us!' you will say.

"I grew to believe that he prayed for me, there, under the dim light from the tall tapers.

"What blessing did he ask on me? I could not tell; but I longed that his prayer might be granted.

"And then, Bernard, at last he rose. He lifted his face from his hands and stood up. Something in his figure seemed so strangely familiar to me, so strangely that, on a sudden, I longed, I craved to see his face.

"He seemed about to retreat through a side door near to the altar; then he paused, appeared to hesitate, then came down the chapel towards me. As he drew near to me—I scarcely knew why—but I hid my face deep in my hands, with a dreadful sense of overwhelming guilt which dyed my cheeks with blood. I shrank—I cowered. I trembled and was afraid. Then I felt a gentle touch on my shoulder. I looked up into the face of the monk.

"Bernard, it was the face of my invisible companion—it was my own face.

"The monk looked down into my eyes searchingly. He recoiled.

"'*Mon démon!*' he whispered in French. '*Mon démon!*'

"For a moment he stood still, like one appalled. Then he turned and abruptly quitted the chapel.

"I started up to follow him, but something held me back. I let him go, and I listened to hear if his tread sounded upon the chapel floor as a human footstep, if his robe rustled as he went.

"Yes. Then he was, indeed, a living man, and it was a human voice which had reached my ears, not a voice of imagination. He was a living man, this double of my body, this antagonist of my soul, this being who called me demon, who fled from me, who, doubtless, hated me. He was a living man.

"I could not sleep that night. This encounter troubled me. I felt that it had a meaning for me which I must discover, that it was not chance which had led me to take this cold road to the sunshine. Something had bound me with an invisible thread, and led me up here into the clouds, where already I—or the likeness of me—dwelt, perhaps had been dwelling for many years. I had looked upon my living wraith, and my living wraith had called me demon.

"How could I sleep?

"Very early I got up. The dawn was bitterly cold, but the snow had ceased, though a coating of ice covered the little lake. How delicate was the dawn here! The gathering, growing light fell upon the rocks, upon the snow, upon the ice of the lake, upon the slate walls of the monastery. And upon each it lay with a pretty purity, a thin refinement, an austerity such as I had never seen before. So, even Nature, it seemed, was purged by the continual prayers of these holy men. She, too, like men, has her lusts, and her hot passions, and her wrath of warfare. She, too, like men, can be edified and tended into grace. Nature among these heights was a virgin, not a wanton, a fit companion for those who are dedicated to virginity.

"I dressed by the window, and went out to see the entrance of the morning. There was nobody about. I had to find my own way. But when I had gained the refectory, I saw a monk standing by the door.

"It was my wraith waiting for me.

"Silently he went before me to the great door of the building. He opened it, and we stepped out upon the rocky plateau on which the snow lay thickly. He closed the door behind us, and motioned me to attend him among the rocks till we were out of sight of the monastery. Then he stopped, and we faced one another, still without a word, the grey light of the wintry dawn clothing us so wearily, so plaintively.

"We gazed at each other, dark face to dark face, brown eyes to brown eyes. The monk's pale hands, my hands, were clenched. The monk's strong lips, my lips, were set. The two souls looked upon each other, there, in the dawn.

"And then at last he spoke in French, and with the beautiful voice I knew.

"'Whence have you come?' he said.

"'From England, father.'

"'From England? Then you live! you live. You are a man, as I am! And I have believed you to be a spirit, some strange spirit of myself, lost to my control, interrupting my prayers with your cries, interrupting my sleep with your desires. You are a man like myself?'

"He stretched out his hand and touched mine.

"'Yes; it is indeed so,' he murmured.

"'And you,' I said in my turn, 'are no spirit. Yet I too believed you to be a wraith of myself, interrupting my sins with your sorrow, interrupting my desires with your prayers. I have seen you. I have imagined you. And now I find you live. What does it mean? For we are as one and yet not as one.'

"'We are as two halves of a strangely-mingled whole,' he answered. 'Do you know what you have done to me?'

"'No, father.'

"'Listen,' he said. 'When a boy I dedicated myself to God. Early, early I dedicated myself, so that I might never know sin. For I had heard that the charm of sin is so great and so terrible that, once it is known, once it is felt, it can never be forgotten. And so it can make the holiest life hideous with its memories. It can intrude into the very sanctuary like a ghost, and murmur its music with the midnight mass. Even at the elevation of the Host will it be present, and stir the heart of the officiator to longing so keen that it is like the Agony of the Garden, the Agony of Christ. There are monks here who weep because they dare not sin, who rage secretly like beasts—because they will not sin.'

"He paused. The grey light grew over the mountains.

"'Knowing this, I resolved that I would never know sin, lest I, too, should suffer so horribly. I threw myself at once into the arms of God. Yet I have suffered—how I have suffered!'

"His face was contorted, and his lips worked. I stood as if under a spell, my eyes upon his face. I had only the desire to hear him. He went on, speaking now in a voice roughened by emotion:

"'For I became like these monks. You'—and he pointed at me with outstretched fingers—'you, my wraith, made in my very likeness, were surely born when I was born, to torment me. For, while I have prayed, I have been conscious of your neglect of prayer as if it were my own. When I have believed, I have been conscious of your unbelief as if it were my own. Whatever I have feebly tried to do for God, has been marred and defaced by all that you have left undone. I have wrestled with you; I have tried to hold you back; I have tried to lead you with me where I want to go, where I must go. All these years I have tried, all these years I have striven. But it has seemed as if God did not choose it. When you have been sinning, I have been agonising. I have lain upon the floor of my cell in the night, and I have torn at my evil heart. For—sometimes—I have longed—how I have longed—to sin your sin.'

"He crossed himself. Sudden tears sprang into his eyes.

"'I have called you my demon,' he cried. 'But you are my cross. Oh, brother, will you not be my crown?'

"His eyes, shadowed with tears, gazed down into mine. Bernard, in that moment, I understood all—my depression, my unreasoning despair, the fancied hatred of others, even my few good impulses, all came from him, from this living holy wraith of my evil self.

"'Will you not be my crown?' he said.

"Bernard, there, in the snow, I fell at his feet. I confessed to him. I received his absolution.

"And, as the light of the dawn grew strong upon the mountains, he, my other self, my wraith, blessed me."

There was a long silence between us. Then I said:

"And now?"

"And now you know why I have changed. That day, as I went down into the land of the sunshine, I made a vow."

"A vow?"

"Yes; to be his crown, not his cross. I soon returned to England. At first I was happy, and then one day my old evil nature came upon me like a giant. I fell again into sin, and, even as I sinned, I saw his face looking into mine, Bernard, pale, pale to the lips, and with eyes—such sad eyes of reproach! Then I thought I was not fit to live, and I tried to kill myself. They saved me, and brought me here."

"Yes; and now, Hubert?"

"Now," he said, "I am so happy. God surely placed me here where I cannot sin. The days pass and the nights, and they are stainless. And he—he comes by night and blesses me. I live for him now, and see always the grey walls of his monastery, his face which shall, at last, be completely mine."

"Good-bye," the doctor said to me as I got into the carriage to drive back to the station. "Yes, he is perfectly happy, happier in his mania, I believe, than you or I in our sanity."

I drove away from that huge home of madness, set in the midst of lovely gardens in a smiling landscape, and I pondered those last words of the doctor's:

"You and I—in our sanity."

And, thinking of the peace that lay on Hubert's face, I compared the so-called mad of the world with the so-called sane—and wondered.

AN EVICTED SPIRIT

Marguerite Merington

Marguerite Merington (1860–1951) was born in Stoke Newington, London, but raised in America after the family emigrated during her early childhood. Merington began her writing career whilst teaching classics at the Normal College (later Hunter College) in New York. Her first work, the drama *Captain Lettarblair*, was performed at the Lyceum Theatre in 1891 with celebrated actor E. H. Sothern in the title role. The play was well received and led Merington to continue her work as a playwright, initially for adults but later for children. She also wrote numerous poems for *Scribner's Magazine* and was invited to edit the correspondence of General Custer, later published as *The Custer Story: The Life and Intimate Letters of General George A. Custer and His Wife Elizabeth* (1950).

One of many pieces of short fiction, "An Evicted Spirit" was first published in March 1899. It appeared in *The Atlantic*, an American periodical, and tells the story of life beyond the veil. Unlike other tales in this collection, the spirit in this text is seen by no one living: she reveals herself only to you, the reader.

I was an only child. In tradition, station, circumstance, my people, by all acknowledgment, were among the leaders of the small provincial town which for generations had fostered our respected family tree, and I, being the only green arboreal shoot from that venerable growth, was the leader of my family. Nature had done much for me: I was good looking, though not unpleasantly aware of it; clever, and strove to value myself only to myself, for my ability, though the very imputation of an effort may point to a not unvarying success. Accordingly, I was looked up to, admired, envied generally, occasionally criticised, though never to my face; in short, I led. Happy I was not wholly, for never in my own life, nor in the lives of those with whom my lot was cast, had I found the illusive ideal quality for which I yearned; but still I lived, vitally always, at times buoyant with the mere ecstasy of being alive; and then one day I died.

The nurse had told me I would recover; the doctor had told my parents I would not. After the first brief agony, when sensation and consciousness met halfway, for myself I did not care; nature has her own fashion of announcing bad tidings to her children.

The watchers stood or knelt about my bed while physical life was ebbing away from me like the sound of a distant bell. Now and again, as those far-away vibrations take on a stronger tone before they fade to nothingness, so for brief moments my strength

revived, but it was the rally that precedes the end. A little acceler-
ated breathing as if something in me were in haste to break away
for a long journey, a little trickle in the throat, and then a large,
firm hand, unseen and inescapable, was laid upon my features,
pressing them gently back from the heightened lines of suffering
to the smooth contours of infancy. Among the watchers life seemed
to be suspended, and the silence to become not merely a negation
of sound, but a fearful and growing entity that at any minute might
take bodily form, seizing the living and engulfing them in some
terrible abyss made up of unfathomable spaces full of silence. Then
the human interruption came in the person of the nurse. Lifting
the curtain of the alcove, to which she had withdrawn discreetly,
she noiselessly approached the doctor as he stood at the foot of the
bed, watch in hand, with his eyes upon my face, and in a matter-of-
fact whisper asked him a question which he answered with a slight
nod, and which formulated my exit from this life.

"Is she dead?" The words struck with a jarring note upon the
tense chord to which the listeners' hearts were strung. My cousin
Ophia shuddered and fell to stifled sobbing; my mother moved to
throw her arms about my frame, but fell forward with hidden face
and aimless outstretched hands; while my father, with an impatient
exclamation, strode noisily from the room, as if death had done
him a personal injury, without offering him a decent opportunity
for the reprisals due a gentleman. Then Ophia, after kissing my
rapidly stiffening lips and hands, led my mother from the room, and
I was left with those to whom death was a professional necessity.

"Is she dead?" For weeks, unwittingly, I had been casting aside,
one by one, the toys with which my consciousness habitually played
in the game I had fancied to be life; for weeks I had been wearing
out the little body that at once had clothed and realised me; and

somewhere about the moment when the doctor had affirmed the nurse's question as he closed his watch, the last of the old familiar ties had ceased to bind me, the dear hands of my people were powerless to stay me, and, shaking itself clear of sensation and the encumbrance of the flesh, my consciousness went marching on alone. There was no break, there was no subversion; it went marching on, as it always had been marching, from unremembered time; on and on to some as yet unapprehended end, inevitable and foreordained; on and on, and ever on; and as it marched the clouds that hitherto had blurred my vision were dispelled, and I began to see.

"She is dead!" The news sped abroad on wings, and hurrying grief's andante came the activity of preparation. All lives are but a series of preliminaries and preparations: for birth, for adolescence, for position, for pleasure, to understand, to make one's self understood, to prolong one's days with honour or enjoyment; in short, all life is but a preparation to live, until we die. But of all the paraphernalia of preparation with which we deck events, none carries more grotesqueness to the disembodied consciousness than our preparations to entertain the great, unwelcome visitor. All other events are relative, having a position in a universal series; for all other catastrophes we have a comparison, an explanation, or a remedy. So long as there is a flicker of life in the newborn child, we can incubate it into fuller life; we lose our money,—there is more money in the world to be scrambled for; our friends are unsuccessful,—we can give them good advice; our neighbour is unhappy in his marriage,—we can say that after all it is his own business, if not indeed his fault; our ideals are shattered,—we become saints or cynics; our nerves are wrecked,—we take to golf or mental therapeutics. But death alone is absolute,—the one situation our little wisdom cannot explain away, the one unquestioned and unanswerable fact in life!

And so at death's coming we hasten to affect external differences, pitifully shrouding ourselves in the dark negations of the colours of life, putting the mottled blackness of crape between our faces and the sky; and is there not also a pathetic expression of remorse in this ceremonial for the dead, a belated payment that Love grudgingly owed life, and, heartbroken, lavishes too prodigally on a memory?

Downstairs, my mother, meek and apathetic, her tears exhausted, was standing as a lay figure to the dressmaker, while my cousin Ophia, being of all least fitted for the task, was composing my obituary notices. "To-day, at her late residence," she wrote. Horrible! I had inherited my father's critical love of language; careless English at all times set my subjective teeth on edge, and now, by the irony of fate, I was made to die "at my late residence." Psychically speaking, I paced the floor. Would no one come to my rescue and snatch the pen from Ophia's hand?

"There, Mis' Stanleymain," said Miss McNulty, the dressmaker, her mouth full of adroitly controlled pins, as she pulled the skirted folds into a stiff flare, "I guess that'll do for now. I'll baste it good and strong for the ceremony, and any little alterations you want I'll fix up for you later on. All you want now is to look prepared, but not conspicuous so that the first thing people say as you come up the aisle is, 'My! what a genteel, simple frock!'"

"I don't care! I don't care!" moaned my mother.

"Of course you don't, dear," rejoined Miss McNulty, dropping the skirt in a dark nimbus about her subject's feet. "I've known trouble myself. Step over it. 'T ain't to be expected you should care at such a time,—not but what that kind is often the fussiest when they commence to take notice again!" she added to herself, as with the dexterity of a juggler she debouched the pins.

The milliner had entered. "I've made you up a Marie Stuart shape, Mis' Stanleymain," she said in a hoarse, sepulchral whisper. "It goes with the deepest bereavement, yet it always looks real dressy." At my mother's protesting little moan, "There, there, my dear, I know just how it strikes you; I can enter into a mourner's feelings, for I come of a burying family," she proudly proclaimed. "Seven years, week in an' week out, I never was a day out of blacks, heavy and lightened, and—Come, Mis' Stanleymain, you can't go bareheaded, you know. Think of *her*! She would have been the first to want you to look your best, and—There, there, dear heart, let me just run down into the kitchen and draw you a cup o' tea!"

Ophia now held out her ridiculous announcements, smudged with tears. "Will you please look at these, cousin Sarah? I never can quite trust my own composition," she explained, with excellent reason. "Our dear one was always so particular; and the young man from the newspaper is waiting,—and newspaper gentlemen are always in such a hurry,—and I don't know whether to say 'taken,' or 'passed away,' or 'called home,' or just"—a sob took the place of the ill-omened word.

But my mother, never critical, was beyond detail, and I certainly should have "passed away" in print, had not my father come whistling down the stairs. "Ask him," said my father's wife, with the nearest approach to sarcasm I ever had heard her gentle voice attain.

With a light laugh, half jocular, half sneering, the head of the family drew the pen through Ophia's delicately illegible tracery, and in his firm hand set forth how on that day, at her father's house, Gillian Stanleymain had died. Then, making the women wince with a joke about its still being his house till the mortgage was foreclosed, he let himself out into the street. At the gate, my old Gordon setter, long banished from my sickroom, came whimpering to him with the pathos of unanswered question in its faithful eyes; but my father only gave the creature an impatient push out of his path, yet did not drive it back, as his wont was, when it followed him.

Our neighbour, Mrs Piper, was the first caller of condolence admitted to the darkened house. Mrs Piper was a large, unwieldy woman, whose habit was to "run in," as she phrased it, in neighbourly fashion, by the servants' door. To-day she slowly and asthmatically climbed the front steps, announcing herself by what I never had suspected her of owning,—a card. Her attire also showed an unusual formality. Long carnelian pendants swung bobbing from her ears, while from her best bonnet she had removed the too gaudy cherries, hitherto its crowning glory, and in their place had pinned at a precarious angle a dingy velvet bow. An old cashmere shawl, that as a child I had been permitted to gaze on at rare and royal intervals, hung from her shoulders, exhaling the conflicting aromas of sandalwood and camphor, its folds adjusted so as skilfully to conceal the strained relations between hooks and eyes at her imaginary waist-line, and as skilfully displaying the bit of old thread lace, pinned with a platter-like cameo, about her neck. Then a remembrance of old laughter came to me as I recalled a saying of Mrs Piper's, made in all good faith, that a "true gentlewoman might always feel well dressed if she only dressed her neck." And there she sat, dear soul, doing my departure homage with her clothes; saying little, but sighing heavily and mopping her broad face, while her chin drew in and out like the pleats of an accordion, as with neighbourliness and comfort written in her every line she held my mother's hand.

216

In contrast to Mrs Piper, the Misses Jenkins, with whom we were on formal terms, now came, with an assumption of intimacy, by the servants' way. "She'll see *us*!" they said, only to find themselves denied; for a day or so before, when my illness was taking a hopeful turn, they had teased my mother's ears and torn her heart by personally conducting her, as it were, through several death-bed scenes, in a study of whose details lay their gruesome dissipation; and thereafter my mother, illogically enough, in her secret heart, held these estimable ladies in part responsible for my demise. Of course they asked permission to "view" my mortal residuum, but again being peremptorily denied, on their way home they at first agreed to mark their displeasure by not coming to my funeral. For such abstention, however, the mortuary habit was too strong with them, so they decided that it really would be too hard upon my memory, since I was not responsible for the slight,—though I would have been quite capable of it, they added, which was true.

"How old do you suppose she was, anyway?" asked Miss Jane of Miss Luella. "She owned to twenty-seven."

"That's what the evening paper said," answered Miss Luella. "I read it over a gentleman's shoulder in the car."

"Pouf! Don't talk to me of the paper!" cried Miss Jane. "You know I won't allow one in the house,—except the Weekly Christian, which never has any news."

"Well, but, sister," rejoined Miss Luella, "I think the paper is right. I dropped into Townley's this afternoon just to see what sort of a casket they were giving the poor child; you know that sort of thing has always had an attraction for me since the dear lieutenant was taken. It's quite an elegant affair,—rosewood trimmed with silver; and the dates were on the plates—and silver wears so well people would never dare engrave a falsehood on it, for fear of being confronted with it on the Judgment Day!"

The "dear lieutenant" was a familiar if unsubstantial figure in our town. A naval officer to whom Miss Luella had been plighted in her youth, he had perished in the civil war; but as the taking of Richmond receded into history he grew more and more shadowy, and for a time was nearly blotted out. Then, lo and behold! all of a sudden his melancholy ghost reappeared, stalking through Miss Luella's conversation, but reconstructed and newly painted with such neat allusions to the "recent war" as to make him quite a jaunty, fin-de-siècle ghost.

Then the acerb sisters agreed that some people had called me good-looking, though for their own part they never could see it. Stylish, ye-es, but that was my clothes. And stuck up! Well, poor thing, one must speak only charitably of the dead, and so saying they stopped at the florist's to punctuate my passing with what they termed a floral piece.

"Should id be an emplem, or should id be chust cud flowers?" Mr Dunkel asked.

"Oh no," cried the ladies with one voice, "*not* cut flowers!" They wanted something superior. It was for one of the first families,—a dear and intimate friend.

"Should de vrend yung or olt be?" was the question.

The ladies looked at each other. "Well," said Miss Jane, with happy tact, "she was young to die."

"I tells you vy. I gif you points. I am an ardist," said the florist. "It should abbrobriate be. To egsamble, for de yung a great variedy of floral emplems is: a wreathe, a gross, an angor"—

"Oh, not an anchor," Miss Luella interposed, "except in the case of a naval officer!"

"Vell, an angor shands on its own endt and a goot shew makes," they were told, "but it gives oder tings abbrobriate for de yung. For de mittel-aged," he continued, "I favours oder emplems; to egsamble, a harbp, or golten gades, or gades achar; but yunger as five or older as fifdy is de same, de grossmutter as de babpy,—a leedle billow done in effer-lasdings mit de vun vord—Resdt!"

My case being presented more explicitly, the artist in floral emblems advised a cross, a wreath, or "Vait!" he said, with sudden inspiration. "I haf id. You vant a pasket mit a tuv berching on de handel like id chust alighted vos,—a tuv mit oudtshpred vinks!" But Miss Jane, being a member of the Audubon Society, objected to the use of a bird in decoration, so the sisters sent the basket, but spared me the dove.

Other visitors came to the house; also written attempts at consolation for the loss of me, most of them sincere, some few perfunctory, some simply idiotic. There were those who told my mother, with curious irrelevance, that a dead sorrow was better than a living one; others assured her—as if they knew!—that I was at peace. Some bade her regard it, not as death, but sleep, which was nonsense, seeing I was just plain dead. And some there were who took upon themselves to answer for the Deity with a smug complacence which I then and there should have denounced, could I but have found a voice or stirred my frozen hand. What came nearest to my consciousness with an approach to pleasure were the offerings from the children I had cared for in the ragged quarter of the town,—not because these were more genuine than the others in their sympathy (most of them spelled it *smypathy*), but because they made my mother smile through her tears. She never will destroy those poor little thumb-marked compositions from the children, full of the sympathy they could not spell.

An old friend came, and begged to take his turn in the night-watches by my side. A success only in extraordinary failure, with poetic talent that persistently refused to fructify, I always had gibed at him—and this was his revenge! It was the nobler in him because he had a physical fear of mortality, this poor lad who tried, but failed, to make himself immortal. I too had had that same fear once, but now it seemed to me fantastic beyond words to find a supernatural horror in the poor little piece of white stillness that had been I, now only asking to be put out of sight! So as he sat beside me in the night I tried to encompass my friend with my psychic presence to his strength and comfort, though the immediate material result to him was only a poem which all the magazines refused.

The nurse and the undertaker were making me ready for the grave. "It's a gloomy profession, yours, Mr Townley," said the nurse.

"No, no, Miss Carr, you mustn't think that," protested Mr Townley. "It has its ups and downs, but it's a nice trade; it's an artistic trade,"—here he bent one of my arms stiffly across my breast, and straightened the other stiffly by my side; "and then, you see, it's steady,—it's steady."

"That's so," said the nurse, gazing at him thoughtfully, for the doctor had family ties, but the undertaker was a bachelor. "It don't affect your spirits in private life, Mr Townley?" she suggested.

"Now, now, Miss Carr, I wouldn't like you to think that of me," she was assured. "In my own home I like my little sing; I like my little joke with the best of 'em. Outside my profession I have the keenest sense of the ridiculous. Why, I don't mind telling you, as between friends, that I take in two of the comic papers! But once I cross the threshold of a house where I've put crape upon the door, I'm a different man. Shoes that don't creak, a face that looks as if it didn't know the shape of a smile, the feelings of the family to be respected—why, though I say it who should not say it, I may go so far as to say I ain't a human being so much as part of an occasion." And indeed the unobtrusive demeanour of the little man suggested that he might be Death's valet, by whom, with all submission, the dread king must not expect to be regarded as a hero.

Skipping back a few paces, he eyed me with a critical approval, which changed quickly to reproach. "Oh, them mourners, them mourners, you never know what they'll do next!" he exclaimed, shaking his head and sighing heavily as one whose patience with humanity had been taxed too far.

"What's the matter?" asked the nurse.

"I'm not disposed to be hard upon mourners," he defended his position. "I make allowance for their feelings; I give 'em all the leeway I can; any little trinket, letters, or flowers they may wish to put in I make no objection to; but—that hair!" and he shook his head at me severely.

Ophia had arranged my hair. Dear heart! she always had longed to do small personal offices for me which I, in my proud isolation, never had suffered from her; but now at the last with loving hands she had dressed my hair as I generally wore it, characteristically putting in the hairpins criss-cross in a way that would have annoyed me greatly, had feeling stayed by me.

"What's the matter with the hair?" asked the nurse. "It looks just as natural."

"That's all very well," the undertaker answered; "but how can I be expected to get the lid down with a pompadour in front and a bun behind?"

"Oh, if that's all," said the nurse, "here, I'll fix it," and with apt hands she loosened and laid flat the coils above my neck, so as to lower my offending head.

And that in part symbolised my life. I had come into the world a naked, round-eyed child, ready to view the world with instinctive truth, but by the imperfect processes of education and the unconscious distortions of the social machine I had become what those about me were,—little better than a frontage on life, a mere façade.

Mr Townley again skipped back a few paces, and, his head on one side like cock robin's, he now surveyed me with entire approbation. "Lovely!" he commented. "Lovely!"

"She does look nice," agreed the nurse.

"Not that I would have had this happen for the world," said the undertaker with a burst of genuine feeling. "I've watched her grow up, child and woman, and it goes to my heart to handle her professionally before her time." And as he took up his hat he added, "I only wish there was some little extra thing I could do that needn't go down upon the bill."

"I'm sure you have done everything in the nicest way," replied the nurse. "But what's your hurry? Stay and talk a bit."

But Mr Townley excused himself with a mournful pleasantness, saying that he had an appointment out of town to "ice a party."

The church services over me came to my consciousness not as an empty form. They did not matter much to me, but for the living they held a timely message of dignified submission to the inevitable, with a hope of better things beyond the objective world. Of course there was no collection taken up, but while the choir was singing, and the congregation trying to sing, Lead, Kindly Light, I, who in life had been proud of my unostentatious charities, now went about the church, a poor little Psyche evicted from the flesh, begging for charity to my memory. And as I looked at the people recalling the intellectual estimates I had formed of them on whose justice I had prided myself, it came to me that after all, while it is a good thing to be invariably just, a day comes when there may be more comfort in remembering that one has been occasionally kind.

Then there was the long drive to the cemetery. I had always liked to lead, and in this my last social function I led; but those who followed me were erect, while I alone lay,—leading, but not of my own volition; the cast-off garment of a woman! Behind me came a long diminuendo line of grief in carriages: the handkerchiefs of those nearest me were wet hard balls with excess of tears, the handkerchiefs in the middle of the procession were wispy rags with modified regret, while some poor relations at the end were almost dry-eyed and actually enjoyed the ride.

At the grave happened one unexpected thing. When "Ashes to ashes" and "dust to dust" was read, Mr Townley stepped neatly forth with a handful of gravel for his accustomed illustration of the rubric; but my father, who was damned by the Weekly Christian as an atheist, put the undertaker on one side, and himself dropped the symbolic earth upon my coffin-lid. Then later he seized a spade from one of the men and helped to fill in the grave, the action bringing out strong lines on his inert good-lookingness. Some of the flowers they put beneath the little mound, and some they laid outside it, and all perished before the sun went down.

That night, for the last time, my consciousness revisited the places that had held the most vital part of my existence. One house, one room, in particular I sought,—the home of a man who had professed himself my most patient and devoted lover. I always had said that I never would allow myself to be married, unless to a great statesman or a genius, yet into my life this man had come with an insistence not lightly to be gainsaid. An average man on a decidedly material plane I thought him; indeed, that very evening, in a curious emotional reaction, he had taken the train to the nearest city to see a popular and silly vaudeville. Yet in my developing consciousness there dawned a question that demanded light. A faint moon ray slid between the bowed shutters of his room, and I saw that everything about the man was clean, from his surroundings to his heart. As he lay there, ruddy, of gigantic strength and stature, he looked, for all his vigorous manhood, like an overgrown child, for he had cried himself to sleep. The salt rheum of sorrow glued his eyelids fast, his nostrils and the corners of his well-shaped mouth were wet, and in his relaxed grasp lay a ridiculous little tintype that he had been clasping so close as to cut the flesh. On his dressing-table I noticed the portrait of his mother,—an eagle-faced woman, imperial in her maternity,—and I recalled how it was said that this man had been a good son to her no less than a father to a brood of younger brothers; then, as I looked at him again, I had a curious apprehension of what manner of child he must have been, and of the child a woman might bear to him, and by degrees illumination came to me. Once, in my wish to lead, almost as much as through my love for the flower, on a wet autumn day, I had made a passionate pilgrimage for the first fringed gentian of the year. On the wet hilltops I had hunted it, in hidden nooks, through bog and bracken, even to the heart of the low-lying valleys; but in vain. And as I returned home, wet, weary, and discouraged, there on a common wayside bank, there at my very door, grew my blue-eyed treasure-trove, awaiting my return. The quest had been worth while for aspiration's sake, but the flower had been growing at my door! So it came to me that this man, had I lived, would have been my husband. He had ridiculed my tenuous studies, burlesquing my psuché, as I called my psychism, into my "sukey," and I had despised his material views of life; but meanwhile a bond had been strengthening between us, for I had touched the spiritual part of him, and he had reached the human quality in me. Yes, had I lived I should have come to love this man well enough even to black his boots—though I might never have told him that, in just so many words. I knew it now—and humanly speaking I was dead. So the little sukey that he had laughed at, but truly loved, bent over him as he lay asleep and gave him a butterfly kiss that he would never feel,—a kiss of revelation and good-bye. Then I went home.

In his study my father sat, though the night was well advanced; but it was not the clever, bad French novel in his hand that kept him from his bed, for he turned no page. The years seemed suddenly to have set their seal upon his frame, and his face was creased, like an insomniac's pillow. I waited by him, my consciousness of the subjective life becoming every moment more distinct. Finally he threw aside his book, and together we went into my mother's room. Her bed was untouched: she was not there. We mounted to my room: she was not there. We looked for her by Ophia: she was not there. We sought her over the house, my father, with growing anxiety, calling her by her name, "Sarah," as he had not done for years, and then by foolish loving names that must have belonged to their courtship days, "Sarahkins" and "Sally." There was no answer. At last we found her in the garret, too enwrapped in an old grief to hear my father's step, as she sat by an open drawer filled with the long-put-away daintiness of a baby's clothes. These never had belonged to me, for, with my abhorrence of sentiment, I had caused the swathings of my infancy to be bestowed on the deserving poor; these had been intended for a child that had come to my parents in their early wedded life, hardly to live an hour,—a loss for which my mother had grieved so over-long that my father had grown impatient; and thus had they drifted apart. Then I had

225

come, the child of psychic unrest, too late to bring them together; nor had I tried,—not as I should have tried,—as now I saw. Nor, as I saw now, had they made me fully understand; for after all, age is so much nearer to youth than is youth to age! So in my lifetime we three had missed one another, but now to-night, though the mortal part of me was lying in a new-made grave, my subjective presence held my parents in a close embrace. Tenderly my father led my mother down to my deserted room, where they sat awhile and talked of me. Their lives had grown too far apart for perfect understanding, but at any rate their childless old age would be sweet with mutual kindliness, like the winter sunshine that melts the snow. And so I left them, while the night wore away in peace.

THE DUCHESS AT PRAYER

Edith Wharton

Born into a wealthy New York family, Edith Wharton (1862–1937) moved in elite circles and was firmly installed in the society life explored in her later fiction. After travelling throughout Europe during Wharton's early years, the family returned to America where Edith was educated by a private governess. Demonstrating a desire to write from an early age, her first volume of poetry, *Verses*, was published privately in her sixteenth year. Wharton did not publish fiction until twenty years later, releasing two short story collections before publishing her first novel, *The Valley of Decision*, in 1902. Her second novel, *The House of Mirth* (1905) was very well received and a successful writing career followed. In 1921, she became the first woman to win the Pulitzer Prize in fiction, which she was awarded for *The Age of Innocence*, a story set in 1870s New York.

Although less frequently discussed than her novels, Wharton wrote a selection of ghost stories for popular periodicals. Many of these tales highlight the loneliness of old age and depict individuals haunted by personal regret. "The Duchess at Prayer" is different. First published in *Scribner's Magazine* (August 1900) this is a story in which there is no regret: the perpetrator of wicked deeds lacks remorse and uncanny occurrences seek to highlight prior wrongs.

I

H ave you ever questioned the long shuttered front of an
old Italian house, that motionless mask, smooth, mute,
equivocal as the face of a priest behind which buzz the
secrets of the confessional? Other houses declare the activities
they shelter; they are the clear expressive cuticle of a life flowing
close to the surface; but the old palace in its narrow street, the
villa on its cypress-hooded hill, are as impenetrable as death. The
tall windows are like blind eyes, the great door is a shut mouth.
Inside there may be sunshine, the scent of myrtles, and a pulse of
life through all the arteries of the huge frame; or a mortal solitude
where bats lodge in the disjointed stones, and the keys rust in
unused doors...

II

From the loggia, with its vanishing frescoes, I looked down an
avenue barred by a ladder of cypress shadows to the ducal escutch-
eon and mutilated vases of the gate. Flat noon lay on the gardens,
on fountains, porticoes and grottoes. Below the terrace, where a
chrome-coloured lichen had sheeted the balustrade as with fine
laminæ of gold, vineyards stooped to the rich valley clasped in
hills. The lower slopes were strewn with white villages like stars

spangling a summer dusk; and beyond these, fold on fold of blue mountain, clear as gauze against the sky. The August air was lifeless, but it seemed light and vivifying after the atmosphere of the shrouded rooms through which I had been led. Their chill was on me and I hugged the sunshine.

"The Duchess's apartments are beyond," said the old man.

He was the oldest man I had ever seen; so sucked back into the past that he seemed more like a memory than a living being. The one trait linking him with the actual was the fixity with which his small saurian eye held the pocket that, as I entered, had yielded a *lira* to the gate keeper's child. He went on, without removing his eye:

"For two hundred years nothing has been changed in the apartments of the Duchess."

"And no one lives here now?"

"No one, sir. The Duke goes to Como for the summer season."

I had moved to the other end of the loggia. Below me, through hanging groves, white roofs and domes flashed like a smile.

"And that's Vicenza?"

"*Proprio!*" The old man extended fingers as lean as the hands fading from the walls behind us. "You see the palace roof over there, just to the left of the Basilica? The one with the row of statues like birds taking flight? That's the Duke's town palace, built by Palladio."

"And does the Duke come there?"

"Never. In winter he goes to Rome."

"And the palace and the villa are always closed?"

"As you see—always."

"How long has this been?"

"Since I can remember."

I looked into his eyes: they were like tarnished metal mirrors reflecting nothing. "That must be a long time," I said, involuntarily.

"A long time," he assented.

I looked down on the gardens. An opulence of dahlias overran the box borders, between cypresses that cut the sunshine like basalt shafts. Bees hung above the lavender; lizards sunned themselves on the benches and slipped through the cracks of the dry basins. Everywhere were vanishing traces of that fantastic horticulture of which our dull age has lost the art. Down the alleys maimed statues stretched their arms like rows of whining beggars; faun-eared terms grinned in the thicket, and above the laurustinus walls rose the mock ruin of a temple, falling into real ruin in the bright disintegrating air. The glare was blinding.

"Let us go in," I said.

The old man pushed open a heavy door, behind which the cold lurked like a knife.

"The Duchess's apartments," he said.

Overhead and around us the same evanescent frescoes, under foot the same scagliola volutes, unrolled themselves in terminably. Ebony cabinets, with colonnades of precious marbles in cunning perspective, alternated down the room with the tarnished efflorescence of gilt consoles supporting Chinese monsters; and from the chimney panel a gentleman in the Spanish habit haughtily ignored us.

"Duke Ercole II.," the old man explained, "by the Genoese Priest."

It was a narrow-browed face, sallow as a wax effigy, high-nosed and cautious-lidded, as though modelled by priestly hands; the lips weak and vain rather than cruel; a quibbling mouth that would have snapped at verbal errors like a lizard catching flies, but had never learned the shape of a round yes or no. One of the Duke's hands rested on the head of a dwarf, a simian creature with pearl earrings and fantastic dress; the other turned the pages of a folio propped on a skull.

"Beyond is the Duchess's bedroom," the old man reminded me.

Here the shutters admitted but two narrow shafts of light, gold bars deepening the subaqueous gloom. On a dais, the bedstead, grim, nuptial, official, lifted its baldachin; a yellow Christ agonised between the curtains, and across the room a lady smiled at us from the chimney breast.

The old man unbarred a shutter and the light touched her face. Such a face it was, with a flicker of laughter over it like the wind on a June meadow, and a singular tender pliancy of mien, as though one of Tiepolo's lenient goddesses had been busked into the stiff sheath of a seventeenth century dress!

"No one has slept here," said the old man, "since the Duchess Violante."

"And she was—?"

"The lady there—first Duchess of Duke Ercole II."

He drew a key from his pocket and unlocked a door at the farther end of the room. "The chapel," he said. "This is the Duchess's balcony." As I turned to follow him the Duchess tossed me a sidelong smile.

I stepped into a grated tribune above a chapel festooned with stucco. Pictures of bituminous saints mouldered between the pilasters; the artificial roses in the altar vases were grey with dust and age, and under the cobwebby rosettes of the vaulting a bird's nest clung. Before the altar stood a row of tattered arm chairs, and I drew back at sight of a figure kneeling near them.

"The Duchess," the old man whispered. "By the Cavaliere Bernini."

It was the image of a woman in furred robes and spreading fraise, her hands lifted, her face addressed to the tabernacle. There was a strangeness in the sight of that immovable presence locked in prayer before an abandoned shrine. Her face was hidden, and I wondered whether it were grief or gratitude that raised her hands and drew her eyes to the altar, where no living prayer joined her marble invocation. I followed my guide down the tribune steps, impatient to see what mystic version of such terrestrial graces the ingenious artist had found—the Cavaliere was master of such arts. The Duchess's attitude was one of transport, as though heavenly airs fluttered her laces and the love locks escaping from her coif. I saw how admirably the sculptor had caught the poise of her head, the tender slope of the shoulder; then I crossed over and looked into her face—it was a frozen horror. Never have hate, revolt, and agony so possessed a human countenance...

The old man crossed himself and shuffled his feet on the marble.

"The Duchess Violante," he repeated.

"The same as in the picture?"

"Eh, the same."

"But the face what does it mean?"

He shrugged his shoulders and turned deaf eyes on me. Then he shot a glance round the sepulchral place, clutched my sleeve and said, close to my ear: "It was not always so."

"What was not?"

"The face—so terrible."

"The Duchess's face?"

"The statue's. It changed after—"

"After?"

"It was put here."

"The statue's face *changed*—?"

He mistook my bewilderment for incredulity and his confidential finger dropped from my sleeve. "Eh, that's the story. I tell what I've heard. What do I know?" He resumed his senile shuffle across the marble. "This is a bad place to stay in—no one comes here. It's too cold. But the gentleman said, *I must see everything!*"

I let the *lire* sound. "So I must—and hear everything. This story, now—from whom did you have it?"

His hand stole back. "One that saw it, by God!"

"That saw it?"

"My grandmother, then. I'm a very old man."

"Your grandmother? Your grandmother was?"

"The Duchess's serving girl, with respect to you."

"Your grandmother? Two hundred years ago?"

"Is it too long ago? That's as God pleases. I am a very old man and she was a very old woman when I was born. When she died she was as black as a miraculous Virgin and her breath whistled like the wind in a keyhole. She told me the story when I was a little boy. She told it to me out there in the garden, on a bench by the fish pond, one summer night of the year she died. It must be true, for I can show you the very bench we sat on..."

III

Noon lay heavier on the gardens; not our live humming warmth, but the stale exhalation of dead summers. The very statues seemed to drowse like watchers by a death bed. Lizards shot out of the cracked soil like flames and the bench in the laurustinus niche was strewn with the blue varnished bodies of dead flies. Before us lay the fish pond, a yellow marble slab above rotting secrets. The villa looked across it, composed as a dead face, with the cypresses flanking it for candles...

IV

"... Impossible, you say, that my mother's mother should have been the Duchess's maid? What do I know? It is so long since anything has happened here that the old things seem nearer, perhaps, than to those who live in cities... But how else did she know about the statue then? Answer me that, sir! That she saw with her eyes, I can swear to, and never smiled again, so she told me, till they put her first child in her arms... for she was taken to wife by the steward's son, Antonio, the same who had carried the letters... But where am I? Ah, well... she was a mere slip, you understand, my grandmother, when the Duchess died, a niece of the upper maid, Nencia, and suffered about the Duchess because of her pranks and the funny songs she knew. It's possible, you think, she may have heard from others what she afterward fancied she had seen herself? How that is, it's not for an unlettered man to say; though indeed I myself seem to have seen many of the things she told me. This is a strange place. No one comes here, nothing changes, and the old memories stand up as distinct as the statues in the garden...

"It began the summer after they came back from the Brenta. Duke Ercole had married the lady from Venice, you must know; it was a gay city, then, I'm told, with laughter and music on the water, and the days slipped by like boats running with the tide. Well, to humour her he took her back the first autumn to the Brenta. Her father, it appears, had a grand palace there, with such gardens, bowling alleys, grottoes and casinos as never were; gondolas bobbing at the water gates, a stable full of gilt coaches, a theatre full of players, and kitchens and offices full of cooks and lackeys to serve up chocolate all day long to the fine ladies in masks and furbelows, with their pet dogs and their blackamoors and their *abates*. Eh! I know it all as if I'd been there, for Nencia, you see, my grandmother's aunt, travelled with the Duchess, and came back with her eyes round as platters, and not a word to say for the rest of the year to any of the lads who'd courted her here in Vicenza.

"What happened there I don't know—my grandmother could never get at the rights of it, for Nencia was mute as a fish where her lady was concerned—but when they came back to Vicenza the Duke ordered the villa set in order; and in the spring he brought the Duchess here and left her. She looked happy enough, my grandmother said, and seemed no object for pity. Perhaps, after all, it was better than being shut up in Vicenza, in the tall painted rooms where priests came and went as softly as cats prowling for birds, and the Duke was forever closeted in his library, talking with learned men. The Duke was a scholar; you noticed he was painted with a book? Well, those that can read 'em make out that they're full of wonderful things; as a man that's been to a fair across the mountains will always tell his people at home it was beyond any thing *they'll* ever see. As for the Duchess, she was all for music, play acting, and young company. The Duke was a silent man, stepping quietly, with his eyes down, as though he'd just come from confession; when the Duchess's lap dog yapped at his heels he danced like a man in a swarm of hornets; when the Duchess laughed he winced as if you'd drawn a diamond across a window pane. And the Duchess was always laughing.

"When she first came to the villa she was very busy laying out the gardens, designing grottoes, planting groves, and planning all manner of agreeable surprises in the way of water jets that drenched you unexpectedly, and hermits in caves, and wild men that jumped at you out of thickets. She had a very pretty taste in such matters, but after awhile she tired of it, and there being no one for her to talk to but her maids and the chaplain—a clumsy man deep in his books—why, she would have strolling players out from Vicenza, mountebanks and fortune tellers from the market place, travelling doctors and astrologers, and all manner of trained animals. Still it could be seen that the poor lady pined for company, and her waiting women, who loved her, were glad when the Cavaliere Ascanio, the Duke's cousin, came to live at the vineyard across the valley—you see the pinkish house over there in the mulberries, with a red roof and a pigeon cote?

"The Cavaliere Ascanio was a cadet of one of the great Venetian houses, *pezzi grossi* of the Golden Book. He had been meant for the Church, I believe, but what! he set fighting above praying and cast in his lot with the captain of the Duke of Mantua's *bravi*, himself a Venetian of good standing, but a little at odds with the law. Well, the next I knew, the Cavaliere was in Venice again, perhaps not in good odour on account of his connection with the gentleman I speak of. Some say he tried to carry off a nun from the convent of Santa Croce; how that may be I can't say; but my grandmother declared he had enemies there, and the end of it was that on some pretext or other the Ten banished him to Vicenza. There, of course, the Duke, being his kinsman, had to show him a civil face; and that was how he first came to the villa.

"He was a fine young man, beautiful as a Saint Sebastian, a rare musician, who sang his own songs to the lute in a way that used to make my grandmother's heart melt and run through her body like mulled wine. He had a good word for everybody, too, and was always dressed in the French fashion, and smelt as sweet as a bean field; and every soul about the place welcomed the sight of him.

"Well, the Duchess, it seemed, welcomed it too; youth will have youth, and laughter turns to laughter; and the two matched each other like the candlesticks on an altar. The Duchess—you've seen her portrait—but to hear my grandmother, sir, it no more approached her than a weed comes up to a rose. The Cavaliere, indeed, as became a poet, paragoned her in his song to all the pagan goddesses of antiquity; and doubtless these were finer to look at than mere women; but so, it seemed, was she; for, to believe my grandmother, she made other women look no more than the big French fashion doll that used to be shown on Ascension days in the Piazza. She was one, at any rate, that needed no outlandish finery to beautify her; whatever dress she wore became her as feathers fit the bird; and her hair didn't get its colour by bleaching on the housetop. It glittered of itself like the threads in an Easter chasuble, and her skin was whiter than fine wheaten bread, and her mouth as sweet as a ripe fig...

"Well, sir, you could no more keep them apart than the bees and the lavender. They were always together, singing, bowling, playing cup and ball, walking in the gardens, visiting the aviaries and petting her grace's trick dogs and monkeys. The Duchess was as gay as a foal, always playing pranks and laughing, tricking out her animals like comedians, disguising herself as a peasant or a nun (you should have seen her one day pass herself off to the chaplain as a mendicant sister), or teaching the lads and girls of the vineyards to dance and sing madrigals together. The Cavaliere had a singular ingenuity in planning such entertainments, and the days were hardly long enough for their diversions. But toward the end of the summer the Duchess fell quiet and would hear only sad music, and the two sat much together in the gazebo at the end of the garden. It was there the Duke found them one day when he drove out from Vicenza in his gilt coach. He came but once or twice a year to the villa, and it was, as my grandmother said, just a part of her poor lady's ill luck to be wearing that day the Venetian habit, which uncovered the shoulders in a way the Duke always scowled at, and her curls loose and powdered with gold. Well, the three drank chocolate in the gazebo, and what happened no one knew, except that the Duke, on taking leave, gave his cousin a seat in his carriage; but the Cavaliere never returned.

"Winter approaching, and the poor lady thus finding herself once more alone, it was surmised among her women that she must fall into a deeper depression of spirits. But far from this being the case, she displayed such cheerfulness and equanimity of humour that my grandmother, for one, was half vexed with her for giving no more thought to the poor young man who, all this time, was eating his heart out in the house across the valley. It is true she quitted her gold-laced gowns and wore a veil over her head; but Nencia would have it she looked the lovelier for the change, and so gave the Duke greater displeasure. Certain it is that the Duke drove out oftener to the villa, and though he found his lady always engaged in some innocent pursuit, such as embroidery or music, or playing games with her young women, yet he always went away with a sour look and a whispered word to the chaplain. Now as to the chaplain, my grandmother owned there had been a time when her grace had not handled him over-wisely. For, according to Nencia, it seems that his reverence, who seldom approached the Duchess, being buried in his library like a mouse in a cheese—well,

one day he made bold to appeal to her for a sum of money, a large
sum, Nencia said, to buy certain tall books, a chest full of them,
that a foreign pedler had brought him; whereupon the Duchess,
who could never abide a book, breaks out at him with a laugh and
a flash of her old spirit—'Holy Mother of God, must I have more
books about me? I was nearly smothered with them in the first
year of my marriage;' and the chaplain turning red at the affront,
she added: 'You may buy them and welcome, my good chaplain,
if you can find the money; but as for me, I am yet seeking a way
to pay for my turquoise necklace, and the statue of Daphne at the
end of the bowling-green, and the Indian parrot that my black
boy brought me last Michaelmas from the Bohemians—so you see
I've no money to waste on trifles;' and as he backs out awkwardly
she tosses at him, over her shoulder: 'You should pray to Saint
Blandina to open the Duke's pocket!' to which he returned, very
quietly, 'Your excellency's suggestion is an admirable one, and
I have already entreated that blessed martyr to open the Duke's
understanding.'

"Thereat, Nencia said (who was standing by), the Duchess
flushed wonderfully red and waved him out of the room; and then
'Quick!' she cried to my grandmother (who was too glad to run on
such errands), 'Call me Antonio, the gardener's boy, to the box
garden; I've a word to say to him about the new clove carnations...'

"Now, I may not have told you, sir, that in the crypt under
the chapel there has stood, for more generations than a man can
count, a stone coffin containing a thigh bone of the blessed Saint
Blandina of Lyons, a relic offered, I've been told, by some great
Duke of France to one of our own dukes when they fought the
Turk together; and the object, ever since, of particular veneration
in this illustrious family. Now, since the Duchess had been left

to herself, it was observed she affected a fervent devotion to this relic, praying often in the chapel and even causing the stone slab that covered the entrance to the crypt to be replaced by a wooden one, that she might at will descend and kneel by the coffin. This was matter of edification to all the household, and should have been peculiarly pleasing to the chaplain; but, with respect to you, he was the kind of man who brings a sour mouth to the eating of the sweetest apple.

"However that may be, the Duchess, when she dismissed him, was seen running to the garden, where she talked earnestly with the boy Antonio about the new clove carnations; and the rest of the day she sat indoors and played sweetly on the virginal. Now Nencia always had it in mind that her Grace had made a mistake in refusing that request of the chaplain's; but she said nothing, for to talk reason to the Duchess was of no more use than praying for rain in a drought.

"Winter came early that year, there was snow on the hills by All Souls, the wind stripped the gardens, and the lemon-trees were nipped in the lemon house. The Duchess kept her room in this black season, sitting over the fire, embroidering, reading books of devotion (which was a thing she had never done), and praying frequently in the chapel. As for the chaplain, it was a place he never set foot in but to say mass in the morning, with the Duchess overhead in the tribune, and the servants aching with rheumatism on the marble floor. The chaplain himself hated the cold, and galloped through the mass like a man with witches after him. The rest of the day he spent in his library, over a brazier, with his eternal books...

"You'll wonder, sir, if I'm ever to get to the gist of the story; and I've gone slowly, I own, for fear of what's coming. Well, the winter was long and hard. When it fell cold the Duke ceased to come out from Vicenza, and not a soul had the Duchess to speak to but her maid servants and the gardeners about the place. Yet it was wonderful, my grandmother said, how she kept her brave colours and her spirits; only it was remarked that she prayed longer in the chapel, where a brazier was kept burning for her all day. When the young are denied their natural pleasures, they turn often enough to religion; and it was a mercy, as my grandmother said, that she, who had scarce a live sinner to speak to, should take such comfort in a dead saint.

"My grandmother seldom saw her that winter, for though she showed a brave front to all, she kept more and more to herself, choosing to have only Nencia about her, and dismissing even her when she went to pray. For her devotion had that mark of true piety, that she wished it not to be observed; so that Nencia had strict orders, on the chaplain's approach, to warn her mistress if she happened to be in prayer.

"Well, the winter passed, and spring was well forward, when my grandmother one evening had a bad fright. That it was her own fault I won't deny, for she'd been down the lime walk with Antonio when her aunt fancied her to be stitching in her chamber; and seeing a sudden light in Nencia's window, she took fright lest her disobedience be found out, and ran up quickly through the laurel grove to the house. Her way lay by the chapel, and as she crept past it, meaning to slip in through the scullery, and groping her way, for the dark had fallen and the moon was scarce up, she heard a crash close behind her, as though someone had dropped from a window of the chapel. The young fool's heart turned over, but she looked round as she ran, and there, sure enough, was a man scuttling across the terrace; and as he doubled the corner of the house my grandmother swore she caught the whisk of the chaplain's skirts. Now that was a strange thing, certainly; for why should the chaplain be getting out of the chapel window when he might have passed through the door? For you may have noticed, sir, there's a door leads from the chapel into the saloon on the ground floor; the only other way out being through the Duchess's tribune.

"Well, my grandmother turned the matter over, and next time she met Antonio in the lime walk (which, by reason of her fright, was not for some days) she laid before him what had happened; but to her surprise he only laughed, and said, 'You little simpleton, he wasn't getting out of the window, he was trying to look in;' and not another word could she get from him.

"So the season moved on to Easter, and news came the Duke had gone to Rome for that holy festivity. His comings and goings made no change at the villa, and yet there was no one there but felt easier to think his yellow face was on the far side of the Apennines, unless, perhaps, it was the chaplain.

"Well, it was one day in May that the Duchess, who had walked long with Nencia on the terrace, rejoicing at the sweetness of the prospect and the pleasant scent of the gilly flowers in the stone vases, the Duchess toward midday withdrew to her rooms, giving orders that her dinner should be served in her bed chamber. My grandmother helped to carry in the dishes, and observed, she said, the singular beauty of the Duchess, who, in honour of the fine weather, had put on a gown of shot silver and hung her bare shoulders with pearls, so that she looked fit to dance at court with an emperor. She had ordered, too, a rare repast for a lady that heeded so little what she ate—jellies, game pastries, fruits in syrup, spiced cakes, and a flagon of Greek wine; and she nodded and clapped her hands as the women set it before her, saying, again and again, I shall eat well to-day.'

"But presently another mood seized her; she turned from the table, called for her rosary, and said to Nencia: 'The fine weather has made me neglect my devotions. I must say a litany before I dine.'

"She ordered the women out and barred the door, as her custom was; and Nencia and my grandmother went down stairs to work in the linen room.

"Now the linen room gives on the courtyard, and suddenly my grandmother saw a strange sight approaching. First up the avenue came the Duke's carriage (whom all thought to be in Rome), and after it, drawn by a long string of mules and oxen, a cart carrying what looked like a kneeling figure wrapped in death-clothes. The strangeness of it struck the girl dumb and the Duke's coach was at the door before she had the wit to cry out that it was coming. Nencia, when she saw it, went white and ran out of the room. My grandmother followed, scared by her face, and the two fled along the corridor to the chapel. On the way they met the chaplain, deep in a book, who asked in surprise where they were running, and when they said, to announce the Duke's arrival, he fell into such astonishment, and asked them so many questions and uttered such ohs and ahs that by the time he let them by the Duke was at their heels. Nencia reached the chapel door first and cried out that the Duke was coming; and before she had a reply he was at her side, with the chaplain following.

"A moment later the door opened and there stood the Duchess. She held her rosary in one hand and had drawn a scarf over her shoulders; but they shone through it like the moon in a mist, and her countenance sparkled with beauty.

"The Duke took her hand with a bow. 'Madam,' he said, 'I could have had no greater happiness than thus to surprise you at your devotions.'

"'My own happiness,' she replied, 'would have been greater had your excellency prolonged it by giving me notice of your arrival.'

"'Had you expected me, Madam,' said he, 'your appearance could scarcely have been more fitted to the occasion. Few ladies of your youth and beauty array themselves to venerate a saint as they would to welcome a lover.'

"'Sir,' she answered, 'having never enjoyed the latter opportunity, I am constrained to make the most of the former.—What's that?' she cried, falling back, and the rosary dropped from her hand.

"There was a loud noise at the other end of the saloon, as of a heavy object being dragged down the passage; and presently a dozen men were seen haling across the threshold the shrouded thing from the oxcart. The Duke waved his hand toward it. 'That,' said he, 'Madam, is a tribute to your extraordinary piety. I have heard with peculiar satisfaction of your devotion to the blessed relics in this chapel, and to commemorate a zeal which neither the rigours of winter nor the sultriness of summer could abate, I have ordered a sculptured image of you, marvellously executed by the Cavaliere Bernini, to be placed before the altar over the entrance to the crypt.'

"The Duchess, who had grown pale, nevertheless smiled playfully at this. 'As to commemorating my piety,' she said. 'I recognise there one of your excellency's pleasantries—'

"'A pleasantry?' the Duke interrupted; and he made a sign to the men, who had now reached the threshold of the chapel. In an instant the wrappings fell from the figure, and there knelt the

Duchess to the life. A cry of wonder rose from all, but the Duchess herself stood whiter than the marble.

"'You will see,' says the Duke, 'this is no pleasantry, but a triumph of the incomparable Bernini's chisel. The likeness was done from your miniature portrait by the divine Elisabetta Sirani, which I sent to the master some six months ago, with what results all must admire.'

"'Six months!' cried the Duchess, and seemed about to fall; but his excellency caught her by the hand.

"'Nothing,' he said, "could better please me than the excessive emotion you display, for true piety is ever modest, and your thanks could not take a form that better became you. And now,' says he to the men, 'let the image be put in place.'

"By this, life seemed to have returned to the Duchess, and she answered him with a deep reverence. 'That I should be overcome by so unexpected a grace, your excellency admits to be natural; but what honours you accord it is my privilege to accept, and I entreat only that in mercy to my modesty the image be placed in the remotest part of the chapel.'

"At that the Duke darkened. 'What! You would have this masterpiece of a renowned chisel, which, I disguise not, cost me the price of a good vineyard in gold pieces, you would have it thrust out of sight like the work of a village stonecutter?'

"'It is my semblance, not the sculptor's work, I desire to conceal.'

"'If you are fit for my house, Madam, you are fit for God's, and entitled to the place of honour in both. Bring the statue forward, you dawdlers!' he called out to the men.

"The Duchess fell back submissively. 'You are right, sir, as always; but I would at least have the image stand on the left of the altar, that, looking up, it may behold your excellency's seat in the tribune.'

"'A pretty thought, Madam, for which I thank you; but I design before long to put my companion image on the other side of the altar; and the wife's place, as you know, is at her husband's right hand.'

"'True, my lord—but, again, if my poor presentment is to have the unmerited honour of kneeling beside yours, why not place both before the altar, where it is our habit to pray in life?'

"'And where, Madam, should we kneel if they took our places? Besides,' says the Duke, still speaking very blandly, 'I have a more particular purpose in placing your image over the entrance to the crypt; for not only would I thereby mark your special devotion to the blessed saint who rests there, but, by sealing up the opening in the pavement, would assure the perpetual preservation of that holy martyr's bones, which hitherto have been too thoughtlessly exposed to sacrilegious attempts.'

"'What attempts, my lord?' cries the Duchess. 'No one enters this chapel without my leave.'

"'So I have understood, and can well believe from what I have learned of your piety; yet at night a malefactor might break in through a window, Madam, and your excellency not know it.'

"'I'm a light sleeper,' said the Duchess.

"The Duke looked at her gravely. 'Indeed?' said he. 'A bad sign at your age. I must see that you are provided with a sleeping draught.'

"The Duchess's eyes filled. 'You would deprive me, then, of the consolation of visiting those venerable relics?'

"'I would have you keep eternal guard over them, knowing no one to whose care they may more fittingly be entrusted.'

"By this the image was brought close to the wooden slab that covered the entrance to the crypt, when the Duchess, springing forward, placed herself in the way.

"'Sir, let the statue be put in place to-morrow, and suffer me, to-night, to say a last prayer beside those holy bones.'

"The Duke stepped instantly to her side. 'Well thought, Madam; I will go down with you now, and we will pray together.'

"'Sir, your long absences have, alas! given me the habit of solitary devotion, and I confess that any presence is distracting.'

"'Madam, I accept your rebuke. Hitherto, it is true, the duties of my station have constrained me to long absences; but henceforward I remain with you while you live. Shall we go down into the crypt together?'

"'No; for I fear for your excellency's ague. The air there is excessively damp.'

"'The more reason you should no longer be exposed to it; and to prevent the intemperance of your zeal I will at once make the place inaccessible.'

"The Duchess at this fell on her knees on the slab, weeping excessively and lifting her hands to heaven.

"'Oh,' she cried, 'you are cruel, sir, to deprive me of access to the sacred relics that have enabled me to support with resignation the solitude to which your excellency's duties have condemned me; and if prayer and meditation give me any authority to pronounce on such matters, suffer me to warn you, sir, that I fear the blessed Saint Blandina will punish us for thus abandoning her venerable remains!'

"The Duke at this seemed to pause, for he was a pious man, and my grandmother thought she saw him exchange a glance with the chaplain; who, stepping timidly forward, with his eyes on the ground, said, 'There is, indeed, much wisdom in her excellency's words, but I would suggest, sir, that her pious wish might be met, and the saint more conspicuously honoured, by transferring the relics from the crypt to a place beneath the altar.'

"'True!' cried the Duke, 'and it shall be done at once.'

"But thereat the Duchess rose to her feet with a terrible look.

"'No,' she cried, 'by the body of God! For it shall not be said that, after your excellency has chosen to deny every request I addressed to him, I owe his consent to the solicitation of another!'

"The chaplain turned red and the Duke yellow, and for a moment neither spoke.

"Then the Duke said, 'Here are words enough, Madam. Do you wish the relics brought up from the crypt?'

"'I wish nothing that I owe to another's intervention!'

"'Put the image in place then,' says the Duke, furiously; and handed her grace to a chair.

"She sat there, my grandmother said, straight as an arrow, her hands locked, her head high, her eyes on the Duke, while the statue was dragged to its place; then she stood up and turned away. As she passed by Nencia, 'Call me Antonio,' she whispered; but before the words were out of her mouth the Duke stepped between them.

"'Madam,' says he, all smiles now, 'I have travelled straight from Rome to bring you the sooner this proof of my esteem. I lay last night at Monselice and have been on the road since daybreak. Will you not invite me to sup?'

"'Surely, my lord,' said the Duchess. 'It shall be laid in the dining parlour within the hour.'

"'Why not in your chamber and at once, Madam? Since I believe it is your custom to sup there.'

"'In my chamber?' says the Duchess, in disorder.

"'Have you anything against it?' he asked.

"'Assuredly not, sir, if you will give me time to prepare myself.'

"'I will wait in your cabinet,' said the Duke.

"At that, said my grandmother, the Duchess gave one look, as the souls in hell may have looked when the gates closed on our Lord; then she called Nencia and passed to her chamber.

"What happened there my grandmother could never learn, but that the Duchess, in great haste, dressed herself with extraordinary splendour, powdering her hair with gold, painting her face and bosom, and covering herself with jewels till she shone like our Lady of Loreto; and hardly were these preparations complete when the Duke entered from the cabinet, followed by the servants, carrying supper. Thereupon the Duchess dismissed Nencia, and what follows my grandmother learned from a pantry lad who brought up the dishes and waited in the cabinet; for only the Duke's body servant entered the bed chamber.

"Well, according to this boy, sir, who was looking and listening with his whole body, as it were, because he had never before been suffered so near the Duchess, it appears that the noble couple sat down in great good humour, the Duchess playfully reproving her husband for his long absence, while the Duke swore that to look so beautiful was the best way of punishing him. In this tone the talk continued, with such gay sallies on the part of the Duchess, such tender advances on the Duke's, that the lad declared they were for all the world like a pair of lovers courting on a summer's night in the vineyard; and so it went till the servant brought in the mulled wine.

"'Ah,' the Duke was saying at that moment, 'this agreeable evening repays me for the many dull ones I have spent away from you; nor do I remember to have enjoyed such laughter since the afternoon last year when we drank chocolate in the gazebo with my cousin Ascanio. And that reminds me,' he said, 'is my cousin in good health?'

"'I have no reports of it,' says the Duchess. 'But your excellency should taste these figs stewed in malmsey'

"'I am in the mood to taste whatever you offer,' said he; and as she helped him to the figs he added, 'If my enjoyment were not complete as it is, I could almost wish my cousin Ascanio were with us. The fellow is rare good company at supper. What do you say, Madam? I hear he's still in the country; shall we send for him to join us?'

"'Ah,' said the Duchess, with a sigh and a languishing look, 'I see your excellency wearies of me already.'

"'I, Madam? Ascanio is a capital good fellow, but to my mind his chief merit at this moment is his absence. It inclines me so tenderly to him, that, by God, I could empty a glass to his good health.'

"With that the Duke caught up his goblet and signed to the servant to fill the Duchess's.

"Here's to the cousin,' he cried, standing, 'who has the good taste to stay away when he's not wanted. I drink to his very long life and you, Madam?'

"At this the Duchess, who had sat staring at him with a changed face, rose also and lifted her glass to her lips.

"'And I to his happy death,' says she in a wild voice; and as she spoke the empty goblet dropped from her hand and she fell face down on the floor.

"The Duke shouted to her women that she had swooned, and they came and lifted her to the bed... She suffered horribly all night, Nencia said, twisting herself like a heretic at the stake, but without a word escaping her. The Duke watched by her, and toward daylight sent for the chaplain; but by this she was unconscious and, her teeth being locked, our Lord's body could not be passed through them.

*

"The Duke announced to his relations that his lady had died after partaking too freely of spiced wine and an omelette of carp's roe, at a supper she had prepared in honour of his return; and the next year he brought home a new Duchess, who gave him a son and five daughters..."

V

The sky had turned to a steel grey, against which the villa stood out sallow and inscrutable. A wind strayed through the gardens, loosening here and there a yellow leaf from the sycamores; and the hills across the valley were purple as thunder clouds.

"And the statue—?" I asked.

"Ah, the statue. Well, sir, this is what my grandmother told me, here on this very bench where we're sitting. The poor child, who worshipped the Duchess as a girl of her years will worship a beautiful kind mistress, spent a night of horror, you may fancy, shut out from her lady's room, hearing the cries that came from it, and seeing, as she crouched in her corner, the women rush to and fro with wild looks, the Duke's lean face in the door, and the chaplain skulking in the antechamber with his eyes on his breviary. No one minded her that night or the next morning; and toward dusk, when it became known the Duchess was no more, the poor girl felt the pious wish to say a prayer for her dead mistress. She crept to the chapel and stole in unobserved. The place was empty and dim, but as she advanced she heard a low moaning, and coming in front of the statue she saw that its face, the day before so sweet and smiling, had the look on it that you know and the moaning seemed to come from its lips. My grandmother turned cold, but something, she said afterward, kept her from calling or shrieking out, and she turned and ran from the place. In the passage she fell in a swoon; and when she came to her senses, in her own chamber, she heard that the Duke had locked the chapel door and forbidden any to set foot there... The place was never opened again till the Duke died, some ten years later; and then it was that the other servants, going in with the new heir, saw for the first time the horror that my grandmother had kept in her bosom..."

"And the crypt?" I asked. "Has it never been opened?"

"Heaven forbid, sir!" cried the old man, crossing himself. "Was it not the Duchess's express wish that the relics should not be disturbed?"

1910

THE STALLS OF
BARCHESTER CATHEDRAL

M. R. James

Montague Rhodes James (1862–1936) is one of the more frequently
anthologised writers in this collection. Regularly spoken about as
the Godfather of the modern ghost story, James was deemed "one
of the few really creative masters in his darksome province" in H.
P. Lovecraft's essay on "Supernatural Horror in Literature" (1927)[*].

Born in Goodnestone, Kent, James came from a family with a
strong Christian faith: his father, Herbert, was an Anglican clergyman and his brother, Sydney, would later become the Archdeacon
of Dudley. Although he did not pursue a clerical career himself,
James's early academic focus on Christian apocrypha perhaps
reflects the family's theological interest. A celebrated antiquarian
and scholar, James enjoyed several high-profile positions, serving
as the provost of King's College, Cambridge (1905–1918) and
Vice-Chancellor for the University (1913–1914). Upon leaving
Cambridge in 1918, James became provost of Eton College, a post
he held until his death.

Whilst tenured at King's College, James began to compose
ghost stories, some of which appeared in popular periodicals

[*]   Howard Philip Lovecraft, "Supernatural Horror in Literature", *The Recluse*,
issued by W. Paul Cook, August 1937.

before publication in edited collections released during James's lifetime. M. R. James remains popular and his work is still regularly anthologised, with stories like "The Mezzotint", "The Tractate Middoth" and "'Oh, Whistle, and I'll Come to You, my Lad'" recently adapted for television.

Sitting alongside "An Uncommon Prayer Book" and "The Treasure of Abbot Thomas", the tale that follows is not the only story in which James blends the theological and the uncanny. First published in April 1910 in the *Contemporary Review* and later reprinted in *More Ghost Stories of An Antiquary* (1911), "The Stalls of Barchester Cathedral" suggests that even the holiest places can harbour evil forces.

T his matter began, as far as I am concerned, with the reading of a notice in the obituary section of the *Gentleman's Magazine* for an early year in the nineteenth century:—

"On February 26th, at his residence in the Cathedral Close of Barchester, the Venerable John Benwell Haynes, D.D., aged 57, Archdeacon of Sowerbridge and Rector of Pickhill and Caudley. He was of ——— College, Cambridge, where, by talent and assiduity, he commanded the esteem of his seniors; and when at the usual time he took his first degree, his name stood high in the list of Wranglers. These academical honours procured for him within a short time a Fellowship of his College. In the year 1783 he received Holy Orders, and was shortly afterwards presented to the perpetual Curacy of Ranxton-sub-Ashe by his friend and patron the late truly venerable Bishop of Lichfield, etc., etc. His speedy preferments, first to a Prebend, and subsequently to the dignity of Precentor in the Cathedral of Barchester, form an eloquent testimony to the respect in which he was held and to his eminent qualifications. He succeeded to the Archdeaconry upon the sudden decease of Dr William Pulteney in 1810. His preaching, ever conformable to the principles of the religion and Church which he adorned, displayed in no ordinary degree, without the least trace of enthusiasm, the attainments of the scholar united with the graces of the Christian. Free from sectarian violence, and informed by the spirit of the truest charity, they will long dwell in the memories of his hearers. (Here an omission.) The productions of his pen include an able defence of Episcopacy, which, though often perused by the author of this tribute to his memory, affords but one additional instance of the want of liberality and enterprise which is a too common characteristic of the publishers of our generation. His published works are confined to a spirited and elegant version of the *Argonautica* of Valerius Flaccus, a volume of *Discourses upon the Several Events in the Life of Joshua*, delivered in his Cathedral, and a number of the charges which he pronounced at various visitations to the clergy of his Archdeaconry. These are distinguished by, etc. The urbanity and hospitality of the subject of these lines will not readily be forgotten by those who enjoyed his acquaintance. His interest in the venerable and awful pile under whose hoary vault he was so punctual an attendant, and particularly in the musical portion of its rites, might be termed filial, and formed a strong and a delightful contrast to the polite indifference displayed by too many of our Cathedral dignitaries at the present time."

The final paragraph, after informing us that Dr Haynes died a bachelor, says:—

"It might have been augured that an existence so placid and benevolent would have been terminated in a ripe old age by a dissolution equally gradual and calm. But how

unsearchable are the workings of Providence! The peaceful
and retired seclusion amid which the honoured evening of
Dr Haynes' life was mellowing to its close was destined to
be disturbed, nay shattered by a tragedy as appalling as it
was unexpected. The morning of the 26th of February"—

But perhaps I shall do better to keep back the remainder of the
narrative until I have told the circumstances which led up to it.
These, as far as they are now accessible, I have derived from
another source.

I had read the obituary notice which I have been quoting, quite
by chance, along with a great many others of the same period. It had
excited some little speculation in my mind, but, beyond thinking
that if I ever had an opportunity of examining the local records of
the period indicated, I would try to remember Dr Haynes, I made
no effort to pursue his case.

Quite lately I was cataloguing the manuscripts in the library of
the college to which he belonged. I had reached the end of the
numbered volumes on the shelves, and I proceeded to ask the
librarian whether there were any more books which he thought I
ought to include in my description. "I don't think there are," he
said, "but we had better come and look at the manuscript class and
make sure. Have you time to do that now?" I had time, and we
went to the library. The presses were opened, and we checked off
the manuscripts. One shelf, we found, remained, of which I had
seen nothing, and we made an examination of its contents. These
consisted for the most part of sermons, bundles of fragmentary
papers, college exercises, *Cyrus*, an epic poem in several books,
the product of a country clergyman's leisure, mathematical tracts
by a deceased professor, and other similar material of a kind with

which I am familiar. I took brief notes of these. Lastly, there was a tin box, which was pulled out and dusted. Its label, much faded, was thus marked: "Papers of the Ven. Archdeacon Haynes. Bequeathed in 1834 by his sister, Miss Letitia Haynes."

I knew at once that the name was one which I had somewhere encountered, and could very soon locate it. "That must be the Archdeacon Haynes who came to a very strange end at Barchester. I've read his obituary in the *Gentleman's Magazine*. May I take the box home? Do you know if there is anything interesting in it?"

The librarian was very willing that I should take the box and examine it at leisure. "I never looked inside it myself," he said, "but I've always been meaning to. I am pretty sure that is the box which our old Master once said ought never to have been accepted by the college. He said that to Martin years ago; and he said also that as long as he had any control over the library it should never be opened. Martin told me about it, and said that he wanted terribly to know what was in it; but the Master was librarian, and always kept the box in the Lodge, so there was no getting at it in his time, and when he died it was taken away by mistake by his heirs, and only returned a few years ago. I can't think why I haven't opened it; but, as I have to go away from Cambridge this afternoon, you had better have first go at it. I think I can trust you not to publish anything undesirable in our catalogue."

I took the box home and examined its contents, and thereafter consulted the librarian as to what should be done about publication; and, since I have his leave to make a story out of it, provided I disguise the identity of the people concerned, I will try what can be done.

The materials are, of course, mainly journals and letters. How much I shall quote and how much epitomise must be determined by considerations of space. The proper understanding of the situation has necessitated a little not very arduous research, which has been greatly facilitated by the excellent illustrations and text of the Barchester volume in Bell's Cathedral Series.

When you enter the choir of Barchester Cathedral now, you pass through a screen of metal and coloured marbles, designed by Sir Gilbert Scott, and find yourself in what I must call a very bare and odiously furnished place. The stalls are modern, without canopies. The seats of the dignitaries and the names of the prebends are preserved, fortunately, and inscribed on small brass plates affixed to the stalls. The organ is in the triforium, and what is seen of the case is Gothic. The reredos and its surroundings are like every other.

Careful engravings of a hundred years ago show a very different state of things. The organ is on a massive classical screen. The stalls are also classical and very massive. There is a baldachino of wood over the altar, with urns upon its corners. Further east is another screen, classical in design, of wood, with a pediment in which is a triangle surrounded by rays, enclosing certain Hebrew letters in gold. Cherubs contemplate these. There is a pulpit with a great sounding-board at the eastern end of the stalls on the north side, and there is a black and white marble pavement. Two ladies and a gentleman are admiring the general effect. The archdeacon's stall then, as now, is next to the bishop's throne at the south-eastern end of the stalls. His house almost faces the western part of the church, and is a fine red-brick building of William the Third's time.

Here Dr Haynes, already a mature man, took up his abode with his sister in the year 1810. The dignity had long been the object of his wishes, but his predecessor refused to depart until he had attained the age of ninety-two. About a week after he had held a modest festival in celebration of that ninety-second birthday there came a morning, late in the year, when Dr Haynes, hurrying cheerfully into his breakfast-room, rubbing his hands and humming a tune, was greeted, and checked in his genial flow of spirits, by the sight of his sister, seated, indeed, in her usual place behind the tea-urn, but bowed forward and sobbing unrestrainedly into her handkerchief. "What, what is the matter? What bad news?" he began. "Oh, Johnny, you've not heard? The poor dear archdeacon!" "The archdeacon, yes. What is it—ill, is he?" "No, no; they found him on the staircase this morning; it is so shocking." "Is it possible! Dear, dear, poor Pulteney! Had there been any seizure?" "They don't think so, and that is almost the worst thing about it. It seems to have been all the fault of that stupid maid of theirs, Jane." Dr Haynes paused. "I don't understand this quite, Letitia. How was the maid at fault?" "Why, as far as I can make out, there was a stair-rod missing, and she never mentioned it, and the poor archdeacon set his foot quite on the edge of the step—you know how slippery that oak is—and it seems he must have fallen almost the whole flight and broken his neck. It *is* so sad for poor Miss Pulteney. Of course, they will get rid of the girl at once. I never liked her." Miss Haynes' grief resumed its sway, but eventually relaxed so far as to permit of her taking some breakfast. Not so her brother, who, after standing in silence before the window for some minutes, left the room, and did not appear again that morning.

I need only add that the careless maidservant was dismissed forthwith, but that the missing stair-rod was very shortly afterwards found *under* the stair-carpet, an additional proof, if any were needed, of extreme stupidity and carelessness on her part.

For a good many years Dr Haynes had been marked out by his ability, which seems to have been really considerable, as the likely successor of Archdeacon Pulteney; and no disappointment was in store for him. He was duly installed, and entered with zeal upon the discharge of those functions which are appropriate to one in his position. A considerable space in his journals is occupied with exclamations upon the confusion in which Archdeacon Pulteney had left the business of his office and the documents appertaining to it. Dues upon Wringham and Barnswood have been uncollected for something like twelve years, and are largely irrecoverable; no visitation has been held for seven years; four chancels are almost past mending. The persons deputised by the archdeacon have been nearly as incapable as himself. It was almost a matter for thankfulness that this state of things had not been permitted to continue; and a letter from a friend confirms this view. "'Ο κατεχων," it says, in rather cruel allusion to the Second Epistle to the Thessalonians, "is removed at last. My poor friend! Upon what a scene of confusion will you be entering! I give you my word that on the last occasion of my crossing his threshold there was no single paper that he could lay hands upon, no syllable of mine that he could hear, and no fact in connection with my business that he could remember. But now, thanks to a negligent maid and a loose stair-carpet, there is some prospect that necessary business will be transacted without a complete loss alike of voice and temper." This letter was tucked into a pocket in the cover of one of the diaries.

There can be no doubt of the new archdeacon's zeal and enthusiasm. "Give me but time to reduce to some semblance of order the innumerable errors and complications with which I am confronted, and I shall gladly and sincerely join with the aged Israelite in the canticle which too many, I fear, pronounce but with their lips." This reflection I find, not in a diary, but in a letter. The doctor's friends seem to have returned his correspondence to his surviving sister. He does not confine himself, however, to reflections. His investigation of the rights and duties of his office were very searching and businesslike, and I find a calculation in one place that a period of three years would just suffice to set the business of the Archdeaconry upon a proper footing.

The estimate appears to have been an exact one. For just three years he is occupied in reforms; but I look in vain at the end of that time for the promised *Nunc dimittis*. He has now found a new sphere of activity. Hitherto his duties have precluded him from more than an occasional attendance at the cathedral services. Now he begins to take an interest in the fabric and the music. Upon his struggles with the organist, an old gentleman who had been in office since 1786, I have no time to dwell; they were not attended with any marked success. More to the purpose is his sudden growth of enthusiasm for the cathedral itself and its furniture. There is a draft of a letter to Sylvanus Urban (which I do not think was ever sent) describing the stall-work in the choir. As I have said, these were of fairly late date—of about the year 1700, in fact.

"The archdeacon's stall, situated at the south-east end, west of the episcopal throne (now so worthily occupied by the truly excellent prelate who adorns the See of Barchester), is distinguished by some curious ornamentation. In addition to the arms of Dean West, by whose efforts the whole of the internal furniture of the choir was completed, the prayer-desk is terminated at the eastern extremity by three small but remarkable statuettes in the grotesque manner. One is an exquisitely modelled figure of a cat, whose crouching posture suggests with admirable spirit the suppleness, vigilance and craft of the redoubted adversary of the genus *Mus*. Opposite to this is a figure seated upon a throne and invested with the attributes of royalty; but it is no earthly monarch whom the carver has sought to portray. His feet are studiously concealed by the long robe in which he is draped; but neither the crown nor the cap which he wears suffices to hide the prick-ears and curving horns which betray his Tartarean origin; and the hand which rests upon his knee is armed with talons of appalling length and sharpness. Between these two figures stands a shape muffled in a long mantle. This might at first sight be mistaken for a monk or 'friar of orders grey,' for the head is cowled, and a knotted cord depends from somewhere about the waist. A slight inspection, however, will lead to a very different conclusion. The knotted cord is quickly seen to be a halter, held by a hand all but concealed within the draperies; while the sunken features and, horrid to relate, the rent flesh upon the cheek-bones, proclaim the King of Terrors. These figures are evidently the production of no unskilled chisel; and should it chance that any of your correspondents are able to throw light upon their origin and significance, my obligations to your valuable miscellany will be largely increased."

There is more description in the paper, and seeing that the wood-work in question has now disappeared, it has a considerable interest. A paragraph at the end is worth quoting:—

"Some late researches among the Chapter accounts have shown me that the carving of the stalls was not, as was very usually reported, the work of Dutch artists, but was executed by a native of this city or district named Austin. The timber was procured from an oak copse in the vicinity, the property of the Dean and Chapter, known as Holywood. After a recent visit to the parish within whose boundaries it is situated, I learned from the aged and truly respectable incumbent that traditions still lingered amongst the inhabitants of the great size and age of the oaks employed to furnish the materials of the stately structure which has been, however imperfectly, described in the above lines. Of one in particular, which stood near the centre of the grove, it is remembered that it was known as the Hanging Oak. The propriety of that title is confirmed by the fact that a quantity of human bones was found in the soil about its roots, and that at certain times of the year it was the custom for those who wished to secure a successful issue to their affairs, whether of love or the ordinary business of life, to suspend from its boughs small images or puppets crudely fashioned of straw, twigs, or the like rustic materials."

So much for the archdeacon's archæological investigations. To return to his career, as it is to be gathered from his diaries:— those of his first three years of hard and careful work show him throughout in high spirits, and doubtless during this time that reputation for hospitality and urbanity which is mentioned in his obituary notice was well deserved. After that, as time goes on, I see a shadow coming over him—destined to develop into utter blackness—which I cannot but think must have been reflected in his outward demeanour. He commits a good deal of his fears and troubles to his diary; there was no other outlet for them. He was unmarried, and his sister was not always with him. But I am much mistaken if he has told all that he might have told. A series of extracts shall be given:—

"Aug. 30th, 1816. The days begin to draw in more perceptibly than ever. Now that the Archdeaconry papers are reduced to order, I must find some further employment for the evening hours of autumn and winter. It is a great blow that Letitia's health will not allow her to stay through these months. Why not go on with my *Defence of Episcopacy*? It may be useful.

"Sept. 15. Letitia has left me for Brighton.

"Oct. 11. Candles lit in the choir for the first time at evening prayers. It came as a shock: I find that I absolutely shrink from the dark season.

"Nov. 17. Much struck by the character of the carving on my desk: I don't know that I had ever carefully noticed it before. My attention was called to it by an accident. During the *Magnificat* I was, I regret to say, almost overcome with sleep. My hand was resting on the back of the carved figure of a cat which is the nearest to me of the three figures on the end of my stall. I was not aware of this, for I was not looking in that direction, until I was startled by what seemed a softness, a feeling as of rather rough and coarse fur, and a sudden movement, as if the creature were twisting round its head to bite me. I regained complete consciousness in an instant, and I have some idea that I must have uttered a suppressed exclamation, for I noticed that Mr Treasurer turned his head quickly in my direction. The impression of the unpleasant feeling was so strong that I found myself rubbing my hand upon my surplice. This accident led me to examine the figures after prayers more carefully than I had done before, and I realised for the first time with what skill they are executed.

"Dec. 6. I do indeed miss Letitia's company. The evenings, after I have worked as long as I can at my *Defence*, are very trying. This house is too large for a lonely man, and visitors are too rare. I get an uncomfortable impression when going to my room that there *is* company of some kind. The fact is (I may as well formulate it to myself) that I hear voices. This, I am well aware, is a common symptom of incipient decay of the brain—and I believe that I should be less disquieted than I am if I had any suspicion that this was the cause. I have none—none whatever, nor is there anything in my family history to give colour to such an idea. Work, diligent work, and a punctual attention to the duties which fall to me is my best remedy, and I have little doubt that it will prove efficacious.

"Jan. 1. My trouble is, I must confess it, increasing upon me. Last night, upon my return after midnight from the Deanery, I lit my candle to go upstairs. I was nearly at the top when something whispered to me, '*Let me wish you a happy New Year.*' I could not be mistaken: it spoke distinctly and with a peculiar emphasis. Had I dropped my candle, as I all but did, I tremble to think what the consequences must have been. As it was, I managed to get up the last flight and was quickly in my room with the door locked, and experienced no other disturbance.

"Jan. 15. I had occasion to come downstairs last night to my workroom for my paper, which I had inadvertently left on my table when I went up to bed. I think I was at the top of the last flight when I had a sudden impression of a

sharp whisper in my ear. '*Take care.*' I clutched the balusters
and naturally looked round at once. Of course, there was
nothing. After a moment I went on—it was no good turning
back—but I had as nearly as possible fallen: a cat—a large
one by the feel of it—slipped between my feet, but again,
of course, I saw nothing. It *may* have been the kitchen cat,
but I do not think it was.

"Feb. 27. A curious thing last night, which I should
like to forget; but as I am not likely to do that, I will put
it down here. I worked in the library from about 9 to 10.
The hall and staircase seemed to me unusually full of what
I can only call movement without sound: by this I mean that
there seemed to be continuous going and coming, and that
whenever I ceased writing to listen, or looked out into the
hall, the stillness was absolutely unbroken. Nor, in going
to my room at an earlier hour than usual—about half-past
ten—was I conscious of anything that I could call a noise. It
so happened that I had told John to come to my room for the
letter to the bishop which I wished to have delivered early
in the morning at the Palace. He was to sit up, therefore,
and come for it when he heard me retire. This I had for
the moment forgotten, though I had intended to carry the
letter with me to my room, but when, as I was winding up
my watch, I heard a slight tap at the door, and a low voice
saying, 'May I come in' (which I most undoubtedly did
hear), I remembered the fact and took up the letter from
my dressing-table, saying: 'Certainly: come in.' No one,
however, answered my summons, and it was now that, as
I strongly suspect, I committed an error: for I opened the
door and held the letter out. There was certainly no one at

that moment in the passage, but in the instant of my standing there the door at the end opened and John appeared
carrying a candle. I asked him whether he had come to the
door earlier; but am satisfied that he had not. I do not like
the situation; but although my senses were very much on
the alert, and though it was some time before I could sleep,
I must allow that I experienced no disturbance of any kind."

With the return of spring, when his sister came to live with him
for some months, Dr Haynes' entries become more cheerful, and,
indeed, no symptom of depression is discernible until the early
part of September, when he was again left alone. And now, indeed,
there is evidence that he was incommoded again, and that more
pressingly. To this I will return in a moment, but I digress to put in
a document which, rightly or wrongly, I believe to have a bearing
on the main question.

The account-books of Dr Haynes, preserved along with his
other papers, show, from a date but little later than that of his insti-
tution as archdeacon, a quarterly payment of £25 to J. L. Nothing
could have been made of this had it stood by itself. But I connect
with it a very dirty and ill-written letter, which, like another that
I have quoted, was in a pocket in the cover of a diary. Of date or
postmark there is no vestige, and the decipherment was not easy.
It appears to run—

"Dr Sr.

I have bein expctin to her off you theis last wicks, and
not Haveing done so must supose you have not got mine
witch was saying how me and my man had met in with bad
times this season all seems to go cross with us on the farm

270

and which way to look for the rent we have no knowledge of it this been the sad case with us if you would have the great [liberality probably, but the exact spelling defies reproduction] to send forty pounds otherwise steps will have to be took which I should not wish. Has you was the Means of me losing my place with Dr Pulteney I think it is only just what I am asking and you know best what I could say if I am Put to it but I do not wish nothing of that unpleasant nature being one that always wish to have everything Pleasant about me.

YOUR OBEDT SERVT,

JANE LEE."

About the time at which I suppose this letter to have been written there is, in fact, a payment of £40 to J. L.

We return to the diary:—

"Oct. 22. At evening prayers, during the Psalms, I had that same experience which I recalled from last year. I was resting my hand on one of the carved figures, as before (I usually avoid that of the cat now), and—I was going to have said a change came over it—but that seems attributing too much importance to what must, after all, be due to some physical affection in myself—at any rate, the wood seemed to become chilly and soft as if made of wet linen. I can assign the moment at which I became sensible of this. The choir were singing the words, *Set thou an ungodly man to be ruler over him and let Satan stand at his right hand.*

"The whispering in my house was more persistent to-night. I seemed not to be rid of it in my room. I have not noticed this before. A nervous man, which I am not, and hope I am not becoming, would have been much annoyed, if not alarmed, by it. The cat was on the stairs to-night. I think it sits there always. There *is* no kitchen cat.

"Nov. 15. Here again I must note a matter I do not understand. I was much troubled in sleep. No definite image presented itself, but I was pursued by the very vivid impression that wet lips were whispering into my ear with great rapidity and emphasis for some time together. After this, I suppose, I fell asleep, but was awakened with a start by a feeling as if a hand were laid on my shoulder. To my intense alarm I found myself standing at the top of the lowest flight of the first staircase. The moon was shining brightly enough through the large window to let me see that there was a large cat on the second or third step. I can make no comment. I crept up to bed again. I do not know how. Yes, mine is a heavy burden. [Then follows a line or two which has been scratched out. I fancy I read something like 'acted for the best.']"

Not long after this it is evident to me that the archdeacon's firmness began to give way under the pressure of these phenomena. I omit as unnecessarily painful and distressing the ejaculations and prayers which, in the months of December and January, appear for the first time and become increasingly frequent. Throughout this time, however, he is obstinate in clinging to his post. Why he did not plead ill-health and take refuge at Bath or Brighton I cannot tell; my impression is that it would have done him no good; that he was a man who, if he had confessed himself beaten by the annoyances, would have succumbed at once, and that he was conscious of this.

He did seek to palliate them by inviting visitors to his house. The result he has noted in this fashion:—

"Jan. 7. I have prevailed on my cousin, Allen, to give me a few days, and he is to occupy the chamber next to mine.

"Jan. 8. A still night. Allen slept well, but complained of the wind. My own experiences were as before: still whispering and whispering: what is it that he wants to say?

"Jan. 9. Allen thinks this a very noisy house. He thinks, too, that my cat is an unusually large and fine specimen, but very wild.

"Jan. 10. Allen and I in the library until 11. He left me twice to see what the maids were doing in the hall: returning the second time he told me he had seen one of them peering through the door at the end of the passage, and said if his wife were here she would soon get them into better order. I asked him what coloured dress the maid wore: he said grey or white. I suppose it would be so.

"Jan. 11. Allen left me to-day. I must be firm."

These words, *I must be firm*, occur again and again on subsequent days; sometimes they are the only entry. In these cases they are in an unusually large hand and dug into the paper in a way which must have broken the pen that wrote them.

Apparently the archdeacon's friends did not remark any change in his behaviour, and this gives one a high idea of his courage and determination. The diary tells us nothing more than I have indicated of the last days of his life. The end of it all must be told in the polished language of the obituary notice:—

"The morning of the 26th of February was cold and tempestuous. At an early hour the servants had occasion to go into
the front hall of the residence occupied by the lamented
subject of these lines. What was their horror upon observing
the form of their beloved and respected master lying upon
the landing of the principal staircase in an attitude which
inspired the gravest fears. Assistance was procured, and an
universal consternation was experienced upon the discovery
that he had been the object of a brutal and murderous attack.
The vertebral column was fractured in more than one place.
This might have been the result of a fall: it appeared that the
stair carpet was loosened at one point. But in addition to this
there were injuries inflicted upon the eyes, nose and mouth,
as if by the agency of some savage animal which, dreadful
to relate, rendered those features unrecognisable. The vital
spark was, it is needless to add, completely extinct, and had
been so, upon the testimony of respectable medical authori-
ties, for several hours. The author or authors of this mysterious outrage are alike buried in mystery, and the most active
conjecture has hitherto failed to suggest a solution of the
melancholy problem afforded by this appalling occurrence."

The writer goes on to reflect upon the probability that the writ-
ings of Mr Shelley, Lord Byron and M. de Voltaire may have
been instrumental in bringing about the disaster, and concludes
by hoping, somewhat vaguely, that this event may "operate as an
example to the rising generation"; but this portion of his remarks
need not be quoted in full.

My reader will probably have drawn much the same conclusion
as I did from the documents before me, as to the responsibility of

Dr Haynes for the death of Dr Pulteney. But the incident connected
with the carved figures upon the archdeacon's stall was a very per-
plexing feature. The conjecture that they had been cut out of the
wood of the hanging oak was not difficult, but seemed impossible
to substantiate. However, I paid a visit to Barchester, partly with the
view of finding out whether there were any relics of the woodwork
to be heard of. I was introduced by one of the canons to the curator of the local museum, who was, my friend said, more likely to
be able to give me information on the point than anyone else. I
told this gentleman of the description of certain carved figures and
arms formerly on the stalls, and asked whether any had survived.
He was able to show me the arms of Dean West and some other
fragments. These, he said, had been got from an old resident, who
had also once owned a figure—perhaps one of those which I was
inquiring for. "There was a very odd thing about that figure," he
went on; "the old man who had it told me that he picked it up in
a wood-yard, whence he had obtained the still extant pieces, and
took it home for his children. On the way home he was fiddling
about with it, and it came in two in his hands, and a bit of paper
dropped out. This he picked up and, just noticing that there was
writing on it, put it into his pocket, and subsequently into a vase
on his mantelpiece. I was at his house not very long ago, and had
picked up the vase and was looking at it. I happened to turn it up to
find the mark, and the paper fell out. The old man, on my handing
it to him, told me the story I have told you, and said I might keep
the paper. It was crumpled and rather torn, so I have mounted it on
a card, which I have here. If you can throw any light on its meaning I shall be very glad, and also, I may say, a good deal surprised."

   He gave me the card. The paper was quite legibly inscribed in
an old hand, and this is what was on it:—

"When I grew in the Wood
I was water'd wth Blood
Now in the Church I stand
Who that touches me with his Hand
If a Bloody hand he bear
I councell him to be ware
Lest he be fetcht away
Whether by night or day,
But chiefly when the wind blows high
In a night of February.

"This I drempt, 26 Febr. A° 1699. JOHN AUSTIN."

"I suppose it is a charm or a spell: wouldn't you call it something of that kind?" said the curator.

"Yes," I said, "I suppose one might. What became of the figure in which it was enclosed?"

"Oh, I forgot," said he. "The old man told me it was so ugly and frightened his children so much that he burnt it."

THE CATHEDRAL CRYPT

John Wyndham

John Wyndham Parkes Lucas Beynon Harris (1903–1969) was a science fiction writer who is perhaps best known for *The Day of the Triffids* (1951) and *The Midwich Cuckoos* (1957). Later adapted for the screen, Harris published these novels under the pen name John Wyndham, one of many pseudonyms used during his career.

Writing as John Beynon Harris, English-born Wyndham placed his early writing in American periodicals, publishing short stories in science fiction magazines like *Wonder Stories* and *Amazing Stories* during the 1930s. In 1935, Wyndham contributed to his first English periodical, selling *The Secret People* (as John Beynon) to *The Passing Show*. *Stowaway to Mars* (1936) soon followed and, after a break from writing during the Second World War, a long writing career ensued.

"The Cathedral Crypt" was published early in Wyndham's career, under the name John Beynon Harris. It first appeared in *Marvel Tales of Science and Fantasy* (March/April 1935) and pairs perfectly with "The Stalls of Barchester Cathedral". Wyndham's story, like that written by James, tells of a malevolent presence in a consecrated place.

"The past seems so close here," Clarissa said, as though she thought aloud. "Somehow it hasn't been allowed to fade into dead history."

Raymond nodded. He did not speak, but she could see that he understood and that he, like herself, felt the weight of antiquity pressing down upon this Spanish city. Half unconsciously she elaborated:

"Most of our cities strive for change, they throw away the past for the sake of progress. And there are a few, like Rome, truly eternal cities which sail majestically on, absorbing change as it comes. But I don't feel that this city is quite like that. Here, the past seems—seems arrogant, as if it were fighting against the present. It is determined to conquer all the new forces. Look at that, for instance."

A car, new and glossy, was standing before the cathedral door. A priest blessed it with upraised hand while he murmured prayers for the safety of the travellers.

"Commending it to the care of God, and the charge of St Christopher," Raymond remarked. "At home they say that the cars empty the churches; here they even bring the car to church. You're right, my dear, the past is not going to give in here without a battle."

The car, with its celestial premium paid, drove on its way, and with it went all sign of the twentieth century. Late sunlight poured upon a scene entirely medieval. It flooded the cathedral's western face, turning it from grey to palest rose, showing it as something which was more than stone upon stone, a thing which lived though it rested eternally. The fragile beauty of living things was built into those Gothic spears which sped heavenward. Such traceries and filigrees, such magnificent aspiration could not absorb men's art and lives, and yet remain mere stone. Something of the builders' souls was swept up to live for ever among the clustered pinnacles.

"It's very, very lovely," Clarissa whispered. "It makes me feel small—and rather frightened."

Over the dark doorways a row of stone saints in their niches stretched across the façade. Above them a rose window stared like a Cyclops' unblinking eye. Higher still, gargoyles leered sunward, keeping their ceaseless watch for devils. The cathedral was a fantasy of faith; spirit had helped to build it no less than hands: a dream in stone on a foundation of souls.

"Yes—that is beauty," Raymond said.

He stepped towards the open doors. Clarissa, on his arm, hung back a little, she did not know why. Beauty can awe, but can it alone send a deeper prick of fear?

"We are going inside?" she asked.

Her husband caught the tone of her voice; he looked at her with a tinge of surprise. He would obey any wish of hers willingly. The world held nothing dearer than Clarissa; she had become even more precious in the three weeks since their marriage.

"You'd rather not? You're tired?"

Clarissa shook away her vague fears; they were a foolishness unworthy of her. Besides, Raymond obviously wanted to go in.

"No. Of course we must look at it. They say the inside is even more beautiful than the outside," she agreed.

But as they walked about the huge, darkening place her uneasiness came creeping back. Ethereal fears clustered within and around her, clinging but impalpable. She fastened to Raymond and his firm reality, trying to share his pleasure in the pictures, shrines and sculptures. Together they gazed up at the huge, shining crucifix slung from the distant roof, but her mind did not follow his words as he admired it. She was thinking how quiet, how lonely it was in this great place. Here and there one or two dim figures moved silently as ghosts, points of light shone in far, dark corners like stars in the blackness of space. There was a sense of peace, but not the peace of tranquillity…

They crossed to the side chapels where Raymond took a lengthy interest in the decorations and furnishing. Some time had passed before he looked up and noticed his wife's pallor.

"What is it? You're not ill, darling?"

"No," she assured him. "No, I'm quite all right."

It was the truth. There was nothing wrong with her save only an overwhelming desire to get back to the familiarities of noises and people.

"Anyhow, we had better go. They'll be wanting to close the place soon," Raymond said. They returned to the central aisle and turned towards the entrance. Now that the sun had set the western end was very dim. The lights were few and feeble, pale candles and a lamp or two; the rose window was no more than a blur; the shape of the doorway, invisible. With misgiving, Raymond hastened his steps. Clarissa clutched his arm more tightly.

"Surely they haven't—" he began, but he left the sentence unfinished as they both saw that the heavy doors were shut.

"They must have overlooked us when we were in that chapel," he said with more cheerfulness than he felt. "I'll try knocking."

But the pounding of his fists against the massive doors was childishly futile. Sledgehammer blows could scarcely have been heard through those solid timbers. Together they shouted. Their voices fled away through the empty arches. The sound, flung from wall to wall, returned to them, a distorted, eerie travesty.

"Don't," implored Clarissa, "don't shout any more—it frightens me."

Raymond stopped at once, but he did not admit in words that he too had felt fearful of the echoes, as though he were disturbing things which should be left to sleep.

"Perhaps there is a smaller door open somewhere," he suggested, but with little hope in his tones.

Their heels clicked sharply on the flagstones as they searched. Clarissa fought down an absurd impulse to walk on tiptoe. Each door they tried seemed equipped with a more loudly clattering latch and more raucously grinding bolts than the last. A few opened, but none of these led into the open.

"Locked," said Raymond disgustedly as they reached the main door once more. "Every single entrance locked. I'm afraid we're prisoners." Half-heartedly he hammered again on the wood.

"But we can't stay here."

There was a piteous sound in Clarissa's voice, like a child imploring not to be left in the dark. He put his arm round her and she pressed thankfully closer.

"We must. There's no help for it. After all, it might be worse. We're together and we're perfectly safe."

"Yes, but—oh, I suppose it's silly to be afraid."

"There's nothing to be afraid of, darling. We can go back into that little chapel and make ourselves as comfortable as we can in there so that we'll forget that all this outer part exists. There are cushions on the benches, and we can use hassocks for pillows. Oh, we might be far worse off."

Raymond woke suddenly at the slight movement of Clarissa in his arms.

"What is it?" he mumbled sleepily.

"Sh—Listen!" she told him.

She watched his face as he obeyed, part fearful lest he should not hear the sound, but in greater part hoping that he would prove it an hallucination. He sat upright.

"Yes, I can hear it. What on earth—?" He glanced at his watch; it showed half-past one. "What can they be doing at this time?"

They listened in silence for some moments. The confused sound down by the entrance clarified into a chant of massive solemnity. No words could reach them, only harmony rising and falling like the surge of long, slow waves.

Raymond half rose. Clarissa seized his arm, her voice imploring:

"No-no, you mustn't, it's—" She stopped, at a loss. There was no word to express her sensation. But it touched him, too, like a warning. He relaxed and dropped back to the seat.

The voices approached slowly. The chant rolled on. Occasionally it would rise from its ululation to a paean and then sink back again to its woeful monotony.

The two in the chapel crept forward until only one high-backed bench hid them from the nave. There they crouched, peering out into the dimness.

The slow procession passed. First the acolytes with swinging censers, behind them a cross bearer, then a single, robed figure leading a dozen brown-habited monks, chanting, their faces uncertainly lit by the candles they carried. Then the Sisters of some black robed Order, their faces gleaming, white as paper out of their sombreness. Two more monks, holding by ropes a lonely nun...

She was young, not ageless like the rest, but the beauty of her face was submerged in anguish. Bright tears of fear and misery poured from her wide eyes, trickling down upon her clothes. She could not brush them away nor hide her face, for her arms were tightly bound behind her back. Now and then her voice rose in a frightened call above the chanting. A weak, thin cry which choked in a tightened throat. She darted glances right and left, twisted to look behind her in hopeless desperation. Twice she hung back, writhing her arms in their cords. The two monks before her pulled on the ropes, dragging her forward. Once she fell to her knees and with lips moving, gazing up at the immense cross in the roof. She implored mercy and forgiveness, but the tugging ropes forced her on.

Clarissa turned horrified eyes to her husband. She saw that he also had understood and knew the rite which was to follow. He murmured something too low for her to catch.

The deliberate procession with its spangle of candles approached the altar. Each row genuflected before it turned away to the left. Despair seemed to snap the last stay of hope in the nun as she passed it, drooping. Raymond leaned further out of the chapel to watch the file disappear into a small doorway. Then he returned to his wife and took her hand. Neither spoke.

Clarissa was too deeply shocked for speech. A nun who had broken her vows—she knew the old punishment for that. They would put her—she shuddered and clutched Raymond's hand the tighter. They couldn't—they couldn't do that! Not now. Centuries ago, perhaps, but not to-day. But the thought of her own words came back to her: "The past seems so close here," she had said. She shuddered again.

Sounds stole out of the little door into the cathedral.

A short, weak scuffle; something between a gasp and a whimper; a voice which spoke in heavy, sonorous tones:

"*In nomime patris, et filii, et spiritus sancti—*"

A muffled clash. The ring of the trowel on the stone. Clarissa fainted.

"They're gone," Raymond was saying. "Come quickly!"

"What—?" Clarissa was still uncertain, bemused.

"Come along. We may be in time to save her yet. There must be a little air in there."

He was pulling Clarissa by the wrist, dragging her after him, out of the chapel, towards the small door.

"But if they should come back—?"

"They've gone, I tell you. I heard them bolt the big doors."

"But—" Clarissa was terrified. If the monks found out that there had been witnesses... What then?

"Hurry or we'll be too late."

Raymond seized a candle from its altar and pulled at the small door. For its size it was heavy, and swung back slowly. He ran down the curving flight of stone steps beyond, Clarissa at his heels. The crypt below was small. One candle sufficed to show all there was to see. The two side walls were smooth, it was the one opposite at which they stared. It showed the shape of two niches long filled in, three more niches, empty and darkly waiting, and one lighter patch of new stones and white mortar.

Raymond set down his candle and ran to the recent work, one

hand fumbling for a knife in his pocket. Clarissa raked at the damp mortar with her finger nails.

"Just enough to let us get a hold on this stone," he muttered as he scraped.

He clenched his strong fingers on its edges. At his first heave it loosened, a second pull, and it fell with a thud at his feet.

But there was another sound in the crypt. They whirled round to stare into the expressionless faces of six monks.

In the morning, only one niche stood empty and darkly waiting.

ANCIENT TOMB IN NORBURY CHURCH

For more Tales of the Weird titles
visit the British Library Shop (shop.bl.uk)

We welcome any suggestions, corrections or feedback you may have, and will
aim to respond to all items addressed to the following:

The Editor (Tales of the Weird), British Library Publishing,
The British Library, 96 Euston Road, London NW1 2DB

We also welcome enquiries through our Twitter account, @BL_Publishing.